Ian Watson was born in Tynes̶[...] English at Balliol College, Ox̶[...] tive fiction stories were stimu̶[...] stay as a lecturer in Japan̶[...] *Under Saturn*, a short story, was pu̶[...] *Worlds* magazine, and since then his stories have appeared in various magazines and anthologies. They have also been published in book form in four previous collections, *The Very Slow Time Machine*, *Sunstroke*, *Slow Birds* and *Evil Water*.

Ian Watson's first novel, *The Embedding*, was published in 1973 and received enormous critical acclaim. His second novel, *The Jonah Kit*, became a British Science Fiction Award winner as well as confirming his position in the front rank of contemporary writers. He has been features editor of the journal *Foundation* since 1975 and a full-time writer since 1976. His most recent novels are *Chekhov's Journey* (1983), *Converts* (1984), *The Book of the River* (1984) and *Queenmagic, Kingmagic* (1986).

By the same author

IAN WATSON

Whores of Babylon

PALADIN
GRAFTON BOOKS
A Division of the Collins Publishing Group

LONDON GLASGOW
TORONTO SYDNEY AUCKLAND

Paladin
Grafton Books
A Division of the Collins Publishing Group
8 Grafton Street, London W1X 3LA

A Paladin Paperback Original 1988

ISBN 0-586-08773-7

Printed and bound in Great Britain by
Collins, Glasgow

Set in Century Schoolbook

By the waters of Babylon we sit down
and weep, when we think of thee,
O America!

Horace Walpole, 1775

Contents

1

In which Alex arrives, and picks up some donkey droppings

When Alex was thirteen, he and the other kids in his age group used to fight with knives. Every Saturday morning for months on end they practised single combat, and pairs, and two-against-one. Alex hated it. The blades were made of stiff rubber but the bruises were real.

The blades had to be of rubber or else he might have got accustomed to not plunging his weapon right home in his opponent's neck or belly. In a genuine fight that sort of delicacy could have been fatal.

At first Alex hadn't seen the point. Their armoury was well stocked with M-16 rifles, pistols, grenades, light and heavy machine guns, mortars, and even rocket launchers. But Mitch, the coach, took the long view. One day the ammunition would run out; whereas they would always have sharp knives.

Alex also learned to throw knives. Steel knives now. *Thuck.* They quivered in the man-shaped target. Mitch had rigged a track to jerk this target along, but to Alex there was something unreal about this kind of target practice. An intruder wasn't going to trundle along in a straight line. And supposing he missed the intruder, Alex would be disarming himself and giving his enemy a present.

He had hated knife practice.

* * *

On Friday afternoons Mitch had tutored the kids in geography. Mitch's favourite map was of military target areas inside America. Primary nuclear targets were marked by solid black spots. Secondary targets were open circles. Some parts of this map were great black splotches as if someone had spilled a bottle of ink.

Oregon, where Alex lived, was almost clean. Portland and another coastal target were secondaries, but otherwise – come nuclear doomsday – the state would be okay, more so than northern California, where other survivalist communities had holed up.

And if doomsday didn't come with a bang, but the world's economic and political systems simply fell apart, plenty of people in Oregon would get by while whole populations elsewhere starved, rioted, looted, and froze.

Alex was brought up to believe in Survival; and in its twin, Collapse.

A few years later Alex had given up on the version of survival as practised at ... At ... At somewhere in the Cascade Range. Alex wouldn't say where exactly. That was his early training coming out. Never lead strangers back to your base.

So here was Alex, in these late days of civilization as we know it, trying to distance himself from Oregon.

What late days?

No doubt when the year 2000 came round it would be a year like any other. Christ wouldn't appear in the sky to rapture all true believers up into the air. No angels would fly down; nor missiles either. Just because a year ended in three zeroes, was that any reason to imagine the Millennium, the end of the world?

Yet though Alex didn't believe this, he still imagined it. Millions of other people must have felt likewise in their various ways. Those who believed in the Rapture. Those who believed in surviving somewhere in the Cascade Range. The planners and the politicians. Ordinary people, grown sick with civilization. Yes, many. Otherwise, would the city of Babylon have been rebuilt?

Alex Winter was a gritty-looking fellow, with unruly wavy hair. His skin seemed to have been sandblasted like some ancient stone statue which sloughed off particles. But it didn't seem as though his skin was diseased, just as though he had recently tramped through a dust storm. For a couple of years while he was in college he had applied an oily skin cream; then he'd given up. He'd decided that his skin simply shed old cells and grew new ones faster than normal.

His face was bold, with a Roman nose and a strong — even jutting — jaw. His eyes were a dull, washed-out blue. His hair was a brindled hue, brown flecked with red, as though every now and then the roots injected a few cells of richer pigment. When he sat, he sat very still and looked determined. When he moved, his motions were often brisk and sudden; though not necessarily effective. With maturity he hoped to reach a compromise between these two states.

He was a sociology drop-out from the University of Oregon at Eugene; concerning which, he reflected how odd was this whole psychological business of reacting against one's home and folks. He had honestly believed that by working his way through school in Eugene he was rebelling — against knife practice and such. He would study the phenomenon of his own upbringing objectively in terms of attitude formation, group dynamics, ideology. He would discover what really made that mountain commune tick. By so doing he would inherit the outside world as a full human being, freed of fear, shrived of doom.

Yet now here he was about to enter a community weirder than any survivalist village, a community designed to find out whether survival *as such* was possible: the survival of any civilization whatever.

Here was Alex escaping from the impending Millennium by altering the date, by rolling back the calendar to the year 323 B.C.

Here he was, approaching the gates of Babylon.

Which of course was much closer to ground zero than he had ever been while in Oregon. On Mitch's target map south-eastern Arizona had been one big black blot.

But Alex didn't care. In his mind a magic bubble enclosed the area which lay ahead. Perhaps at last he had overcome his upbringing.

Unless on a far more fundamental level he had finally submitted to it.

We'll see, he thought.

And it is Alex who is writing this account. In Greek, on hinged boards coated with beeswax.

They crossed the Arizona desert awakening from a daze, their minds buzzing with the common tongue, the universal language: Greek.

Forty passengers rode the hovercraft; and their brains still frothed and simmered from all the speed-teaching. For a week they had been drugged and hypnotized and interfaced with computers. Even sleep had been invaded. Recorded voices had squeaked at high speed like whistling dolphins.

By the time the passengers arrived at Babylon, they'd been told, their heads would have cleared. A deep sediment of Greek would have settled to the bottoms of their minds. Their ordinary consciousness would be lucid, clear, and Attic.

A couple of Sahuaro cacti flashed by, towering amidst the scrub. The dead-looking ocotillo and brittle-bushes resembled corals on a sea floor so long drained that most things had turned to dust. Or so it seemed, after the lushness of Oregon. Ahead, not even scrub. A whole swathe of desert was as barren and pockmarked as the moon, as though the landscape had been deliberately scoured to produce a no-man's-land between the native vegetation of America and that of Babylon. But Alex remembered that this was the old Luke-Williams Air Force Gunnery Range. Rockets and cannon shells and tracer rounds had pruned the plant life in years gone by.

Next door to the range was another empty segment of the state, the Papago Indian Reservation. In the north of this the grazing had failed. The nearer sod-roofed adobe villages of Hickiwan and Vaya Chin were abandoned years since. This Alex recalled from the briefing before the language lessons began in earnest. He recalled, but it meant little to him.

In the far distance he noticed jagged mountains which looked un-Babylonian. If the copper smelters had still been burning away full blast at Ajo down there in the south-west, he mightn't have been able to see those peaks at all on account of sulphuric smoke hazing the sky.

The Ajo open-cast mines, once run by the Phelps Dodge Corporation; the US Air Force; the Papago Indians – these things meant nothing much. They were part of America, not Babylonia; and America lay behind the travellers.

Their hovercraft followed the concrete ribbon of the road which once gave access to the construction site. No cars or buses might use this now. It was closed; no longer a modern highway. They flew a few inches above it. The gale of air supporting the hovercraft beneath, and the wind from the tail fans, swept the concrete clear of grit. Yet they did not touch it. They were disconnected, just as they were disconnected from America. The voices babbling in their brains disoriented them. But already, as promised, these voices were becoming quieter, dropping beneath the horizon of awareness.

'Alex – '

Deborah was saying something to him in Greek, in ancient Greek with an enriched vocabulary which linguists had cannibalized from modern Greek.

He nodded, but paid little attention. Nothing that they could say at the moment meant anything. They were still in transition.

He did wish a relationship to flower between himself and Deborah. When they first met a spark had flown, a connection had formed, a tenuous bridge had been built. He was certain of the spark, the bridge; before drugs and hypnosis drowned him and her. No doubting it. He wished they might be friends and lovers. He felt sure she wished this, too. Here they were, sitting side by side, almost touching. But he sat very still. Whatever they felt for each other was dwarfed by what was going to happen. They couldn't relate as the people they had been; only as the people they would become.

Was that the last Sahuaro before Babylon? The cactus stood brokenly, wooden ribs exposed, savaged by lightning or by a cannon shell.

A solitary jackrabbit took off, terrified by the roar of the hovercraft. The animal's sides flashed from tan to white as it dodged left and right to confuse its enemy. Not that the enemy was interested. Abruptly the rabbit halted and faced north, to drain the heat of flight out of its enormous ears.

* * *

14

Deborah Tate: of medium height, and definitely graceful, though unusually so. Her shoulders sloped
remarkably. This was the first physical characteristic
of Deborah's which had struck Alex: that strange,
almost alien swoop of the shoulders sloping down from
a long, vase-like neck. She was like some African
tribal woman whose neck had been stretched, and her
shoulders pressed down by brass neck-bands. Such
African beauties could not, of course, support their
skulls unaided upon the stretched vertebrae, not without a column of strong metal to brace the neck. Yet
Deborah's white skin soared unaided. So in a way she
looked almost unhuman, as though she was a woman
from another star; her neck and shoulders a perfect
touch-sculpture. Since no one else had stared at her
wonderingly Alex had concluded that her neck and
shoulders somehow conformed to some ideal pattern
within himself: the geometry of some personal emotional equation.

Her eyes were glossy dark; her hair raven dark and
strong, cut close in a thick helmet-cut with a protective
black tongue teasing her nape. She wore a loose white
poncho blouse of linen over a long white linen robe
from which the tips of leather sandals and her toes
peeped out. Her arms were bare, with copper bangles
at the wrists.

In her Greek costume she looked chaste. But she
had already hinted that once in Babylon she would
soon go to sit in the Temple of Love to wait for any
stranger to come along and toss a coin in her lap. Old
man, youngster, ugly or handsome, skinny or fat, clean
or filthy, she must go with him and lie with him.
Every woman of Babylon was obliged to do so sometime before she reached the age of thirty; a custom
which could prove inconvenient if the woman was ugly

– she might spend weeks waiting. Presumably one of the priests might then bribe a beggar to cast the coin.

The prospect seemed to fascinate Deborah.

Maybe she only spoke of it to Alex, back at the university, in the hope that the stranger might be him? So that she could experience the frisson of excitement and trepidation, then avoid the reality?

Alex already knew that it would not be he who threw that coin in her lap, with the head of King Alexander stamped on it. Not he; not yet. To do so would be untrue to Babylon. He hoped she understood this.

Later on, though – presuming that they both became Babylonian citizens – maybe he would bid for Deborah before the auction block in the marriage market of Babylon. (For that was also a custom, if a woman had no dowry.) Maybe.

Alex was already sure that he would become a citizen at the end of the first trial month. He would enter Babel Tower to be taught Babylonian, lying drugged and hypnotized in some deep stone chamber. He would emerge, to grow his hair long, and wear a turban and perfume, and flourish a jaunty walking stick.

He wouldn't simply be some Greek-speaking tourist who departed again, delighted or disgusted, to be debriefed by the university psychologists. Babylon still needed tens of thousands more citizens. The city had been completed only five years ago. Alex would be one of those citizens; he would belong.

'There's a drumming in my ears,' Deborah said softly in Greek.

Alex touched her hand lightly; only lightly, and quickly. 'It'll fade. It'll pass.'

Maybe that was the wrong response? Maybe she spoke of her excitement so as to share it with him?

But how could there be right things or wrong things to say on this journey? Silence was best. The other passengers were mostly absorbed in themselves, as if gathering strength to hoist a great rock, to shoulder a whole new world. There was very little tourist chatter; only the dying hum in all their skulls.

She said, in Greek:

> 'My tongue freezes into silence,
> And a gentle fire courses through my flesh;
> My eyes see nothing,
> And there's a drumming in my ears . . .'

Alex imagined for a moment that she was echoing his own thoughts in rapport. But no; surely she was quoting poetry. Yes, that was it. She was reciting one of Sappho's love songs. Seventh-century Sappho; no anachronism there.

The skull hum had all but disappeared; so why the drumming in her ears? Was it for him? – or for Babylon? – or for the temple of Ishtar, the sacred brothel?

Deborah came from New York, opposite point of the compass to Alex. Perhaps New York gave her something of a prior lien on Babylon? Her mundane background was computer operator. Also, hopeful actress; but already that particular dream had died, to be replaced by the desire to live a role at last.

That was about all Alex knew of her earlier life; and he had told her just as little of his own. Arriving ten days earlier at the hypermodern township of Heuristics south of Casa Grande on Interstate 8, all the new arrivals put their pasts behind them. Their purpose: to confront the future which was written in the past, but not in their own personal past.

He and she had flown into Sky Harbor Airport, Phoenix, to be bussed out together with thirty or so other people to the University of the Future in the desert at Heuristics. It wasn't entirely by chance that they had sat together on the bus, but it was only on the bus that they had mentioned their previous lives.

Heuristics: as a name this sounded no more nor less capricious than the names of several other townships thereabouts. Such as Aztec. And Mecca. Salome, and Bagdad. Yet of course *'heuristics'* meant the art of asking questions, a word from the ancient Greek, as Alex now well knew.

Being hypermodern, the township of Heuristics was mainly invisible; just as the future was invisible? Heuristics was mostly underground, with window-ceilings. This highly energy-conservative design also served to hide the actual extent of the university, which might have been smaller or very much larger than the actual oasis of glass, the array of twinkling lakes which would have been visible from the air: a chequerboard of mirages or mirrors. Mirrors, more like. The University of the Future was indeed a many-faceted mirror reflecting the past into the future. Though what did it show of its graduates' faces? Alex did not know yet. By the time he did know, would he wear the same countenance as before? Would Deborah?

'Look,' she said in Greek.

Everyone in Babylon spoke Greek to begin with. Greek was the world language used by travellers. It was the English of its day. For this was the epoch of Alexander the Great, and these were the last days of his reign. Alex's namesake lay dying of fever even now in the palace of Nebuchadnezzar.

'Look, Alex!'

Ahead to east and west fields fuzzed the desert with rich greens. Canal water glinted, webbing irrigated farmland . . .

Babylonia did not actually trespass upon the Papago Indian Reservation, but it came quite close, the further to remove itself from modern civilization: from the rumbling, farting commercial entrails of Arizona. Were the Papagos — those weavers of bright baskets — not now retrenched deep within their heartland, surviving on welfare, with their few starving cattle cropping the last arid pasture, they might well have been incensed to behold the greenery of Babylonia and to guess how much money was spent on piping water underground from the flood-control reservoir on the Gila River outside Gila Bend. However, it was a fifty-mile walk from the nearest Papago village to Babylon. The Indians still held their wasteland in perpetuity. The border between Babylonia and Papaguería remained sacrosanct, inviolate; except to buzzards.

Realistically — Alex told himself — Babylon made not one jot of difference to the neighbouring Indians. If there had been no Babylon, the money certainly wouldn't have been spent on piping a river into Papaguería. So there was no injustice.

Why then did the thought cross his mind? Was he, the trained survivor, suffering a twinge of liberal conscience?

If so he was a fool. Unprepared for the Babylonian experience.

Besides, there were only four or five thousand Papago Indians. There were thirty or forty times as many Babylonians. Probably some of the more go-ahead Indians were already basket-weavers or herdsmen in Babylonia.

At last! Far off Alex spied the city walls with the Tower of Babel rising behind.

This time he did clasp Deborah's hand. When he let go she shook her wrist as though a fly had settled on it. Her copper bangles rattled.

* * *

The fields running up to the outer wall were patchworks of leeks and onions, turnips and cabbages. Dykes, shaded by date palms, divided the fields. (Big, mature palms – of which there were thousands – must have been transplanted here full-grown.) Dozens of men and women laboured at a leisurely pace, a few cranking hand pumps, most carrying and emptying water-pots. The women wore loose cotton or flannel smocks, belted at the waist. The men were mainly stripped to their loincloths.

The Euphrates flowed citywards close by, bearing coracles, some with a single donkey tethered aboard, others giant boats with three or four donkeys penned on them in addition to passengers and cargoes of produce, wine-casks, or goats. From atop the great brick citadel a few guards eyed and counted the river traffic.

Coracles weren't the handiest of boats. Even with oars fore and aft and with a central mast dangling sail to trim the course, these perfectly round craft tended to spin in the current like waltzer cars at a funfair.

Yet this was how goods arrived in town from upstream Babylonia, dizzily water-borne. Then the skin hulls were stripped off the stick frames and loaded on to the donkeys to be carried back north. The donkeys munched up the straw padding of the boats to sustain them on the return journey; while the sticks were sold as kindling.

It all made sense.

The Euphrates made a return journey, too. Once well out of sight of the city and the southern Babylonian estates, the bulk of the water was filtered and cleaned and pumped through underground pipelines back to its source some twenty miles north of Babylon. From there, topped up with extra water from Gila

Bend, the river recommenced its course down through verdant Babylonia.

Alex was aware that visitors should never allude to this arrangement, nor to the buried nuclear power source which would run the pumps automatically for at least the next fifty years. Citizens of Babylon ignored the origin of the Euphrates; forgot it. According to the laws of Hammurabi, the penalty for broaching the forbidden topic was enslavement to a temple on grounds of blasphemy. Or worse: the Greek visitors had been told that an offender could legally be executed.

Thus actually the broad Euphrates flowed all the way from distant Armenia, and onward down to the sea.

Am I mad? wondered Alex momentarily. *Are we all mad, who come here?*

No! The pretence regarding the river was a logical lunacy. It aimed to challenge the greater lunacies: of time, decay, decadence, and the death of civilization. It was only one item in a much greater pretence; a pretence so grand that it readily became reality.

Enough said, regarding the false Euphrates. The true Euphrates.

Was Alex mad? Or would he be mad only once he became a Babylonian?

No. He had been mad previously. The rest of the world was mad. It had been mad for years, waiting for the end.

Now Alex would be sane.

And now the hovercraft had arrived at its destination. The road of concrete had disappeared a while since, giving way to a road of dirt.

In the lee of the outer walls below the looming citadel, the craft settled on its skirts. Its engines died. The dust swirled and settled. The passengers disembarked.

An avenue led onward and inward, tunnelling between wall and citadel. Down this avenue they could see the more massive inner walls pierced by the Ishtar Gate. But before they could proceed, a squad of soldiers spilled out of a guardroom and barred the way with spears. These were local soldiers, robed and bearded; not Macedonians.

'What's wrong?'

'Their corporal's counting us,' said Deborah. 'That's all.'

It wasn't quite all. Even when the corporal had finished totalling the new arrivals, his men still blocked the way. The corporal glanced impatiently along the avenue. Soon a small group of Greeks, no more than half a dozen, hastened into view, shepherded by a couple of spearmen. The Greeks trotted along the avenue, then headed for the waiting hovercraft. The soldiers all dropped back into shelter, though otherwise none of them acted as though the twentieth-century machine existed. The craft quickly roared to life, reinflating its skirts and whipping up clouds of dust which covered all the waiting visitors.

They had arrived neat and clean, but now, as the craft swung round and departed, suddenly they were as travel-stained as though they had walked the whole way to Babylon – across all of Asia Minor, Cilicia, Cappadocia, down through Mesopotamia.

'Shit,' one voice said loudly in English – and a soldier's spear jerked as if to impale the word. For English was a dead language; it hadn't yet been born.

The corporal stepped forward. 'Now you enter Babylon, Gate of God,' he called out in Greek.

The newcomers had to stop once again outside the Ishtar Gate, not because of soldiers but simply to admire.

The massive inner wall of baked brick rose impregnably from the steeply sloping scarp of a deep canal-moat lined with burnt brick and bitumen. A bridge of removable planks led across to the gate, its towers gorgeously enamelled and decorated. At top and bottom were friezes of rosettes like spinning chariot wheels. In between, against a bright turquoise background, beasts in glazed, moulded brick stood out one above the other: white and blue bulls with yellow horns and hooves, and dragons.

The dragons' bodies were covered with scales. Their hind legs were those of a bird of prey; their forelegs were feline. Tails were tipped with scorpion stings; heads sported the double horns of the Arabian viper. Mane and scaly claws and forked tongue were a golden brown; the rest was creamy white. The dragons stepped forth proudly, quivering with alertness; though at the same time they looked somewhat pea-brained.

Alex's thoughts were sharp and clear. They were as luminous as that brickwork. He felt that he ought to perform a sacrifice of thanksgiving to some long-forgotten resurrected god. To Shamash, perhaps, whose sun beat down. It would only be polite.

'Rejoice,' said Deborah. 'We have come.'

She sounded like Philippides after his marathon run to Athens when the tide of the Persians had been turned, a hundred and sixty-odd years ago now. There were already so many layers of history; of rise and fall . . .

So many layers. For Babylon the Magnificent, the Babylon of Hammurabi the compiler of laws and builder of canals, fell to the pugnacious, greedy, uncultured (and perhaps maligned) Kassites, who let the city fall into neglect. After a while that first Babylon was totally destroyed by the Assyrian Sennacherib. His soldiers killed every man, woman and child in the city, smashed the houses down, and even diverted a major canal to flood the ruins.

Less than a hundred years later, the Chaldeans – who destroyed the overstretched Assyrians with Persian help – rebuilt Babylon as their own capital. Before long the city, under Nebuchadnezzar, was even more splendid than ever.

Yet curiously, these Chaldeans failed to quite live in the present. Certainly their intelligentsia – priests and scribes – failed. Amidst sumptuous new palaces and temples, and even as they were building astronomical observatories to study the planets and the stars, they were also digging nostalgically in the old ruins for clay books and record tablets. With these texts as their guide, the Chaldeans began affectedly to copy the past in dress, speech, and custom. (Perhaps that was why, according to some Greeks, King Nebuchadnezzar had tried to collect and destroy all old records!)

Soon the Persians, former allies, attacked and overthrew the Chaldean Empire; slowly Babylon crumbled away into ruins and wreckage. Or more exactly, Darius the Great adorned the city; then his heir Xerxes taxed it savagely to pay for his Greek wars, eventually sacking and wrecking the city when it rebelled. But by the time of Darius III Babylon was back in business.

Presently, Alexander of Macedon overthrew the Persians (and put a torch to the winter palace of the Persian kings). But then something new in history happened. Alexander conceived the dream of ruling the whole world. He unified the Macedonians and Persians; the first world empire was organized with a common language and a common economy, centred upon Babylon. Babylon rose again as capital of the known world.

Briefly, oh so briefly. For in the palace of Nebuchadnezzar Alex's namesake lay a-dying, at the age of thirty-three.

This was the end of Babylon yet again; the last days of rekindled glory. Rise and fall. Rise and fall. And final fall. Ahead, dust and ashes; and the unknowable future.

What future? The future of Rome, currently a town of no great note. The future of Byzantium. The future of the Holy Roman Empire. Of the Spanish Empire. The British Empire. The Third Reich. The Stars and Stripes.

Dust and ashes. Buried monuments. Bones. Amnesia.

Meanwhile, what rough village in the Congo or the South Seas or Patagonia was slouching towards the future to become the new capital of human life?

Which indeed? – when there was no room left in the world for new golden hordes to gather, no lost forsaken hills for barbarians to sweep invigoratingly down from?

Where was the new birthplace of power and splendour? Could there be such a thing? Must the latest Babylons – of New York and Moscow, Tokyo and Peking – make way in their turn? And if so, make way for what?

What were the dynamics of decline and fall? Where was the elixir of immortality? How, as the years rolled by, could the present be perpetuated into the future so that change did not sweep away all that one knew? What did the social psyche know which the futurologists knew not?

To answer such questions was Babylon rebuilt in the Arizona desert and rekindled with life, gloriously poised on its final precipice with Alexander forever dying of a fever in the palace.

Had the history of Babylon happened in quite the order that Alex remembered? Maybe; maybe not! He had trouble sorting it all out in his head. So many ups and downs, before the final downer. Undoubtedly the sequence was more complicated.

That didn't matter. Babylon had been rebuilt synchronously, simultaneously, with the city of Hammurabi and the city of Nebuchadnezzar and that of Alexander coexisting in time. Here in the rekindled Babylon the great buildings of all the different epochs occurred together.

Thus the city questioned time itself; time, the reaper of human dreams.

Babylon was no Disneyworld. It was no utopian archology. It was no experimental community which wilfully turned its back on the twentieth century in fanciful pursuit of an ancient lifestyle. If it were merely one of these, would the American government have underwritten the huge initial cost, equivalent to that of a manned space station? Would it have exempted Babylonia from state and federal law?

Space! Perhaps the future Babylon, the new centre of civilization – if any – would be in space . . . one day, with the people of the asteroids and moons as the new, rich, vigorous barbarians. While earth itself would be a ruin.

In the meantime Babylon was the most ambitious, most important project regarding the future of civilization as one knew it.

Perhaps.

And perhaps the university at Heuristics was a monstrous folly and its Babylon a different sort of folly; more akin to the follies built by rich English gentry in their landscape gardens in the eighteenth century? Though much vaster; and not merely a façade, but a fully functioning ancient city.

Was the autumn of a culture marked by vast, capricious building projects? By exercises in architectural metaphysics, designed to stem the tide of time? By schemes reeking of immortalist religious yearnings masquerading as something else? (Call this the Ozymandias Syndrome!) Was Babylon the psychic salvation of the American dream, or the very symbol of its decay?

Alex wasn't entirely sure. He hoped to find out.

'Come on!'

Deborah was the first to pass through the Ishtar Gate. Alex followed close behind.

He felt, oddly, as though he was entering his own head; and that once in, he might never find his way out again. But then, he doubted he would ever want to leave.

The Processional Way, also known as Victory Street, stretched straight as an arrow into the distance. Its centre was paved with white limestone flags and the edges with slabs of milky-veined red breccia. On both sides the street was hemmed by high, blue-glazed walls. Snarling lions in red, white and yellow tiles marched along both walls out from the heart of the city.

The wall of lions on the right cut off any view of Nebuchadnezzar's palace and the Rainbow Gardens. But that was no big disappointment. Before he could tackle the greater wonders Alex felt that he needed to come to terms with the common streets, the populace. No survivalist should be without immediate food and lodgings. First establish your base. Explore outwards in concentric circles. Gawping could come later. Unobtrusively he patted the pouch of shekels under his tunic.

So when they reached the end of the lion walls, where Victory Street crossed the Libil-hegalla canal, he glanced only briefly back at the south face of Neb's palace, which was now exposed to view. He merely registered the colonnaded tiers clad in so many trees and flowering shrubs. Like a camera he snapped the scene, but didn't develop it. As yet he had no real context for that palace. No experiential framework, as they say.

The rest of the party stopped on the bridge and stared. But not Deborah. She understood.

One thing which did catch Alex's eye and numb him for a while, however, was the sight of the Tower of Babel half a mile to the south-west. The sprawling base wasn't visible, but most of the upper circuits were. Babel looked enormous, far bigger than he had imagined. The air seemed to shimmer and ripple around the tower as though the whole of the district containing it – indeed, the very fabric of the city – was somehow warped and distorted to accommodate such bulk. To Alex's eye the tower looked less a Babylonian ziggurat than the building as painted by Brueghel.

Once across the bridge, Alex and Deborah plunged down one of the side streets. The street soon branched, putting out side shoots rigidly to right and left like an espaliered peach tree. Their progress was no plunge now, but a sidle through increasing numbers of Babylonians going about their business. The main triumphal thoroughfare had been fairly deserted. After all, it led only to the exit. No doubt on feast days people processed there, but otherwise their feet – mostly bare feet – left the broad, well-paved avenue alone.

These narrow side streets, the veins of the city, were

surfaced not with flagstones but with compacted rubbish – just as if strips had been cut from a bulldozed refuse dump and laid between the blank house walls. Strips which were excessively, generously thick. The road level – a gastronomic rather than a geological stratum composed of dried apple cores, cabbage stalks, gnawed ribs of pork, fish bones, date stones, pot fragments, rags, bits of old rush matting – rode knee- to waist-high above the doors of houses. Side-steps were hewn to give access to the homes; and Alex wondered whether his notion that these streets consisted of strips cut from a refuse dump and laid like pastry lattice on the cheesecake of the city was quite so absurd. So much solidified rubbish couldn't have accumulated and risen tide-high in only five years. More like fifty years. And while on the subject of tides, what a mess there would be if the Euphrates ever broke its banks and flooded the city! Water would pour down these steps cut from ancient dreck, into every doorway.

Babylon, it seemed, had been rebuilt as a *used* city, a second-hand city, even though its civic structures gleamed.

The dominant odour of these streets was a kind of vegetarian halitosis: armpit of Brussels sprouts, with a soupçon of donkey dung and urine. This might be perfectly comforting and friendly, were you a rabbit. The meaty and fishy elements must be scavenged nightly by stray cats and dogs – by rats too? – or bare feet would tread upon a lawn of maggots.

Had rats been introduced? Had they gravitated mysteriously across the intervening desert sands, scenting the Hamelin of new pickings without fear of poison bait?

The nostrils of Babylon's passing citizenry did not, by and large, twitch to the aroma of their native paths busily and appreciatively like bunnies'. If the flesh of the streets exhaled a compost-heap body odour, a fair number of passers-by — those who were modestly prosperous enough — deployed a whole battery of counter-smells, an olfactory palette of aromatic gums, fragrant oils, musk, sandalwood, patchouli.

Many men wore only a kilt, striding along stripped to the waist. (A few owned no more than a breech-clout.) Others sported cloaks fastened at the shoulder with a duffel peg; one or two, who walked arrogantly, boasted embroidered robes. Some men were clean-shaven but many wore beards, often stylishly waved. Wavy hair fell loosely over some men's shoulders, though turbans were also popular, and one saw the occasional fez. Richly robed fellows swung walking sticks jauntily.

Women were in smocks or loose, ankle-length shawls. Their hairstyles varied: plaited and coiled like a turban, or done up in a bun. Some buns were huge, and netted in a snood. Some faces were lavishly painted. Kids raced along the street almost naked, boys and girls alike; but then they still were alike, except beneath the *cache-sexe* of their abbreviated loincloths.

'We'll have to visit a perfume vendor, too,' said Alex. 'Before long, eh? Shall we?'

Deborah wrinkled her nose, for a moment just like a rabbit. 'Greeks don't wear perfume,' she said. 'It's effete.'

He was sure she was teasing. 'I bet they do here, Deb. I just bet they do.'

Hitherto all the whitewashed house façades had been blankly private save for the single vaulted arch-way which gave access sunkenly into shadows; and then only on the side of the street which faced the cooler north. Yet the walls, which continued on from one building to the next, weren't featureless. They were built in a saw-tooth style, in and out, in and out, so that the sunshine – where it reached into the street – cast bands of brightness and shadow. The walls on the sunny side were a chiaroscuro of slats like a long louvred window set on its side, as though a sudden jerk on a rope running the length of the houses might have swung all the bands of clay bricks at once, rendering the interiors breezy and visible.

Realistically, of course, in that unlikely event the houses would just have tumbled down – as indeed their highest elevations seemed already to be doing bit by bit, resulting in frayed, crumbling crenellated battlements up top.

One house was scaffolded precariously with poles and rope. Builders were hauling up baskets of clay from a damp greasy mound tipped in the street, partly blocking it. The men were repairing a section of slumped roof and parapet wall. Grown-up kids playing mud pies, for real.

'I bet they guarantee those repairs at least till the next thunderstorm,' said Alex, nodding aloft. 'Albeit a year from now.'

'Adobe's a *good* building material. It'll outlast steel and glass.'

'Should they slap it on while it's wet?'

'Become a builder. Find out.'

He nudged her. 'Talking of men wearing perfume,' he whispered, 'I hear the local Macedonians have all gone Persian.'

'So?'

'You said that was effete. You seemed to disapprove.'

Briefly Deborah looked confused, but then she laughed. 'Look, Alex, where I come from – *came* from, I mean – guys could bathe in asses' milk, should they find a convenient ass. And many did. They could wear bones through their noses and raspberry jam on their cheeks. It only bothers me as a visiting Greek lady, see? If it attracts you, do it. Find yourself.'

Oh, I will, he thought – and felt ashamed, of naivety. Not for the first time it occurred to him how his own home community had been fairly puritanical in its codes of behaviour . . . But wasn't Babylon, too, in its own way? A woman who murdered her husband for the love of another man wasn't just locked away. She was impaled alive. Supposedly.

Obviously a law like that wasn't carried out to the letter.

Or was it?

A crashing and clanging issued from the next doorway. A pall of fumes arose from the house's hidden courtyard, smutting the blue sky overhead; Alex concluded that this particular building must house a factory or a smithy. (Unless, which was less likely, the place was on fire within and the frenzied occupants were trying to beat out the flames with swords and chains and hammers.) No other sign gave notice of a workshop. No clay tablet trodden with duck's-foot cuneiform letters was inset by the door. How did the locals know where a place was? Or whose place was whose?

From here on much of the rest of the street was sky-soiled on the north-facing side; and more intermittent Nibelungish din soon reached his ears from within the walls. Half a dozen houses – not all quite in a row – were anonymous foundries or blacksmiths'.

'This must be the Street of the Smiths, but how does anybody find the right Mr Smith? I don't see any signs.'

'I guess,' said Deborah, 'if you have business here, you already know.'

'That isn't much help to a newcomer.'

'Why should there be signs on everything? The thing

itself is its sign.' She waggled her hand. 'Do you need signs on your fingers telling you which is which? If so, you're in trouble. And so is anyone with you.'

Alex experienced a quick chill of implied threat. He said nonchalantly, 'There mightn't be any signs, but have you noticed how everyone's walking in the same direction? That's been true of all streets since the bridge. No one going the opposite way.'

'Isn't it obvious?' she asked. 'With streets so narrow?'

Again Alex felt he had suffered a minor defeat. Too many of these, he feared, might erase Deborah from his life – like a message rendered nonsensical by too many errors.

He was rescued from discomfiture by donkeys. (And Deborah, one moment cool and languid, was panicked the next by these same beasts, as David Copperfield's Aunt Betsy Trotwood would be goaded into a tizz, a passion, by the mischievous antics of donkey boys and their wicked quadrupeds, two thousand and some years later.)

Laden with swaying bundles, a gang of donkeys – the only *team* work was that imposed by the confines of the houses – came at a canter, buffeting pedestrians out of the way while urchin muleteers played a hopeless game of tag behind, trying to catch hold of tails and avoid the hammer kicks of hooves which would surely ensue. Further up the street one incompetent lad still sprawled amidst the slippery mound of clay which had created a bottleneck, causing separation of boys from donkeys, and donkeys from their braying senses.

The leading donkey sideswiped Alex with its swaggery flanks, which were both belly-bountiful in their own right, like those of some huge hairy child suffering from kwashiorkor, and swollen besides by bundles of trader's booty tarpaulined under a sheep fleece. A small package of dirty cloth tied with cord slipped out from under the fleece, to fall at his feet.

Without really thinking, while confusion mounted and loud Babylonian curses erupted everywhere and while the next donkey blundered heavily past, Alex snatched the package up. Otherwise it would be squashed down into the deep litter of other rags and tatters of bedding and cabbage stalks, wouldn't it?

Now two other beasts were trying to run abreast, crowding the street from wall to wall. Perhaps this was the fault of the kilted man squeezed between their necks, trying to wrestle them both to a halt; he was being dragged along. The people ahead of this donkey duo took to their heels, encouraging the animals to do likewise.

'Help!' cried Deborah, doing nothing to escape. Why not? Maybe this was beneath the dignity of an elegant Greek lady.

Alex seized his chance, and her hand (his other hand gripping the packet) and dragged her in flight as far as the next intersection, which luckily was close at hand. They ducked down a different street just as hooves thudded by – the runaway pair pursued in turn by yet more beasts, then by squealing urchins, finally by a foul-looking burly fellow swearing and lashing a whip at the urchins' backs.

Enjoying the sensation of leading Deborah, Alex hurried her more than halfway down this street of refuge before she dug her heels in, out of breath or tired of playing that role. She gazed at him wide-eyed. Angry? Exhilarated?

In purest Attic Greek she said, 'Wow. I could use a drink.'

No one else had dodged up this particular thorough-fare to escape the stampede, though the way had been completely clear. Now, as if some unseen Babylonian traffic controller had waved a flag, the street began filling with folk from ahead.

'We appear to be facing the wrong way,' said Alex.

'I doubt if it damn well matters. Much. Might get our toes stubbed.'

'Won't get impaled for jaywalking, you mean?' He winked.

People crowded by.

'God, you do construct cages around yourself.'

He slipped briefly into English, and joked, 'Well, we *are* looking for bars.'

She looked shocked, insulted, on the point of marching off alone. Perhaps high-born ladies did not walk these streets alone; so she stayed.

'Sorry, Deb. I'll ask directions to the nearest beer shop, or wine palace, or whatever.'

The man he chose to ask – a short, dark, Hispanic type – was kilted and bare-chested but wore leather sandals, so obviously wasn't riff-raff. What else he was was betokened by his tattooed forehead. He wore there the sun-disc mark of Shamash. The sides of the man's head were shaved, and the curious quiff of hair which remained on his crown made him resemble a sun-browned version of the comic-strip French detective boy Tintin. Alex stepped in his way.

'Excuse me.'

'I'm busy.' The man spoke gruffly, thrust past, and continued on his way. He smelled of sandalwood.

'You just asked a slave,' said Deborah.

'So?'

'A temple slave.'

'Obviously he wasn't *my* slave.'

'A slave.' She repeated the word, to savour it. 'A real honest-to-goodness slave.'

'That's right. The old country has reintroduced slavery. White slavery; not just black.'

She looked defiant. 'What old country?'

'Okay, we'll pretend it doesn't exist. Not yet.'

It. He'd found himself unable – reluctant – to mention the name America. Another tattooed slave passed. The man spat irritably as they stared at him.

All of a sudden Alex really saw these people in the street, not just witnessing but experiencing them.

Slaves. People owned by other people, as you own a horse or a dog. Though horses did not wear scent . . .

Was everyone in Babylon – tattooed or untattooed – equally a slave? All slaves to a dream, to an almighty pretence, a fabrication? Were the visiting free Greeks all applicants to a curiously fulfilling kind of slavery – no matter whether they were fated to prosper here, or to fall on hard times?

'I guess,' mused Alex, 'if they were just phoney slaves, that would make the whole place phoney.'

What if the slaves ran away? Would soldiers hunt them down in the desert, using dogs to track and spears to chivvy? Could one escape across a state line from Babylonia into America and be free again?

America didn't yet exist. America was unknown. Any state line was a fault line in time, behind which all Babylonia had slumped into the past, had submerged itself like a whale sounding deep into the abyss of history. How could one even imagine escaping from the belly of such a whale? Because it had dived, the whale would survive – emotionally at least – whilst the surface of America would wither under the scorching rays of the eternal, epoch-mocking sun, Shamash, who judged and condemned all human actions, who sent kingdom after kingdom into the empty hollow darkness which was the afterlife, and which also was posterity.

'I guess,' said Alex, 'some people might give up their freedom gladly – so they can become authentic. Maybe people do this all the time. You're a little interested in that too, eh?'

She didn't answer; perhaps because he had not really expected an answer. Instead she began walking on down the rest of the street, which was temporarily clear again. He caught up. They turned the corner and almost tripped over a beggar, a barefoot bundle of rags.

'Alms,' croaked the creature. He instantly recognized Greeks, and begged in Greek.

This wasn't an American beggar, some bagman or hobo on a park bench. This was an Asiatic, ancient, timeless beggar. Not a scrap of spare fat on him. More like a monkey with bad teeth. A herpes sore adorned his lower lip.

Alex addressed the beggar: 'Greetings! Can you direct us to a taverna?'

'Good God,' protested Deborah. But Alex didn't intend to follow the man's directions, into some thieves' kitchen. He was simply curious. He wanted to prove the man a masquerade. He wanted the man to wink.

No, that's a lie. Alex wanted him *not* to wink; so that this was all for real.

The beggar stank. He couldn't afford perfume or any oily alkaline soap. Could such a person ever spare a coin to toss upon a woman's loins in the temple of Ishtar? Only if someone else gave it to him. Only if someone else expressly paid him to go there and choose a particular woman. Alex toyed briefly with this thought, tormenting himself.

The man grinned evilly, yellow-toothed. He held his palm higher, more urgently. Like a monkey, for peanuts. The motion revealed a knife stuffed inside a

37

band of cloth round his waist. The beggar wore those rags not for warmth or for decency's sake – Babylon was a hot city – but to hide a weapon. Alex hadn't bargained for this. (Was Mitch right, after all?)

Deborah dragged on Alex's arm, hauling him away.

Slaves. Beggars. These people weren't extras on some back lot. They were the big scene, just as much as King Alexander. They were the action.

And there was no camera.

Unless . . . maybe tiny, hidden lenses were watching everywhere, indistinguishable from a speckle on a wall.

This street was wider than the last, but people still made their way in only one direction. Abruptly a chariot clattered down the thoroughfare, its horse whipped on by a Macedonian officer wearing bronze breastplate and skirt of leather thongs, his helmet hard-crested like the skull of an extinct Corythosaurus. Pedestrians scattered to the walls to avoid being trampled. No one seemed to mind.

After a while, they did find a bar-restaurant. Wide windows, open on to the street, disgorged smells of honeyed barley-cake, bean soup, goat stew, horsemeat steaks. Sample meals stood on the brick counter within. Behind, the kitchen was a smoky den, though open to the sky.

Patrons squatted on stools at low tables. Most drank pots of beer. A couple of men were sucking wine from jars through long filter-tubes, for all the world like opium smokers puffing on hookahs.

Alex ordered honey cakes with a side dish of dates, and beers. They found vacant stools in a far corner, and settled.

The beer, sweetly sour, also tasted of dates. Too

many sweet things? No; right now this was good for their blood sugar.

'Well, well,' he said.

He remembered the packet which he'd picked up, and later stuffed into his sleeve. He produced it.

'What's that?'

'It fell off one of those damn donkeys.'

'And you kept it?'

'I forgot.'

'But that makes you a thief!'

'Hardly! It's just a pack of rag.'

'So why did you take it?'

'I'll return the damn thing.'

'How? Who to? That's a lie. Why didn't you return it right away?'

'What is this? My trial? Now who's constructing cages?'

'Why didn't you give it back?'

'We were avoiding being trampled, remember?'

'You had time to pick it up. You could have done a citizen a favour.'

'Mightn't be worth giving back.' Circumspectly, Alex untied the twine and unfolded the soiled cloth.

Inside nestled a black plastic box containing a cassette tape. Hastily, Alex covered it.

'Oh my God, what's that doing here?' she whispered.

'Dunno,' he whispered. 'It might be a computer program. Or results.'

'Why?'

'Because everything's being watched and recorded and measured. By the university. We're all bits of information.'

'You'd better get rid of it. Chuck it in the next canal.'

'It has to be valuable. This is fate, destiny. Don't look a gift donkey in the mouth.'

'Valuable to you?' She shook her head. 'Uh-uh. That

isn't why we're here – not to start playing power games with the system.' She shuddered. 'You fool. Even knowing about that thing makes me a criminal as well. I don't want to know about it. I don't want to be speared. Or enslaved.'

'Not even enslaved for one day?'

'That thing's no use to you.'

'It's useful to someone.'

'Maybe it's just blank.'

'And someone wants to copy something? Steal some knowledge, smuggle it out? In which case, returning this to its owner mightn't have been a bright idea. It might have been a damn dangerous idea.'

'How, if you hadn't opened it?'

'I might have felt the shape inside. That overseer with the whip might have thought I had. We might have been followed and murdered.'

Deborah whistled softly. 'You've really persuaded yourself. You must be mad. Will you please get rid of the thing?'

'I can't do that. This is important – but who to? You're in on it too, you know. You're involved.'

'Oh no I'm not. You don't bind me – with a bit of tape.'

I do, he thought, *if I don't throw the tape away. Which I won't do.*

So I must be mad, must I? Alex must be mad? Maybe so. There had to be something a bit schizoid about becoming a Babylonian.

Inside his sleeve Alex clutched the wrapped cassette, though not so fiercely as to crack the twentieth-century plastic case.

'Let's get another beer,' he suggested. 'Let's loosen up. Or should we try the wine?'

'Shit,' she said; referring precisely to what?

* * *

Later, they found rooms in a sprawling three-storey inn between Sin Street and Marduk Street, near the Greek Theatre.

The inn was called 'Between the Skin Shops'. On one side was a reeking fuller's and tanner's, where cloth fresh from the weaver's was cleaned and thickened in solutions of alkaline ash obtained from combusted reeds; and where pigskins were steeped in baths of alum and gallnut, bated with dung, and tanned with oil. On the other side stood a striptease parlour. Two kinds of skin, each of a different stripe. Thus the servant, who showed them upstairs, explained amusedly.

Alex's room was small and bare with a window overlooking the central earthen courtyard, where a quartet of donkeys wandered aimlessly and from which a solitary date palm rose, its uppermost fronds shading part of the roof. A curtain of reeds, tied to one side with cord, hung in the window. Alex could carry his straw pallet up to the roof if he liked to sleep out under the stars. Many guests did, to enjoy the cool of the night; the rooms could get stuffy. Otherwise, his lodging contained a wooden chest with no lock, a pisspot – the toilet proper was downstairs, a platform over a pit, though with the luxury of a bitumen seat – and several small lamps of sesame oil standing on a shelf: shoe-shaped lamps with the wick sticking up through an eyelet hole on top. A handful of sulphur matches lay in a roughly hollowed-out stone.

The public rooms downstairs all had doors of reeds, but guests' doors were stout wood. The first thing Alex did when his door was shut was to take a good Greek knife from inside his tunic and cut a brick loose low down the dingiest wall. He prised the clay brick out, scraped a hole behind, and pushed the wrapped cassette inside. He replaced the brick, swept the scrapings into a little pile, then pissed in the pot, carefully soaked a nub of cloth and used hot urine to make mud to seal around his excavation. He felt quite proud of his guile. The result would pass casual scrutiny. He scuffed the rest of the evidence around the floor, and rubbed his hands clean.

He lay down on his pallet and slept.

At the evening meal downstairs he and Deborah encountered half a dozen fellow-guests. The meal was taken in a large chamber with spiral columns support-ing the weight of the floor above; though not entirely. A quarter of the dining room was open to a darkening though unthreatening sky.

Four of the other guests were traders from Upper Babylonia, due to tramp home next morning, leading their mokes. The traders conversed in Babylonian and mostly ignored the visitors. One other guest was a well-fleshed muscular black man who described him-self whimsically as a Nubian, though his Greek vowels spoke of Georgia or Alabama. The last guest was an Indian, from actual India, far fringe of Persian trade. This man, Gupta, spoke Greek thanks to Alexander's conquering armies. He and the Nubian, Nabu, had arrived in Babylon a week or so earlier.

Over supper Alex warmed to Nabu, though he dis-trusted skinny brown Gupta, whose eyes darted shift-ily, often in Deborah's direction. Gupta seemed to be at once evasive and snoopy, the sort of person who would sneak into your room while you were out – just by accident, of course! the wrong door! When animated (as he was later) his dark eyes shone, his neat white teeth flashed, and his tongue was a pink rose petal. Otherwise his features remained furtively anonymous, a mask of bland characterlessness. Yet all the while

42

he watched, and kept his ears cocked. Oddly, Deborah seemed to prefer him to the wholesome Nubian.

The meal consisted of unleavened bread, thick lentil soup dished out with a terracotta ladle, followed by tough roast mutton and lumpy turnip, with figs and yoghurt for afters. The guests ate with bone spoons and single-pronged bone forks, out of pottery bowls and from wooden platters. Two torches, of reeds dipped in bitumen, quickly burned all the moths they attracted through the open gap. A chorus of frogs croaked from a garden pool in some other house.

Serving at table was a middle-aged woman with peculiar habits. While they ate she shuffled around the circuit of the walls, halted, shuffled six paces onward, halted, all the while muttering to herself, 'Hummum, hummum, um-hum, um,' like someone engaged in a strange penance. Periodically she darted in to the diners to hover over them, inspecting, before returning to her previous station. Alex figured her for an obsessional neurotic, captive of innumerable phobias. She wore several amulets on strings around her neck: little clay figures of a goat, a dog, and a drum.

'Ah'm goin' to become a scribe,' confided Nabu, patting his belly affably. 'It's a fine life, a scribe's. Ah've seen 'em goin' about their lesser business, and ah bet there's lots of big important business too.'

Deborah looked derisive.

'Compiling the records of the city.' Alex gave an approving nod. Information was power.

'What kind of records?' asked Gupta quickly. 'How do you know there are any records?'

'Yes,' said Deborah. 'The only records might be the price of yesterday's cucumbers.'

'Brothers, sister,' said Nabu, 'we all know there have to be records of a different sort; though we don't speak of it. Otherwise, why are we all here?'

'Mum-mum, mum-mum,' muttered the serving woman. She darted closer. 'Mum!' she said emphatically, warningly.

Abruptly Gupta's hand snaked out. He caught the woman's robe, forcing her to bend.

'Ha ha!' he exclaimed. 'You sound hungry. Don't you get your dinner till we finish? Do you get the scraps?' With two fingers of his free hand, chopstick-style, he snatched up a small hard onion left in his soup bowl. Nimbly, two other fingers prised the woman's mouth open and in popped the onion. Then Gupta released her.

She scuttled directly to the nearest flambeau and spat the onion on to the heart of burning tarry rushes. Then she resumed her progress, silently. One of the Babylonians said something, pointed, and all four chortled.

'What you do that for, man?' cried Nabu.

Deborah looked alert, excited; and it was to her that Gupta said, 'I did it so that I could peep inside her mouth.'

'Are you a doctor?' asked Deborah.

'No. Though I could have been. That woman hasn't said a comprehensible word in my hearing in the last ten days. Now I know why.'

'How, if you aren't a doctor?'

'Anyone could see, respected lady, that her tongue has been torn out at the root!'

'What?'

'Ha ha. My little joke.' His eyes shone. 'I fooled you, did I not? You don't mind that. It doesn't offend you. It thrills you, yes?' He stuck his own tongue out of his mouth, arching it up towards his nose. The top of his tongue tickled the tip of his nose. Abruptly as a toad's or a chameleon's, his tongue withdrew.

'In my country,' said Gupta, 'we do many wonderful

44

things with our tongues. Some wise men divide, with a knife, the left and right side of the tongue. They stick their two tongues separately up their two nostrils and, deprived of oxygen, they meditate. Other wise men swallow their tongues for ten minutes. Yes, right down the throat! Then they disgorge. Of course, first you have to spend months and years stropping your tongue like the leather belt on which you sharpen a knife – so as to lengthen it. I'm not a doctor, splendid lady, but a magician. A magician needs to know a lot about the body. Sometimes he must hide things inside it and be able to retrieve them at will. I can hide a big pearl behind my eyeball. Sometimes a magician must bend and flex unbelievably. Yes, the wonders of the body! All its hidden secrets! Your own body is a wonder, graceful lady. Your neck is the upraised white gorge of a goose as it honks at heaven; your shoulders are its breasts. I could teach you to swallow all manner of long objects. Stiff snakes, steel blades, hollow bamboos all the way down to your belly.'

Deborah smirked.

Gupta switched his attention to Alex. 'Do you want something hidden, sir? Gupta can hide it for you.'

Alex felt himself flush.

'Anywhere at all!' Gupta clapped his hands; but summoned no sudden jewel or genie. 'I can hide it in full view of your face and you'll not notice. In fact,' (and he showed his hands, front and back, both bare), 'see, I've already hidden it.'

If Gupta had seemed shifty to begin with, now he was bold; as though earlier he had been busy furtively rearranging circumstances in the dining room by the power of glance alone, and now everything was to his satisfaction.

'What was it that I hid? Ah, that is the mystic secret.'

Alex said, 'I used to be a juggler. I juggled with knives. I tossed knives at targets representing people who were acting offensive.'

Nabu hastily intervened: 'Say, Gupta, can you give us a jugglin' show?'

But the Indian continued staring at Alex with a mixture of resentment, eccentric hilarity, and – yes – licence to do as he pleased.

'What is hidden? Where, and why? Gupta always knows the secrets. He looks,' (saying which he scanned Deborah) 'with eyes which see through walls, through reeds, through bricks. Through stones, through cloth, through skin.'

Had the Indian, by hideous chance, been in that same street when the donkeys bolted? Had he spied Alex pick up the packet; and remembered him? Or was mind-reading from facial tics and flushes another of his tricks?

Whichever, Alex decided he had better dig out the cassette from its hiding place as soon as the light was adequate next morning. He would keep it about his person till he found somewhere out in the city to hide it. A loose stone somewhere, a hole; maybe in the grounds of some temple.

'That's enough,' said Nabu. 'Just you quit teasing, upsetting these good folk. Just cut it out.'

'*I'm* not upset,' said Deborah.

'Of course you aren't,' agreed Gupta. 'And isn't your companion the clever one with knives, who knows how to *cut* things out?'

'Um-hum, MUM,' said the serving woman.

2

In which Alex makes holy love, and meets a hairdresser

A roar of anger woke Alex out of a confused dream. Oh yes, he had just pushed the plunger which primed the bomb which would blow up the whole world exactly an hour later. Why had he done so? It had something to do with a message which he either had or hadn't received. He felt nobly, coolly tragic to be the one who had to destroy so much hope and beauty and love. He heard Deborah call out, scrambled from his pallet, clutched a cloth about him and rushed from his room down the corridor in the direction of disputing voices. He was still half asleep.

Nabu's incensed voice boomed from an open door: 'Ah say it's disgustin'!'

'Not if it's his custom!' (Deborah's voice.)

'Why leave this door open? So everyone could see him?'

Alex hove to in the doorway. Nabu and Deborah were just inside, she seeming to restrain him. Gupta sat stark naked on the bare clay floor in the clear morning light, his legs loosely crossed. One hand was occupied down by his bum, the other hovered by his mouth. A little glossy black box lay open before him, and from it up to his lips snaked a thin strip of . . .

Gupta was busy feeding Alex's unravelled tape into his mouth, eating it! The other end of the tape emerged from his anus, teased out by twitches of his fingers. Brown-stained, fouled.

Alex staggered against the doorpost. Gupta had slunk into his room while he slept and stolen the cassette. Now he was . . . besmirching it.

The Indian nodded to Alex. 'Good morning! Have you lost something?' he enquired adenoidally, around the contents of his mouth.

Before Alex could betray himself, Nabu burst out, 'This here is hygiene, Indian-style! This is how you clean out your bowels! You spend all night swallowin' a cord of towelling – till you excrete it! Then you pull to and fro vigorously. You leave your door open so everyone can watch you. It makes me sick.'

Deborah started to giggle.

With a few rippling heaves of Gupta's Adam's apple and a slow pass of his hand, within moments the Indian was crumpling something like a tapeworm in his palm; and his mouth was empty. Swiftly Gupta wound the long thin worm around his fingers and tucked it neatly into the black box.

'Actually,' he said in a prim voice, 'it is a silk ribbon, nothing more.' He whisked his other hand from behind him. 'Here is a second ribbon. Both quite clean. Ha ha, my little joke! They were never joined together inside me. You saw them as one single ribbon, Nabu, because the other day I told you how some wise men in my country, who can control their inner motions, clean out their guts by swallowing a very long bit of towel and passing it right through them like the snake of Kundalini.'

Gupta adjusted his sitting position into a tighter lotus, hiding his genitals. 'Isn't it remarkable what you can see – when actually there is nothing to see? And conversely!'

Alex saw that the black box was lacquer, not plastic. The tape wasn't a tape. It was wider than a tape. It was, as Gupta had said, ribbon. He sighed his pent breath out.

A predatory brown bird with beady eyes, Gupta scried him. 'You saw something of intimate interest too, hmm, Alex?'

'I had a nightmare. I got a bit confused.'

'Dear me, and on your first night in Babylon!'

'Not a good omen,' said Deborah light-heartedly.

'No, dear lady, a dream is not an omen. People in Babylon pay scant attention to dreams, unless a professional interprets them. But then, the Babylonians are themselves a dream, are they not? I know how to interpret dreams, Alex. You have brought your nightmare to the right room.'

'If you interpret dreams,' said Alex harshly, 'do you interpret Babylon too?' Was Gupta a trained observer, masquerading as this sleazy fakir?

'Ah! Here we come to the nub. The intimate something which you thought you saw is perhaps connected with how this city is evaluated?' Gupta wound the other ribbon tight and placed it with its twin. Together, the two ribbons looked just like a couple of tape spools. 'Connected with how Babylon is understood, both from within and from without? Am I getting close?'

Or was Gupta an agent, not of the university, but of some other interested party? Some foreign government?

'Rubbish,' said Alex, answering both himself and Gupta too.

The Indian chuckled. 'Today you should visit the temple of Marduk. There you should pray for victory.'

'Pray?' Alex repeated in astonishment.

'Yes. Prayer is simply a means of fixing the mind. Marduk is god of war. You must pray for victory, over the fear that destroys.'

Yeah, *that* was the nightmare, all right. The whole world being destroyed. Alex remembered now.

With the cassette duly recovered from its hiding place in the wall — of course Gupta hadn't stolen it! — and with the slim packet now tucked into his loincloth under his tunic, Alex shared a breakfast of porridge with the others. Sparrows twittered and bounced along the wall-top fringing blue sky, hoping later to descend and peck bowls clean before the mad serving woman could hum the bowls away.

'Are you going to Marduk's temple?' Deborah asked Alex.

'No.' Yet the precincts of a temple were precisely where he had thought of hiding the tape. 'Yes. Maybe.'

'Let me be your guide,' offered Gupta. 'Yours too, fair lady.'

'We'll go alone,' said Alex.

Deborah cocked an eyebrow. '*We* will?'

If Deborah was with him, how could he hide the tape successfully? Damn the tape! This business was becoming obsessional. Witness his hallucination that Gupta had been eating the tape, performing an intestinal Indian rope trick with it. But until he had deposited the thing somewhere secret, he couldn't relax.

Had Gupta somehow *made* him see what he imagined he saw?

If Alex went on his own to the temple, Gupta would contrive to be Deborah's guide for the day; of that he felt sure. What might Deborah inadvertently reveal to Gupta about Alex's secret, and hers? About their mutual bond?

Courage, he thought. *Victory*.

'Sorry, Deb,' he said. 'I guess a guy has to pray

alone. Can we meet up afterwards? Take in lunch; see some sights? We could meet . . .' He had no idea where.

'At the main exit from the temple on to the river road,' Gupta suggested helpfully.

'Yes. There.' Alex rose.

'When?' asked Deborah; which was a good omen.

'Don't forget,' said Gupta, 'that much of the city takes a siesta in the early afternoon.'

Looking pointedly at Deborah, not Gupta, Alex named the hour of rendezvous.

Nabu rubbed a porridge smear from his lower lip and stood up too. 'I'll walk along with you, Alex.'

'No, don't bother. I'll find the temple.'

'Suit yourself, friend. Suit your own sweet self.' Offended, the sunbelt Nubian stomped off.

The route, described by the doorkeeper of the inn, was easy. Alex forged south through minor streets – of leather-workers and mat-makers, coppersmiths and confectioners – till he struck the main cross-thoroughfare, Marduk Street. This was a vast paved boulevard mainly lined with high windowless houses. As he strode along, with the sun at his back, the shining bulk of Babel Tower ahead seemed to tug at him once more as though the great spiral structure was indeed distorting the geometry of the city, building more space in its heart, just as the sides of a whirlpool open up extra surface space in the waters which the whirlpool perturbs.

The turbaned, stick-twirling Babylonians who were strolling along – upper-crust people for the most part – hardly gave Babel a glance, but it was almost with difficulty that Alex himself finally veered off south-wards along the Processional Way. This he followed until he reached the long approach road leading west to the temple of the god of victory.

51

Vaulted bazaars opened off either side, thronged hives of commerce where sacks of corn and sesame seeds, boxes of dried fish, bundles of reeds, skins and wool and cheeses were changing hands. Porters rushed to and fro, cursed by merchants and factors. Several auctions were simultaneously in full swing, in addition to the individual business of bargaining. So much complex bustle deterred Alex from wandering under the vaults and soon he arrived in the temple forecourt, hoping to find it less crowded than the precincts.

It did prove to be; though only by comparison and due to the sizable acreage of the forecourt, where numerous vendors were peddling incense and oil and bleating lambs, bowls of wine, rissoles, and amulets to the steady trickle of citizens who made their way through one or other of several gates in the walls surrounding the court. These walls, enamelled blue and yellow, were high, though distance eventually dwarfed them. Those were smooth, firm walls with no loose bricks, naked to public view.

The temple itself looked complicated, with potential nooks and crannies. Broad ramps sloped steeply upward, zigzagging and bisecting one another, circuiting the tower-tipped tiers of the dun-coloured edifice which was the colour of dried blood. Up these ramps climbed worshippers, while others descended. Could all these people really be intent on prayer? To a god of war? Or did they wish only to exercise themselves and admire the view from the summit?

Impelled by curiosity, Alex accosted one departing worshipper, bearded and turbaned, swinging an ornate ivory-handled walking stick.

'Excuse me, Sir. I'm a visitor. Do you really worship the god of war here?' (Or is it only to 'fix your mind' for the day?)

The man flushed angrily. 'Fool!' he snarled, and shoved Alex aside.

Another, older man heard this exchange. He approached, smiling in wry apology, and stood twiddling his own bull-headed, bronze-bound stick.

'Perhaps, Greek, it is purer to worship gods who don't exist?' he offered cryptically. 'Perhaps worshipping them *causes* them to exist? On the other hand, where else can you innocently worship war in these late days? Maybe these worshippers are simply searching for their own lost innocence – the innocence of the beast, which does not ask whether the sun will rise tomorrow. Or even whether tomorrow will exist.'

'Yes? Go on.'

The old man had a time-lined, dusty face, as though dirt had entered the many cracks and ingrained itself. Alex felt that he was looking at an aged version of himself.

Fondling the bronze bull in his hand, the man said, 'The beast knows nothing of tomorrow. Yesterday is already erased. All is now, the present, the moment. The moment repeats itself for ever.Thus the beast and his kind endure for a million years. In place of history they possess instinct. But perhaps, Greek, the gods of war destroy empires – with all their records and monuments – every so often, otherwise the weight of memory would cripple us beneath its burden? We wouldn't have the energy for new enterprises; which are really the same old enterprises, forgotten then rekindled.'

What was Alex to make of this? Was the old man a philosopher, a fantasist, a fool? Or a futurologist? Was he saying that the world, and civilization, had to be destroyed – so that the world could continue? That America must fall into decay so that the empire of Amazonia or Ashanti could arise? Surely he was forgetting about all the nuclear missiles poised in their silos, cradled in their submarines? Was it possible that society could simply collapse, and the missiles remain where they were, rusting, unfireable?

Alex didn't dare phrase such questions here, only a few hundred paces from Marduk's temple.

The old man executed a little skip around his walking stick.

'And perhaps, Greek,' he said, 'Marduk has nothing to do with war. Don't assume that you're wise, merely because you're a foreigner. What happens elsewhere is mirrored here. What happens here is mirrored elsewhere. You're here to discover Babylon. Babylon isn't here to discover you.'

He winked, and began to stride off in sprightly style.

'Thank you for your courtesy, sir!' Alex called after him.

'My pleasure. My whim.'

'How do you mean, "Babylon isn't here to discover me"?'

The man wagged a finger. 'You Greeks have a saying: Know Thyself. Explore thyself. You're quite wrong. Your own life has no purpose and no goal – though of course the world would be purposeless without any people in it. Accumulate information, my boy! Forget about generalities and principles! Compile the list of whatever happens to you – never try to sum that list up.'

Wagging his hand in farewell, the man went on his way, leaving Alex baffled. Maybe that had been his mischievous intention: to call Alex a fool at much greater length than the other man, and more circuitously.

On the subject of circuits, the zigzag ramps of the temple awaited. Alex still had to hide the tape, which might be packed with information, or might be blank.

* * *

He stood puffing at the summit of the temple. His heart beat fast, and the package still pressed against his bowels.

He had passed too many people on the way. One intersection of the ramps had been occupied by a great cage of tiny scampering monkeys with inquisitive bright eyes. A lower intersection had opened into the heart of the temple, ruddily lamplit and shadowy, where shapes of magi moved beneath looming fearsome statues and where linen curtains concealed musicians – he heard kettledrums beating softly, harps rippling like waterfalls, the whistling of an ocarina, entertainment for Marduk while the god's brazen nostrils inhaled the reek of charring flesh and blood. Within, the geometric temple was a cavern, its pillars resembling stalagmites. Hiding places abounded, but also places from which hidden figures could easily spy whatever he did. You would have to be a habitué to hide anything safely there.

So he rested at the summit for a while, taking in the view: the sprawling, walled suburbs over the water to the west where garden green glinted amidst houses; the bend of the Euphrates to the south, with the Borsippa canal forking off into farmland; the road to Nippur to the east.

Behind him a terracotta dragon – like those at the Ishtar Gate, but rampant – reared to half his height again, a spade gripped in one claw to support it. Spade and dragon: symbols of Marduk. Lower down the ramps he had passed terracotta statues of lions, too. A spiky lightning rod rose highest. He kept his back to the dragon, letting it block the view to the north where the Tower of Babel pulled at his mind.

Defeated, yet feeling that none the less he had scaled a peak, he descended the ramps again.

* * *

Emerging from the courtyard by the west gate, he soon found himself upon the river road a few hundred cubits south of the great stone bridge. People of many nationalities passed by, as though the port of the world was here. He saw Arabs, Armenians, Indians, fellow-Greeks (of course); even a Chinese face. He soon spotted Deborah leaning on the balustrade of the corniche, alone. Before he could reach her, to his exasperation Gupta appeared up steps from the quays below, grinning.

'Greetings, Alex! Did you find what you were seeking? Or did you lose it? Ha ha! Did you pray for guidance? If so, here I am.'

Alex realized that he had quite forgotten to pray. Well, that wasn't true. He never had any intention of praying; but maybe he ought to have done so . . .

'Hi, Alex,' said Deb.

'What's down below?' he asked her, making no effort to look over for himself. Big coracles were spinning inshore to tie up.

How the ungainly craft avoided dashing themselves against the piers of the bridge upstream was a puzzle, unless the answer was that the water obligingly funnelled them through. That was the only bridge over the Euphrates, and it was crowded with traffic passing between old city and new. From stout pier to stout pier stretched rows of planks. (Every night – as Alex later learned – the central sections were lifted and stacked ashore under guard. You did not build a bridge for your enemies to cross! Yet this was in the very heart of Babylon. Was the heart sick, divided against itself? Or was this a bridge between two hemispheres of the Babylonian brain; and every night when the city slept did it dream two separate dreams: the dream of the past, and the dream of the future?)

'What's down there, Deb?'

'Tunnels to the bazaars,' she told him. 'The crews unload, then break up their boats, and drive their donkeys through the tunnels. Tunnels are what's down there. And one weeping rabbi.'

'A who?' Now Alex did lean over the balustrade. Immediately he saw the bearded figure who was facing the wall, skullcap on his crown, prayer shawl around his shoulders, the black box of a phylactery fastened with ribbon to his forehead like a container for buttons, comfits, or pills; with his back to the boats and donkeys and baskets of fruit and skins of wine and crans of fish, with tears running down his cheeks.

'He comes here every morning,' said Gupta, 'to mourn the ruin of the temple of Solomon. Many more Jews camp out on the quay road on festival days. They want nothing to do with pagan rites.'

'That's crazy.'

'How is it crazy?'

'Why should people pretend to be Jews, or rabbis?'

'They *are* Jews,' said Deborah sharply. 'He *is* a rabbi.'

'Oh,' said Alex.

They lunched on fish cakes from a stall. While they were licking their fingers clean afterwards, Gupta said, 'Let's visit the Wonder Cabinet of Mankind.' He glanced at the high, hot sun. 'This afternoon, after siesta?' Indeed, traffic was already beginning to thin out. It was past noon. People were returning home.

'Shall we? I'd like to show you both the famous Wonder Cabinet. Though if I built a cabinet myself, ha ha, it would have different sorts of wonders in it!'

'Wonders which vanish before your very eyes. Like soap bubbles,' suggested Alex.

'Shall we?' pressed Gupta.

'Yes,' said Deborah.

* * *

They returned to Between The Skin Shops and sought their cool rooms.

During his siesta Alex dreamed: that the missiles had all flown, the bombs had all fallen. Russia and America were no more; Europe and China had been wiped off the map. Man-made plagues raged elsewhere. It was the collapse, the end of technological culture, of global governments.

Somehow Babylon survived. Here in the loneliest corner of the American desert – though there was no longer any 'America' – Babylon remained intact, entire. Untouched. And continued being Babylon.

It was as though all the power released by the warheads had torn a hole in the continuum of time and space; had scrambled the clock of the sun and the calendar of the moon; and had sucked this ancient city from out of a previous era to deposit it in the future, as the only future which remained.

Babylon thrived. The Euphrates flowed round and round. Seasons passed; then decades. Eventually the Babylonians began to colonize what was once America. They knew nothing, any longer, of the customs or speech of the dead America or of the dead twentieth century. They knew only Babylonian ways. Long hair and perfume; coracles and ziggurats; Ishtar and Marduk. Yes, Marduk had won a great, much-prayed-for victory.

But elsewhere, far away, was a new Assyrian wolf or a second Alexander marshalling his forces in Angola or Argentina, to collide with Babylon once more?

The Wonder Cabinet of Mankind occupied one corner of the backside of the royal palace. This was the first museum in the history of the world, opened to the general public by Nebuchadnezzar.

'Ha ha,' laughed Gupta, 'behold the wonders of the world!'

The long dim gallery with its spiral roof supports was full of antiquities; amongst which were clay tablets and cylinders, inscriptions from Ur, stone bowls and figurines of Aramaic weather gods, Kassite clubs, Mesopotamian statuary, foundation stones of antique temples, reliefs, stelae, Theban obelisks, mace-heads and cudgels, jewellery, breastplates, bric-à-brac. And so on, and on. The three were the only visitors.

'What marvels!' cried Gupta. It was hard to tell whether he was fascinated or sarcastic.

Perhaps the curator – a dour antiquity himself, armed with a feather duster – thought Gupta was pouring scorn. He trudged over, flicking at pots and ancient stones.

He addressed Deborah and Alex, ignoring the raucous Indian: 'Here is the whole span of time, Greeks.'

For a moment Alex believed him; for gone was the Rome of the Caesars, and the Rome of the popes. Gone was the crucifix; gone was the mosque. Gone, the Renaissance. Gone, the space age. They were *not*, as yet. So they had never been.

Deborah must have felt it deeply too.

'Isn't it strange?' she murmured. 'There's so much that isn't here.'

'Almost everything we ever thought important isn't here,' said Alex, glad that she had apparently stepped outside her role – under the influence not of the living city, but of dead stones.

'And yet,' she continued, 'this world's just as full, with all its own ancient history stretching way behind it.'

He tried to match himself to her mood. 'And the future – the culmination of the past – had hardly begun when this museum was opened. Had it, now?

What a fantasy that future seems! What a fever dream. Of men like gods flying through the sky and through space, and wielding bolts of lightning, and sending their thoughts and pictures from place to place in an instant. It's as though mythology lies ahead, not behind.'

'The *whole* span of time,' repeated the curator with emphasis.

Alex whispered to Deborah, 'Imagine that there's such a thing as a twentieth century. Then skip on, another thousand years. What a puny thing the twentieth century would seem. Because A hadn't happened yet. Or B, or Gamma – which is so goddamn important, so crucial to history that it changes everything absolutely. Visitors from the stars, immortality, I don't know what. Then a thousand years later A, B, and Gamma will have been totally dwarfed by Delta and Omega . . .'

She stared wildly around the Wonder Cabinet. 'To believe that this is the whole span! To know it in your very soul! Why, this frees us from time's water wheel. We shall swim with the flood of years instead of being drowned.'

'That's why we were sent to Babylon,' he said. 'Sent by a world which *isn't here*, and never has been.' *Give or take*, he thought, *a certain computer tape . . .*

'Now you see it, now you don't,' quipped Gupta.

'The whole span,' the curator intoned, as if those were the only words he knew; as though he were a guardian golem equipped with the simplest of responses – plus a feather duster.

'Sent to learn how not to drown.' Alex sighed.

Yes indeed: there were wonders here, though the wonder did not reside in the worn old clubs and obelisks, in the clay and bronze of this first museum – as opposed to, say, steam engines or Saturn rockets or computers. The wonder dawned when you entered a frame of mind in which such things as rockets, satellites, wrist computers and heart transplants were simply *equal* to cudgels and breastplates; when you saw the twentieth century through the other end of the telescope of time. *That* was to grasp the real, far future.

Alex thought to himself: we have built us an alien city, as if on Mars. We built it to alienate us from the big dipper of the present, which seemed about to fly apart. As soon as Babylon is no longer alien to us we can start to redeem the future. We can purge it of its threat. We can know it – not by Delphi methods or computer projections, world models or algorithms rooted in the present. Not by reason. But emotionally.

Then, too, he might begin to understand his own emotions. Particularly his emotions towards Deborah, whatever those might be.

'While we were asleep this afternoon,' he confided – thus joining his sleep to hers – 'I dreamt of war.'

'If you visit Marduk,' exclaimed Gupta brightly, 'what else do you expect?'

The magic moment was gone.

Deborah laughed giddily. 'That's enough junk for one afternoon. Let's get out of here.'

Gupta took her by the arm.

Outside, she was again a visiting Greek lady. She detached herself from Gupta, and walked on her own.

Next morning, despite summons by gong, Deborah did not present herself for her breakfast porridge. The four traders had departed with their donkeys the day before, and only one new guest had replaced them: a liverish, abrupt woman of indeterminate age who had parked a hand-barrow hutch of speckled hens in the courtyard.

She sat there in the dining room, pecking at her porridge with a spoon; Nabu was there too – though for all the conversation he made, he might well have swallowed his own tongue, Gupta fashion; and Gupta also, wreathed in vague smiles; and of course the humming serving woman patrolled.

Alex pushed his empty bowl aside. 'Deborah must have slept in. I'd better rouse her.'

'Aha,' said Gupta. 'She has gone. Off to the temple of Ishtar at dawn. Bright and early, rise and shine.'

'You're joking.'

'Certainly not. I was up and about too, doing my yogic exercises to remain sprightly.'

'At least you didn't hare off after her,' grunted Nabu. 'Give her a head start, eh?'

'Why should I pursue her? I am not a stranger to her, Nabu. I do not qualify for her favours this morning. Actually,' (and he leered at Alex) 'I dare say that she went so early so that she could experience sitting outside the temple a while. Few men hunt for a fuck in the early morning, unless already abed with a receptacle for their dawn erection. Ha ha, their own cockcrow! At a busier hour, I dare say a woman of her calibre would be snapped up speedily. Maybe it was modesty which sent her out early. Who knows?'

'Excuse me.' Alex left in haste.

Unfortunately, the Libil-hegalla canal interrupted his beeline towards Ishtar's temple. He arrived at a platform between two warehouses overlooking the wide, murky water; a cul-de-sac. Several coracles were being poled along: one laden with cabbages, another with chairs, a third with sheepskins. In both directions until the waterway bent out of sight the backs of buildings plunged down into it, some with loading bays. From the mouths of pipes in many walls brown stains drooled into the water – which did not, however, smell unwholesome, since the canal flowed along at a leisurely though perceptible rate.

He had forgotten about the canal. Now he recollected how he and Deborah had crossed it by a minor bridge to arrive at the street where their lodgings were. That bridge was out of sight – probably to the north – one way or the other, but which? How to reach it, rather than another dead end? These back streets might run at right angles for the most part; they were still a maze.

Frustrated, he retraced his steps quickly back to Sin Street, then hastened southwards to the junction with Marduk Street, which bridged the canal. Soon he plunged into the quarter – or rather the triangle with a curved hypotenuse – defined by Marduk Street, the canal, and the Processional Way.

He calmed down and walked more slowly. What precisely was he intending to do? Watch, like a voyeur? Toss a coin of his own into her lap? No, that was against custom. He already knew Deborah (though not carnally). Gupta had pointed that out, damn his tricks.

Interfere? Dissuade?

Ridiculous!

Why should he do anything? Why shouldn't he amuse himself instead by visiting the Greek Theatre or the Hanging Gardens? Or spend a whole day exploring the new city over the river? What business of his was it, anyway?

He continued walking on towards the Ishtar temple. A couple of times he sought to confirm his route by asking tradesmen. The first tradesman obliged, with a sly wink.

Later on, the second man he asked said frostily, 'There are strip shows in the Greek Theatre quarter.

Macedonians throng them. The girls are obliging. Wait till evening.' Obviously this particular pious citizen disapproved of the visitor's seeming – or unseemly – haste to avail himself of a famous delight of Babylon.

'I know there are!' barked Alex. 'Damn it, my inn's right next to one.'

'Perhaps you're too mean to pay a proper price? Do you think, stranger, you can buy with a copper what is more precious than gold? You can; but it shall do your soul no good! Maybe you're frightened of catching a disease which will make your urine burn and foam? Or is your urgency that of Priapus?'

Alex was on the point of protesting at these insults when it occurred to him that the man might want to goad him into an accusation, and a quarrel on the street – with who knew what results?

He simply said, 'I arranged to meet a friend there.'

Reluctantly the fellow conceded some directions. These turned out to be lies; by the time Alex realized, more time had gone by.

In a spacious courtyard shaded by cedars of Lebanon many reed mats were arranged in rows upon the soil, separated by gangways of straw.

Some thirty women sat waiting here and there, cross-legged or with their knees drawn up, the laps of their plain gowns forming for each a begging bowl. None of their faces was painted but each wore a band of plaited gold cord round her head. The temple building was a hall of glazed brick with high clerestory windows, resembling the nave of an early church; cloisters sprouted to one side.

Deborah wasn't among the waiting women. Alex could already see as much from the gateway, where two spearmen stood guard: one facing the courtyard, one with his back to it; both impassive. At this still early hour only a couple of men were treading the gangways, assessing the women who waited politely, patiently, never ogling or flashing smiles, neither dropping their gaze nor deploying it enticingly; so far as Alex could see from where he stood.

After a while one of the men shrugged, tossed down a coin, and said something. The woman before him rose. Together they headed for the temple hall, side by side. The other man completed his circuit – dubiously, by no means as eager as the sparrows which hopped anxiously about – and made his way towards the gate just as Alex finally strayed inside.

Encountering Alex, the man drawled in Greek, 'A homely dumpling. A horse. A mouse. A slut. An urchin. A grandmother. Someone who looks just like my sister. Acne. A pox of freckles. And three whom I already know! Oh dear. I wish there was a temple with boys. Last night my friend told me he had seen a girl just like a boy arrive as they were closing for the night. He was lying, japing me! Or else he meant that urchin. Maybe he did mean her. Her nose is runny. I'm sure I'd catch a rheum.'

The fellow reeked of patchouli. His eyes looked drugged, the pupils dilated. His hair was dandified, oiled and waved. His nose was somewhat crooked, as though it had once been broken. He was as smoothly clean-shaven as a woman; which made Alex conscious of his own two-day growth.

The soldier who faced inward began to pay attention. 'Here, you,' he said, or something equivalent in Babylonian.

Alex hastened to put a couple more paces between himself and the presumed pederast.

The man continued speaking Greek: 'What is it, my bold bullyboy?' He minced nearer to the soldier till finally he reached out a finger and softly tapped the spear point; then he ran his fingertip down the blade.

The soldier rapped out a string of Babylonian.

In mock alarm the fellow darted back, and clutched Alex's arm. 'My dear, he tells me I can't leave until I've chosen! Or else he'll tickle my ribs with that sharp tool of his.'

Alex shook himself free. He felt oppressed – not naïvely disgusted so much as threatened. On the other hand, here was someone who seemed able to play the system and get away with it.

Unless, in addition to all else, the fellow was an exhibitionist and a masochist; albeit a cautious masochist, perhaps, who came early to the temple when male visitors of more straightforward tastes were less likely to gang up on him.

Suddenly inspired, Alex said, 'You'd like to be sitting on one of those mats, wouldn't you?'

Whether this was accurate or not, the dandy growled quite venomously, 'Oh, my *dear*!' He swiftly recovered his composure. 'Heigh-ho, it'll have to be the urchin, then. I'm sure I'll sneeze in a rag for a fortnight.'

Back he went, to cast a coin and say something. The skinny figure who arose at his bidding hardly came up to his chest.

It occurred to Alex that presumably he also couldn't leave the courtyard till he had made a choice. So he walked around the gangways slowly, though his heart beat fast. What if Deborah emerged from the temple hall? What if she only just now *arrived* at the gateway? He felt nakedly exposed, which was ridiculous, considering his role and the women's – wasn't it?

Most of the women had put their hair up in tight buns, fastened by hairpins of silver or copper or plain bone – depending upon their social status, no doubt, otherwise it might have been hard to tell a high lady from an alewife, since they all wore simple gowns and no cosmetics. A few women had straw tangled in their hair, so these must have stayed overnight sleeping in the courtyard or the cloisters; or maybe these were women who had stayed for many nights and tired of performing a thoroughly scrupulous toilet.

Actually, the pederast's description had been quite slanderous.

Quite; not entirely. Here was the spotty dumpling. Here was the horse, angular and bony. However, the freckled redhead was a comely girl. And here was a young tanned bosomy blonde, though she was plump and greasy. And here, a handsome strong-looking Negress with skin of polished ebony over rippling muscles; she could probably bend iron bars, clutching them in her ivory teeth.

No, the pederast wouldn't have liked a strong woman. Or a bosomy one.

Surely this was a disgusting way to assess people? But did he not, at the same time, assess himself? Did he not assess the criteria by which he chose to judge – and thus discover those private criteria which under ordinary circumstances would never have such free rein to express themselves?

No, the pederast wouldn't have liked this one . . . Thus Alex shifted the blame, away from himself.

If the fellow was a boy-lover, why did he come to a woman's temple? Homosexuality couldn't be illegal in Babylon. Alexander the Great had loved men as well as women. 'Greek love' and all that . . .

Probably the pederast could have satisfied himself elsewhere, except that his tastes ran to the boyish rather than to actual young men. Perhaps he disliked the physical inconveniences involved (as Alex imagined them).

Alex felt increasingly confused, and tried to concentrate. Should he choose the 'obvious' tanned blonde? Or the horsy woman who was definitely ugly; though why should her body be ugly too? Lying with her might prove an alien, disconcerting experience for both of them. There was a certain deft familiarity about the joining of bodies accustomed to such manoeuvres; and Alex, while not particularly accustomed, was nevertheless not wholly unaccustomed. The ugly woman might be unused to lovemaking. Contrariwise, she might be far more sensual; whereas beauty might be frigid. She might be wiser in the ways of Babylon, if not in the arts of love. Ought he to seek the familiar? No.

He was glad Deborah wasn't here; though several more women were turning up now, and in their wake more men.

Why was he glad? Was he happy that her tryst had arranged itself quickly? Relieved that she hadn't seen him? Glad for whose sake?

He realized that this temple could teach people of themselves: of their mixed emotions, false chivalries, sanctimonious shams, egotisms, lusts and illusions – so that they could at last learn love, affection, joy? Ishtar's temple could expose and disorder your emotional routines as a way station to a future which must be grasped emotionally, before all else.

When he made his choice it was by accident. Out of the corner of his eye he caught a glimpse of Deborah emerging from the hall accompanied by a tall, robed, black-bearded man, wearing a beehive of a turban, who inclined his head and then walked off, swinging a walking stick.

Alex was at the end of a row of mats, standing before someone who might have been the pederast's 'mouse'. A little mouse with shortish brown hair and small, ordinary features; neither beautiful nor otherwise. She looked to be in her late teens.

Burrowing, he found the first coin to hand. Without inspecting it, he dropped it in her lap. 'You,' he said.

With a faint smile, she said, 'You must say, "In the name of the goddess".'

'In the name of the goddess.'

She rose smoothly, holding his coin, which proved to be silver.

Perhaps this was how a choice should be made at the temple of Ishtar, ideally. At random. Literally by the toss of a coin. With the value of the coin determined likewise.

Let Deborah — who was heading away across the courtyard — make what she would of his choice. If she noticed. She seemed preoccupied; perhaps she was taking pains not to stare at him.

As the mouse stepped ahead of Alex he noticed in her hair, short though it was, a golden pin.

Inside the temple, light filtered softly from the high clerestory windows. Private chambers resembling a row of confessionals occupied one side of the nave. Richly brocaded curtains were drawn across the few which were occupied — one, doubtless, by the pederast and his urchin. No noises penetrated the heavy curtains. In each of the open chambers he saw a couch, a ewer of water, a bowl, a towel. Wine and fruit; and a little oil lamp burning.

Alex's mouse led him down towards the altar. An old woman was sweeping the floor and whistling. Another old woman was replenishing with clean linen and fresh water the chamber which Deborah and her lover must just have used. Perhaps every woman who entered the temple became a priestess for a while; for at the unattended altar the mouse herself deposited the silver coin in a great golden bowl half full of other coins. A cauldron of sandalwood chips and incense smouldered beside it. She knelt and prayed briefly, whispering in Babylonian. What did she pray for? Gentleness on his part? Or that she would not become pregnant?

She led him to an open booth flanked by other open booths. They entered; Alex closed the curtains. Facing each other in the faint lamplight, they undressed. For a moment he imagined her at a high-school function; or in church, in Smalltown, USA. Instead, she was the whore of Babylon.

Her breasts were small but pointy. Her hips were narrow; her pubes were shaved, making her seem more naked and much younger. Her armpits were hairy, though.

Then he forgot about high schools and churches as their bodies met.

The meeting was fairly satisfactory. He entered her without much difficulty and came quickly inside her, then held her tight while his penis remained fiercely sensitive and moved only slightly, which she in turn seemed to find exciting. Gradually he built a rhythm again. He did not ejaculate a second time but she definitely reached a climax of her own, sighing instead of crying out.

Afterwards he stroked her hair and the golden pin. 'What did you pray for at the altar?' he asked.

'For you, Greek,' she replied. 'I prayed for you.'

Should he ask more questions? No . . . they had already exchanged, in a different way, sufficient information about one another. Soon she began to move in a manner suggesting that she wished to disentangle and leave. He rose. 'Some wine?'

She shook her head slightly. Shifting off the couch, she plunged her hand in the ewer several times, dabbed water on her sex and thighs and patted dry with the towel. She began to dress.

Alex, too. He took up his loincloth, quite forgetting how carefully he had taken it off and folded it so as to conceal the package within. The package flew out on to the floor at her feet. To his horror she swooped, picked it up, felt it.

'What's this, Greek? An amulet to protect your loins?'

'No, no.'

Her fingers danced slightly – hardly at all – and the cloth flopped open, exposing the plastic case.

Her eyes widened. 'Holy Ishtar!'

'Give me that! Don't look at it!'

'Don't look? One glance is enough.' She didn't hand it back. 'What a funny little wound-up scroll inside. Well, well.'

'A scroll. That's right. Of ribbon. It *is* a sort of amulet.'

Her nails tapped the plastic. 'Oh no it isn't. You know what it is, and I know what it is. There's nothing *right* about it, that's for sure.' She didn't shrink away or seem scared. 'How did you come by it?'

'I found it.'

'Where?'

'It fell off a donkey.'

She laughed with delight. 'Oh yes, it fell off a passing donkey – right into your private parts!'

'Something like that. I didn't know what to do with it. I was going to hide it somewhere. It must be important, to be here in Babylon. Who is it important to? And why?'

'Look, Greek . . . What is your name, anyway?'

'Alex.'

'How imperial. Mine's Thessany.' She stuck out a hand, though not the hand holding the tape. 'Hullo.'

How odd to shake hands shortly after copulating nakedly, bodies hand in glove.

'I don't suppose people often swop names here, Thessany?'

'I don't imagine they do. But everything has suddenly altered for us, hasn't it?'

'It needn't.'

'Oh, it must. And it has. You see, Alex, I'm by way of being a high-born lady.' She looked wryly amused, as though remembering other times, other places. 'That gives me certain expectations and ambitions. Lots of restless yearnings! I think I'll take a glass of wine, after all.'

Alex poured, into two goblets of dark-blue glass inlaid with white festoons. The wine tasted superior.

'I take it that your ladyship isn't married?'

'Not quite yet.'

'You will be?'

She nodded. 'I suppose I must. A married woman has more opportunities for intrigue.'

'But aren't there punishments?'

'For intrigue? Failure is the punishment.'

'No, I mean for having affairs.'

'Only if you poison your husband for love of another man, or chop him up. Otherwise, that's up to your husband. He can thrash you if he cares to; or dares to. Alternatively you can conduct an affair under Ishtar's roof and protection. Mentioning no names, but it *has* happened. That can prove costly. These old bags who do the tidying are real mnemonists. Try to pull the wool over Ishtar's eyes and you'll soon find that the goddess isn't satisfied with a single coin. It'll be five; and of gold.'

'That's a bit corrupt!'

'No it isn't, it's religious. Religions always gather money. Religions sell goods: salvation, forgiveness, blessings, victory. But who mentioned affairs? Not I, my dear Alex! I spoke of intrigue, which is often far more interesting. So it seems, to my comparatively unenlightened young flesh.'

Was that a reproach? Had he failed to satisfy? Maybe the satisfactions she sought were something else entirely.

I thought of her as Mouse, mused Alex. *How wrong can one be?*

'You'll soon be married,' he said, 'and so you came here first.' Yet she hadn't been a virgin; not as he understood virgins.

He didn't need to voice his query. She grinned. 'I had a kind of affair with a fellow when I was thirteen; I looked younger. The man in question was here today.'

'He took that urchin girl!'

'Probably he's still busy taking her. Yes, I had a precocious affair. Then other interests intervened. I came here to remind myself of past sensations, soon to be my lot again.'

'How was the reminder?'

'Okay. Quite acceptable.' She flexed her fingers. 'Frankly, it's better on my own; then my brain really schemes. But this way I can scheme other sorts of things.'

Alex forbore to comment on her assessment of him as lover. 'Didn't your other, um, lover run risks seducing a high-bred girl of thirteen?' he asked.

How ridiculous to call that perverted dandy a lover! Thessany's experiences with the pervert had undoubtedly been something quite other than a love affair.

'Risks? Risks are delicious.'

Thirteen . . . When Thessany was thirteen Babylon had only just opened its gates; or not long previously.

Presumably her parents had brought her here, to become instantly high-bred.

'Do you know who it is you'll marry?'

'A man. Never mind who.'

'And that man needs to ask permission from your father?'

'Naturally.'

'So who is Daddy? What's his status? Is he Inspector of Coracles – or President of the Perfume Guild? Costermonger to the Court of Alexander? Official Procurer of Pillows?'

Thessany sniggered. 'Let's return to the intrigue at hand. If we wish to discover the secret of this little scroll' (which she still held on to), 'we'll need to keep in touch, right? Where are you staying?'

'An inn called Between the Skin Shops.' He held out his hand for the cassette, but what she handed him instead was her empty goblet.

'If this little box fell out of your jockstrap in the street you could get into fearful trouble. Or supposing some official spy searched your room; or somebody might waylay you, pretending to be a robber. Possession of this scroll puts you in a vulnerable position, my Alex. Whereas *I* have plenty of places where I can hide things.'

'Why should a spy . . . ? Oh, I see. You're blackmailing me.'

'Do pour me some more wine, will you? You're uncouth. First you bed me; now you let me parch with thirst.'

He refilled her goblet, then his own, of which he drank deep.

'I ought to toss the wretched thing in a canal.'

'Oh no! That wouldn't do at all. You could be destroying Babylonian government property.'

'So you'll take charge of it, eh?'

Alex felt very reluctant to yield control of the tape. To his annoyance he realized that it had become a kind of idiot talisman for him. Other people wore mystic amulets of all sorts round their necks; he wore a cassette tape stuffed in his waistband. In a way the tape amounted to the same thing as an amulet. He couldn't read any information magnetically encoded on it; a computer tape couldn't be decoded for another two thousand years and more. That made it a magical object, which tied him mystically to that distant future twentieth century which he had abandoned either permanently or temporarily. The tape had become an irrational key to his personal time machine. He feared to surrender it – even while yearning to become a true Babylonian, which was another sort of surrender.

He squared up to Thessany: 'If you keep it, that puts *you* in a delicate position, not me! Surely you don't want me to have a hold over you?'

So far she had avoided telling him her father's name or occupation or address . . .

'Tush, does the worm turn? I think I shall entrust the object to my friend Moriel, for safekeeping and research.'

'Who's Moriel?'

'Why, the man I was speaking about a while ago.'

The pederast! Or paedophile, whatever he was.

'Him? He's *reliable?* He nearly collected a spear in his guts just recently. I want nothing to do with a type like that.'

'A type like that can be very trustworthy and useful. He doesn't wish certain irregularities in his conduct highlighted. Yes, he's ideal.'

'He seems the very acme of self-advertisement!'

'Oh, within limits. He's also rather good at self-preservation. Never oversteps the bounds. Not so far! He'll make an excellent go-between. He has all the right instincts, finely honed. He's a hairdresser, which gives him entrée to all kinds of circles. You'll find his salon in the inner city, junction of Esagila Street and Qasr Lane.' She drained her wine. 'Let's hasten, and await him in the courtyard. We'll find some quiet alley, to pass the package ever so discreetly.'

'I'd rather know how to get in touch with you directly.'

'No doubt. The essence of a good intrigue, however, is an impeccable go-between. Someone who can procure items of interest – rumour, scandal, secret news. Someone with naughty connections.'

'Maybe Moriel has already left.'

'I rather doubt that.'

When they intercepted Moriel, the hairdresser's behaviour no longer seemed so outrageous. His eyes looked less drugged. No doubt he had successfully discharged certain pent-up excesses.

They adjourned to a nearby alleyway littered with fresh turnip peelings. Thessany negotiated. The cassette, wrapped in its cloth, was exchanged. Thessany packed Alex off in one direction and herself went the opposite way, leaving Moriel lingering on the spot, brooding. Alex was thus prevented from doubling back to trail Thessany homeward, if homeward was where she was heading. He returned to the inn, wondering how soon he would see Deborah.

In the yard Gupta stood chatting with the landlord, a rotund, bald, squinty man called Kamberchanian, obviously Armenian. Kamberchanian also owned the neighbouring striptease parlour, and abominated the fulling and tanning business on the other side of his inn. It was his ambition to buy those premises and transform them dramatically into a costly furrier's, thus eradicating the smells of alkali, ash, alum, and dung which tended to invade both of his own premises when the wind was in the wrong direction. Such odd smells made some guests doubt the quality of cuisine at the inn, and had even put occasional customers off his girls. These discriminating patrons of the skin shop – the sort whom Kamberchanian forever hoped to attract – conceived strange fancies that there was some symbolic connection between the unveiling which the girls performed and the removal of flesh, fat, and hair from animal skins next door but one. A spectre of mortality haunted Kamberchanian's entertainments and their intimate aftermaths.

All this had emerged when mine host joined his guests for supper the previous evening in the hostelry.

A fanciful ambition, Kamberchanian's! Here was the wrong part of town for a costly furrier's.

Gupta made a beeline for Alex: 'Ah, I was just gleaning some business tips. Did you enjoy yourself?'

Alex only grunted.

'Do tell Uncle Gupta!'

'That's my own affair.'

'So are the charming Deborah's affairs her own. The moment she came back she packed up and left.'

'You aren't serious!'

'Never more so. Old Kamber was most distressed. A real loss of clientele. The lady had class. He planned to offer her lucrative employment. The dear chap does nurse fantasies of grandeur. No concept of reality – even though his hands are plunged in reality daily! Come to think of it, maybe that's why his girls stick with him loyally. He inspires affection. Confidence! That's why I was quizzing him about opportunities, even though I take whatever he says with a pinch of salt. Prosperity, like a full purse, is here today and gone tomorrow. Like beauty. Like innocence.'

'Where did she go to, Gupta?'

'I haven't the faintest idea.'

Alex felt chilled. 'You didn't make any effort to keep in touch?'

'That, Alex, is your little game; not mine.'

'I think you're lying.'

'Maybe I am; maybe I'm not. Now you see it . . . now it is all illusion.'

'I think you know very well where she went.'

'In general terms I do. She went somewhere else inside Babylon. No doubt we shall all bump into one another, tomorrow or in ten months' time.'

That man who bedded Deborah at the temple! Deborah and he had made an arrangement – who else could it be? – and she had gone to him.

Alex tried to call to mind an exact image of the man:

Mature, muscular, not stout. Tall, with a wavy black beard and a beehive turban. Expensively robed. The wood of his walking stick, which he had flourished with easy aplomb, had been inlaid with ivory in a spiral pattern . . . or was Alex confusing that with another fine walking stick he had spotted en route to the temple before that lying hostile tradesman misdirected him? The two memories melded inconveniently in his mind.

How could he trace Deborah's man?

Oh, that was easy. He couldn't himself. But Thessany would have noticed the man, particularly one so distinguished-looking. Most likely she already knew who he was. And how about Moriel? Maybe Moriel trimmed and waved the man's beard professionally?

Did he really wish to ask a favour of Moriel? One which would no doubt be faithfully reported back to Thessany? Did he want to give Thessany an extra hold over him? To present her with a hostage to fortune in the shape of Deborah?

But then he saw a way. Deborah knew about the scroll; the tape. Wasn't Alex forever dropping the damn thing? She might mention the enigma of the tape to the man with the beehive turban, who must be a fellow of consequence. Alex had to be sure who that man was, and whether Deborah had gone to him.

No need to mention that he harboured any special feelings for Deborah! She was a mere acquaintance, who had spotted the cassette by accident. But what a coup it would be to spin a web of intrigue around absconded Deborah, just as Thessany had spun one around him. Alex perceived that he ought to pick up tips from Thessany – as Gupta had from Kamberchanian – so as to triumph in Babylon, particularly in an affair of the heart. Which this was indubitably; a consuming affair. Always providing that he hid his true feelings from Thessany!

It might also be a smart idea to change his lodgings. Why should Thessany know where Alex lived, and not vice versa? If she could keep in touch with him through Moriel, why, so could he with her.

Alas! Deborah might tire of her Babylonian beau, or he of her. She might return to Between The Skin Shops. Alex had to stay put.

'What a lengthy meditation,' Gupta said. 'Now you've lost something else, namely Deborah.'

'Something else? What else did I ever lose?'

'You feared you'd lost something yesterday morning, eh? In the case of your lady friend, though, I can see you have a clue. You have let your *mind* search for her in the maze of Babylon. Yes, you've spied a thread leading through a labyrinth, a sticky silken thread such as cunning little spiders weave.'

This accurate sally inflamed Alex's suspicions. Thessany had hinted at the existence of official spies; and Gupta was dangling bait too assiduously. For a com-

79

parative newcomer the Indian was surprisingly adroit. He might have arrived at Kamberchanian's inn only a dozen days before, but did that prove him a total tenderfoot in the city?

Had Nabu actually come to Babylon in the same party as Gupta? It was worth asking the Nubian.

Another thought occurred: Deborah had seemed to enjoy the way Gupta carried on. Could she have said anything to him about Alex's tape? (To the extent that the tape was Alex's any longer!)

'Yet then, sir, that cunning little spider wraps the fly up in a package and drags it to her lair!'

No confiding in Gupta! Ten times no.

Alex said, in an offhand way, 'She might have left a note in my room.' This was a proposition which Gupta could hardly have the gall to contradict – even if he *had* been into Alex's room during his absence, even if he *had* noted how a brick had been prised out of the wall.

'I'll pop upstairs and see. You carry on milking Kamberchanian's brains.'

First Alex checked his room in case there was a note, which there wasn't; then he went along to Nabu's room.

Nabu was inside, stripped to his loincloth, performing press-ups.

'Okay if I come in?'

'Sure.' The Nubian jumped up and began towelling himself. 'I reckon I might become a wrestler rather than a scribe.'

Alex shut the door. 'Deborah has gone.'

'Sorry to hear it. She was one nice lady. I guess you and Gupta managed to piss her off.'

Alex shrugged. 'I'm sorry you thought I was brushing you off yesterday. I wasn't, honestly. Can I ask you something?'

'Can't stop you. So you just go ahead.'

'You and Gupta both checked in here on the same day.'

'Right.'

'Did you travel to Babylon together?'

'We did not.'

'You're sure?'

"Course I'm fucking sure. What of it?'

'I think Gupta might have been here for a long time already.'

'What, in this inn?'

'Of course not! In the city.'

'Doing what?'

'A bit of spying.'

Nabu went to the window and looked down into the yard. 'He's chatting up Mr Kamber right now. Is that what you mean by spying?'

'He said he's asking him for business tips.'

'So why's he asking Mr Kamber for business tips if he ain't a greenhorn? Man, you're paranoid.'

Alex smiled thinly. 'All survivalists are paranoid. This city's founded on paranoia.'

'What a load of bullshit.'

'No it isn't. Babylon's all about survival. Surviving in Babylon isn't a big naïve romp.'

'Like me, huh? Big and naïve?'

'What I mean is, you can get corrupted, trapped, destroyed. There'll be government spies.'

'Sent by whose government?'

'Babylon's. And from elsewhere. You know, like Greece and India and Carthage.' Alex grinned lopsidedly. 'Surviving could be a tough business.'

'Depends on your attitude, boy. Way you're headed right now, you'll end up in some alley with your skull cracked open. Take some friendly advice. Relax.'

'Relax? That's rich, from someone who just worked himself into a lather.'

'And who did I hurt in the process? Not a living soul.'

Alex said incoherently, 'Babylon's my skull. That's what I'll crack. This city's my skull.'

'Play skull-games by all means,' retorted Nabu, 'but leave me out of them.'

Coincidentally, Nabu checked out of the inn later that very day and Alex never saw him again, except perhaps once – in the distance, at Babylon Fair in the fields beyond the Adad Gate, when he noticed a black man oiled and nearly nude save for a *cache-sexe* and studded leather thongs on ankles and wrists. The Negro was limbering and primping and flexing muscles of black volcanic rock, like some darker, mobile, more plastic version of the diorite column on Palace Street on which were inscribed, in ten thousand cuneiform signs, the laws of Hammurabi, moral sanctions for a city which honoured their elegant phrasing more than it did their substance. (Yet in Babylon punishments could be savage and sudden, as Alex was subsequently to discover. Sometimes, too, justice consisted not in the enforcement but in the remission of harsh penalties.)

Only this one possible future sighting of the Nubian, outside a boxing or a wrestling booth. Alex had not ventured down the temporary avenue of hucksters, haruspices, prestidigitators, saltimbanques, and well-patronized mountebanks to investigate more closely.

In a nutshell – like some burly Hop-o'-my-Thumb floating away to be captured by fairies or by an enchanted frog family residing in the marshes, who appeared in human form only once a year, at the fair – Nabu vanished from his life that afternoon.

3

In which Alex is careless with his shekels, and becomes an omen

Days hastened by. Alex's unshaven jowls became more decently bearded. Wandering as the whim took him, he explored the whole of the Etemenanki district, then the new city over the water. Back in his home area he visited the Greek Theatre one afternoon and took in a performance of Euripides' *Andromeda*, once lost, now found again.

The braggings of Andromeda's mother about her daughter's loveliness had rubbed salt into sea-god Poseidon's soul, so he had unleashed a monster on the land. To buy Poseidon off, the maiden was chained to a cliff as a meal for the sea-dragon.

While the masked players down on the proscenium enacted this drama, Alex pondered its relevance to himself.

Was Deborah Andromeda? Was the man with the beehive turban Poseidon? Or was that man the monster?

Was Alex Perseus? Brave Perseus who rescued Andromeda (leaving his famous winged horse offstage)?

The mass of spectators on the circuits of stone seats were rowdily appreciative, as though they were at a boxing match. They ate and drank. They applauded and catcalled. Even when the chorus were dancing their most stately, graceful routines, these interludes were punctuated by whistles from the audience –

perhaps endorsing or deploring fine points of choreography? But they also hushed at tragic moments when certain solos were sung, to the accompaniment of a single flute; and one of Andromeda's solos burned itself into Alex's heart. (Later he bought a copy of the speech from a drama scribe.)

ANDROMEDA (*in chains*):
> Like the real Helen who never sailed to Troy
> So that men and ships followed a ghost
> And Priam's son loved a ghost in bed,
> A hallucination sent by gods to craze men,
> Or by one goddess to save that selfsame Helen
> From Paris's lust and from the blood debt
> Of all the foolish heroes, and the ruin
> Of great Troy for ever . . .
> I am sacrificed for a phantom too,
> The phantom of my father's pride,
> Which irked an even more potent phantom,
> Poseidon, figment of a sick imagination,
> My sire's. But my death will be real
> If the sea-dragon that ravages these shores
> Is real; if it is not a guise for pirates
> Who plunder, and can be bought off
> With a chained virgin's blood
> – Of pierced maidenhead!
> Who could rescue me from this cruel rock
> Unless he be a pirate too, of another stripe?
> For what are heroes but pirates by another name
> Who wage war on fate (or fatal circumstance)
> And pluck from time the mantle of distinction,
> Stealing from the gods the flame of immortality,
> Robbing even the grave of its boon, oblivion?
> Do not heroes seize the high ground of history
> There to erect their image, their phallus
> Of power to procreate not sons and daughters
> But a name, the name of hero
> Before which women must weep and pray?
> And yet my soul yearns for a hero
> – Just as, enchained, made vulnerable,
> I yearn also for a pirate to pluck me,

For then at least this will be over
When I will be a virgin prize no more.
And if the dragon-pirate and the hero
Could perhaps kill each other mutually
Leaving nearby for me to grasp
The hero's fallen blooded sword
And the pirate's sharp sea-serpent tooth
To saw my chains and shatter them
I could break free, escape, and be myself:
A priestess in some greensward temple
Close by a private fountain, where no
Intruder phantom god lurks and leers
To step out from the shade in shepherd's guise
Or rise from the depths disguised as a naiad
With budding breasts and tresses of gold,
Before revealing – himself. But I am torn
In my heart between the fear of ravage
– And the fear of rescue from ravage;
And the desire for both these fates
Which my father taught me long ago
And my mother too, conspiring with him
Every time she combed my hair out
And anointed me with fragrant oils.
I hear a growling on the shore, the clutch
Of claws – or are those boots and weapons
Of a man? I hear a sighing in the air,
A rushing fall, as if a horse could gallop
Through the clouds, its hooves beating
Blue-black bruises in their fleece
From which the raindrops fall
Which are the tears of heaven.
Who comes from the sea? Who comes
From the sky? A god? A man? A beast? A hero?
Or my own faint fears, shameful that they are,
The beating of my own heart in my breast,
The blood pounding in the bonds that hold me
Tight as a lover's embrace . . .

A few days before that performance of *Andromeda*
Alex had made his way to the junction of Esagila
Street and Qasr Lane, half fearing to find no hair
salon there; perhaps half hoping not to.

But sure enough, Moriel's premises were present in the shape of a substantial corner house. Archways, equipped with stout night shutters, opened upon a ground-floor barber shop and an adjacent beauty parlour. A sign, in Greek and cuneiform, announced: QUALITY PRIVATE ROOMS UPSTAIRS. BY APPOINTMENT.

Outside the barber's a tattooed slave with a sword through his belt was minding a snuffling grey mare hitched to a buggy-style chariot. Other clientele must have arrived on foot; a pair of bearded barbers and a couple of bearded coiffeurs were busily tending male and female heads in the adjoining salons. Clients sat on wooden thrones; the barbers and coiffeurs stood on low stools. The establishment was well stocked with bottles of oil and perfume, pots of unguents, ivory combs, copper tweezers, bronze scissors, manicure sets, mussel shells cradling rouge and kohl, razors, alum sticks, camel-hair brushes, basins, mirrors, curling tongs and little charcoal braziers to heat them.

Alex hung about outside while a barber put final touches to a fellow's waved, oiled crown. The man admired himself, then paid the barber and reclaimed his hickory walking stick from an urn. Alex nipped inside and ascended the vacant throne.

'Your pleasure, lord?'

'Er . . . a haircut.'

'A cut? Your hair isn't long, so how can I cut it?'

'Maybe I ought to have a shave.'

The barber sandpapered his palm against Alex's cheek. 'The opposite, I should have thought, lord! Though if a shaved style pleases you . . .'

'It pleases your master, Moriel. Actually, it was him I came to see. Could he attend to me?'

'He is busy, lord. He never plies his skills downstairs. One usually makes an appointment.'

'I believe he'll see me, if you'll kindly mention my name: Alex the Greek.'

'Did I not say he is otherwise occupied, Lord Alex?'

But just then, through a reed door, Moriel himself descended. He held the reeds well aside and bowed low several times, to usher a fine lady whose red hair was a high, coiling bonfire. She too bowed low to avoid mussing her coiffure in collision with the lintel. Escorted by Moriel she minced out to the buggy, where the slave handed her aboard.

As the proprietor returned, Alex leapt up. 'Excuse me, Moriel!'

'Oh, it's the regal namesake himself! What an honour; and so soon after we last met. By sheerest coincidence I have five teeny minutes to spare. Do come up.'

Moriel led the way upstairs and along a corridor to one particular airy room where gauze was stretched across the window for privacy, and as a fly net.

Mirrors and bowls, bottles, jars and combs abounded. The combs were all of silver here, the bowls of fine china. A small army of gold and silver hairgrips lay upon one shelf. On another shelf were bizarre constructions of copper wire, frameworks for future rococo coiffures. Murals decorated the plaster of three walls: plump harem odalisques bathed in marble fountains, reclined sybaritically on divans, titivated themselves amidst flowing drapery.

The client's throne up here was a softly cushioned one, the woodwork gilded.

'To what do I owe the pleasure? Far too soon, you know, to have solved our little puzzle – which calls for extreme discretion. And isn't it indiscreet to arrive here without warning during business hours?'

'Perhaps; but there's something you should know.'

And Alex expounded a version of events which

linked the 'little scroll' and Deborah and the man he had seen at the temple of Ishtar.

Moriel caressed his eunuch-smooth chin. 'Hmm. Interesting.'

'You probably saw that man. You were there too.'

'Ah no, I fancy not. I was distracted much of the time. A veil was drawn over me.'

'Think!'

Moriel recollected. 'How could I ever forget such an outstanding priestess of Ishtar as you describe? My fingers would have positively itched to do her hair for her . . . unless of course I was besotted at the time through inhaling some exotic powder.'

'Did you see her or not?'

'Alas. Incidentally, whom are you more concerned about: him, or her?'

'Both,' said Alex hastily, 'in case she tells him.'

'Ah yes, during pillow talk what secrets spill out! So I'm told; and so I know, from experience. You might suppose that those who share *my* pillow are too green and unripe to spill much; at least by way of tasty secrets. But ah, theirs are often the most delicious little cherry secrets. I love to pluck the first secret of all; and sometimes, to my astonishment, I open a juvenile snake pit where all manner of corrupt – and would-be so – fruits lurk, fermenting; to mix one's metaphors.'

'Do I have to listen to all this? If we only have five teeny minutes!'

'Oh, but you should. Perhaps Thessany is – was – one such snake pit; and perhaps, on the other hand, not . . . I have only the merest clues as to who the man you describe might have been. I shall pursue those clues assiduously. I find myself intrigued – as our mutual friend would say. Now, kindly be off with you. Await a message.'

* * *

When Alex returned to the inn from the theatre Hummum the serving woman handed him a letter: two hinged beeswaxed boards sealed with a blob of wax which was stamped with what he took at first to be a tiny picture of ram's horns. Or cuckold's.

'Who delivered this?'

'Mum-um! UM!' responded Hummum vigorously.

On closer inspection he concluded that the seal imprint was a stylized head of hair. Hastily he returned to his room, broke the seal, opened the boards. The message, scribed in Greek capitals, ran as follows:

DEAR BOY!

I SHALL NEED TO PAY SOME BRIBES TO SECURE INFORMATION. CREDITORS BOTHER ME, FOR PERFUMES AND COSTLY UNGUENTS RENDERED, TILL MY NOBLEST CUSTOMERS SETTLE THEIR ACCOUNTS. SUCH IS THE WAY OF THE NOBLE, ALAS! MY BARBERS DEMAND THEIR SALARIES, NONE THE LESS. I ALSO NEED TO PAY AN OUTRAGEOUS FINE ON ACCOUNT OF A TRUMPED-UP CHARGE. OUR MUTUAL FRIEND IS AWAY FROM TOWN VISITING HER AUNT'S LANDS AT BORSIPPA. SHE WILL SURELY REIMBURSE YOU, SINCE OUR MUTUAL INTERESTS ARE INVOLVED. A MESSENGER WILL CALL AT BREAKFAST TIME TOMORROW. HE MAY BRING NEWS ABOUT THE OTHER MATTER. GIVE HIM SEVEN SILVER SHEKELS.

YOUR FRIEND, M.

Which 'other matter' did Moriel mean? The cassette? Or Deborah? Which? It was unclear.

Seven silver shekels. Alex had arrived in Babylon with twenty shekels in his purse. Twenty shekels was the cost of a cheap, decrepit slave; so he'd heard. (A strong, young, handsome slave could cost ninety.) The poorest-paid labourer earned ten shekels a year. Already Alex had spent a couple of shekels, and given one to Thessany at the temple. Presumably he owed Kamberchanian a shekel or more for lodgings. If he paid Moriel seven more ... Momentarily the cold hollow clutch of impending poverty gripped his guts.

Was he being diddled? He had already parted with the 'little scroll'. He decided not to hand over any money.

Next morning he gobbled his porridge quickly, then loitered in the courtyard pretending to admire the lone date palm, on which perched a couple of pigeons. A scraggy black cat admired the pigeons, too, from its hiding place behind a wooden water-butt. Hoping that the birds might descend into its jaws, it darted aggrieved glances at Alex.

A boy hesitated in the entrance; headed for Alex. He was barefoot, and otherwise bare apart from a brief raggy kilt. Ten or eleven years old, black-mop-headed, cooked brown by the sun and basted with dirt streaks as though he had been rolling sweatily in dust.

'You're from Moriel?'

The boy nodded.

'You have some news for me?'

Another nod.

'So tell me.'

'Master Moriel said you must first give me some money.' The boy skipped back a pace as though he suspected that Alex, hearing this, might grab him by the arm.

Alex shrugged. 'First tell me the news.'

'Master Moriel said: when you give me the money, that will prove who you are. He told me how much. You pay me, and we will see if it is the same sum. Otherwise you might be anybody.'

'The landlord can easily assure you who I am. Shall I summon him?'

The boy shook his head. 'Master Kamberchanian is well known for his fantasies, sir.'

One of the pigeons flapped down. The cat wriggled a while, then made an abortive rush. The bird clattered aloft unscathed, and shat from on high.

'I have to hurry back,' said the boy. 'I *do* have important news, which might soon be too late. But who is it for?'

'It's for *me*.' Alex began to sidle around in the hope of blocking the boy's exit; the boy glanced behind him and retreated.

'This news will not wait, sir.'

'Seven silver shekels. That was how much.'

'But where are they? I don't see seven shekels.'

Exasperated, Alex counted out the money, which the boy accepted with cautious, outstretched palm. As soon as he had all seven coins they vanished up and under his kilt.

'You must hasten, sir, to the Festival Temple outside the north wall. There you will see the Greek woman and find out who the man is. The matter of the scroll is being pursued. Seven shekels will unlock a secret door. That's all.' And before Alex could question him, the boy fled.

'Wait!'

From the doorway to the dining room Gupta eyed Alex with interest. He clapped his hands. 'You have made a boy disappear! Taking your money with him. That's a good trick.'

'Now I'm disappearing too.' Alex headed for the entrance, but then slowed his steps. The doorkeeper had gone off somewhere. Time was of the essence; and what was the quickest route? Much as he loathed to involve the Indian in this affair, Gupta would probably tell him the truth; whereas casual strangers might misdirect!

'Gupta! I'm not inviting you to accompany me, do you understand?'

'Impeccably, sahib.'

'Can you tell me the quickest way to the Festival Temple? Please?'

'Easy. Cut along Sin Street all the way. Pass through Sin Gate. A bridge crosses the moat. A road leads north-west to the temple. You can't miss it.'

Nodding his thanks, Alex hurried off.

Sin, of course, was the moon-god; just as Shamash was the sun, and Ishtar, Venus. Sin was supposedly a wise old man with a lapis lazuli beard who wore an enormous turban. Sin also measured time, and since time maps out history Sin was a repository of wisdom whom other gods consulted once a month when Sin was at his brightest. The moon-god was also the enemy of night-time criminality.

As Alex hastened northwards along the street he noted signs of other sins. Early though it was, several fellows squatted or wandered vacantly, looking drugged. Was hereabouts where Moriel obtained illicit pharmaceutical exotica such as aphrodisiacs? Nor was Kamberchanian's the only striptease parlour in the vicinity. Yet might it not be that such establishments were located here under the aegis of Sin's watchful moon-eye as a way of emphasizing that in Babylon there was nothing evil about them whatsoever?

At Sin Gate a spear-toting guard halted Alex.

'Where are you going, Greek?'

'Just to the Festival Temple.'

'You aren't a citizen.'

'No, not yet.'

'Quarter of a shekel exit tax.'

Angrily Alex paid over the bronze coin. The guard produced a waxed tablet from a leather pocket.

'Name? Date of entry? Address of lodgings?'

Fretting, Alex told him. Curling one arm round his

spear for balance, the guard painstakingly inscribed the information in the wax with a bronze nib.

'Can I go through? I'm in a hurry, man.'

'Wait.' The guard inscribed a copy below, then snapped the tablet in half. He handed the lower part to Alex. 'Present this on your return. Don't lose it or you'll have to pay tax again.'

'Great. Thanks.' Alex sped through the gate, which was decorated with green rosettes and white sickle moons bobbing like boats on wavy blue water.

Sin Bridge led to a Y-fork of dusty roads, both stretching away through patchwork fields of vegetables. The temple was obvious a quarter of a mile down the left-hand road: a ziggurat glazed green like a great artichoke. A small crowd bustled about the entrance, where several chariots were parked.

Even as Alex set out from the bridge people were boarding the vehicles, horses were being unhitched. A chariot departed in the direction of the citadel further west; occupants of other chariots still conversed. He started to run.

Deborah was sitting in a chariot waiting to be pulled by a black stallion. She wore a white sari and was intent on her companion: the man with the giant turban. That grandee's robes were sumptuous, glittering with gold thread.

Alex slowed from a sprint. The meeting had to seem spontaneous. He could hardly race up screaming Deborah's name. But now the grandee gathered his reins. Presumably the stallion would canter off, too, towards the Ishtar Gate. To cut on to the westerly route Alex left the road and waded hastily through rows of cabbages. Reins slapped rump; the chariot started to roll.

He was still short of intercepting when the stallion trotted by. He raised a hand in salute, assuming a look of surprise and pleasure; or so he hoped.

Deborah spotted Alex and favoured him with a smile and a vague wave. She didn't ask her escort to halt the chariot.

The hell with that! The chariot wasn't exactly racing along. Alex gained the road and jogged behind, hoping to convey an impression of voluntary exercise. He let the vehicle pull well ahead. Deborah glanced back once. As soon as the chariot passed out of sight through the gap between outer wall and citadel, he hared forward.

Reaching that gap, he could see the chariot already crossing the bridge before the Ishtar Gate. A guard blocked his way. Hastily Alex thrust the half-tablet at the man.

'Hang on, Greek! This here's a Sin Gate receipt.'

'So?'

'You have to return by the same gate.'

'I'll pay again!' Alex scrabbled in his purse for another quarter-shekel, which he thrust at the guard.

'Oh Shamash! Now I need to write another tablet.'

The chariot had passed through the gate. At this rate there'd be no hope of catching up. Alex thought of racing off; imagined a spear in his back; despaired.

'Forget it! I'll go back by Sin Gate.' He reached for his coin, which had vanished deep in the guard's clenched paw.

'You've already paid me.' The soldier was enjoying himself now.

'I've changed my mind.'

'People like you make our jobs a misery.'

'Is this how you treat foreign guests? The money doesn't go to you. Why should *you* care?'

The guard whistled to himself out of tune.

'Oh, I see. There's a rake-off.'

'Goes to the upkeep of the gate. To the splendour of Ishtar, Greek!'

'Where do you spend it? In her temple? Or up on Sin Street?'

Reluctantly the guard disgorged the coin from between the lips of his fingers. 'I'll remember you.'

Alex snatched his money and headed back in the direction of the temple. The previous members of the crowd who had no chariots were now returning city-wards afoot. He passed several whose looks he didn't care for before encountering a likely pair: one big and fat, the other small and skinny. Bearded Laurel and bearded Hardy, kilted and bare to the waist. The Mesopotamian – or hippopotamian – Hardy's breasts wobbled as he walked.

'Excuse me, sirs; please favour me with an answer?'

'A pleasure,' puffed Hardy, who looked relieved to halt.

'Can you tell me what was happening just now at that temple?'

'I can, and I will. This year's it's Sin's turn to give a bride to Marduk for the sacred marriage. Sin's priest Shazar and the bride-to-be were sacrificing on neutral ground. Entrails were being divined, and other omens. Oil on water. Drift of smoke.'

'All excellent,' said Laurel tersely.

'Was Sin's priest the man with the giant turban?'

A nod.

'The woman in white was the bride-to-be?'

'Just so.'

'What a bride!' exclaimed Hardy. 'She will justly be hailed the most beauteous woman in all of Babylon. She'll deserve all her honours and gifts. For a whole year she'll be the radiant symbol of our city: the belle of Babylon – and quite right too.'

Rather like winning a Miss World contest, thought Alex . . .

Ollie Hardy slapped his belly so that it danced. 'For

twelve months she warms the god's bed with her loveliness – though vulgar eyes drink in the fullness of that naked beauty only once, at the climax of her wedding. That'll be something for sore eyes and empty bellies: Belle and Shazar's feast! Should you be so lucky as to be invited. As to when: in one month's time. This particular bride isn't yet Babylonian, though all the omens say she will be. Since King Alexander's coming we find nothing amiss in a new-comer as the bride of Marduk; but first she has to be initiated in our ways, in Babel.'

Deborah, the bride of Marduk? First she had gone to the temple of Ishtar; now somehow she had found a way to give herself to the whole city . . . in what was apparently a most profitable transaction. She was going to marry the very *power* of the city – as far as the state religion went – and she knew about the tape.

'What happens when her year's up?' he asked.

'Off to the Underworld with her,' said Stan Laurel.

'Unless,' Ollie corrected him, 'she is with child by the god. In which case she remains till she gives birth; then away with her. Her child grows up to be a priest or priestess.'

'And when did that last happen?' demanded Stan. 'Not with the last five brides.'

'Maybe Marduk doesn't want a brat from a wife he owes to some rival god. Maybe he consults the moon to know when not to lie with his love.'

'Maybe.'

'Maybe he finds twelve months with the same wife quite enough.'

'Maybe.'

'Hey, you aren't suggesting the bride gets *murdered* at the end of a year?'

'That would be sacrifice,' said Stan, 'not murder.'

'Well, sacrificed?'

'Certainly not in public,' said Ollie. 'She simply goes. Down to the Underworld. The lady vanishes. Expires with joy. A new bride; and the city is renewed. Good day, Greek.' And off he waddled, with his Stan.

Alex trudged back towards Sin Gate, cutting across the fields, thinking furiously.

Why had Moriel sent him on this wild-goose chase instead of simply telling him the facts? Why send him too late? Was it all done to tease him? So that an actual sighting of Deborah would fuel his obsession?

Was Deborah's life in danger in a year's time? Surely she knew the rules of the game? Maybe she didn't.

If only Alex could rescue Deborah, as Perseus rescued Andromeda. If only he had a winged horse to ride upon. A cassette tape (conceivably blank, in somebody else's possession) did not make a very adequate substitute.

Be damned to what the hairdresser had said about arriving at his salon uninvited! Alex decided to go there right away to remonstrate and demand some answers.

The guard on Sin Gate admitted Alex back into Babylon without any further nuisances arising. He soon left Sin Street and veered through the busy minor streets of the Ninnah district, aiming for the inner city.

On the way he passed an oil presser's, a brewery, a slaughterhouse, then a brick-works set amidst stacks of finished bricks, mounds of rubble, and a sludge-hill of mud. Dirty smoke ascended from the sky-maws of the kilns. His journey was by turns slippery, heady, bloody, sooty and dusty, then slippery once more. It occurred to him that he must be close to Prosperity

Canal, the Libil-hegalla. Sure enough he soon sighted water and laden coracles, and not long after reached the same bridge on the Processional Way where he had paused an apparent age ago, numbed by the sight of Babel. He crossed the Way and entered the inner city. Soon he arrived at Moriel's corner.

Opposite the salon was a seal-cutter's shop, its counter displaying blanks of rock crystal and chalcedony. Alex lurked outside this shop for fifteen minutes, observing the salon. A dandy gent arrived; a dandy lady left.

Then who should drive up, chauffeured in a buggy-chariot, but Thessany! Thessany, who was away visiting her aunt at Borsippa. Alex dashed across Esagila Street.

'Hey!'

'Oh, it's you.' Pink and mauve face-paint hid any blushes. 'Say nothing here.'

'I'll say one thing. You're supposed to be at Borsippa.'

'Am I? In that case I must have come back early. Let's go upstairs and talk. I'm rather glad to see you.'

'Really?'

The chauffeur was burly, russet-bearded and bare-chested (apart from a hirsute red tangle). He wasn't tattooed, nor was his scalp cropped of kinky red hair, so he must be an independent paid servant. Maybe Thessany's father was aware of her delinquent whims and wouldn't let her have a slave, who could presumably be ordered to obey any weird commands. Leaving the servant in charge of horse and vehicle, Thessany shooed Alex indoors and upstairs.

'Mori!' she called. The hairdresser poked his head out through a reed door, registering Alex's presence as one might greet a slice of lemon in the mouth. 'Use the blue room,' he said, and ducked back. Thessany led Alex along to a chamber walled with mirrors and turquoise tiles and equipped for hairdressing. She skipped to occupy the throne-chair and gestured Alex to bring the footstool round in front. Alex preferred to stand.

'What an intrigue this could be!' she enthused. 'The bride-to-be of Marduk is involved.'

'So I've discovered, at needless cost to my feet and purse.'

'You've brought sheer delight into my life, Alex the Greek.'

'One thing I didn't discover is what happens to a bride when her year is up.'

'Who knows?' she said airily. 'I wonder what would happen if that little scroll of ours was found in the possession of the god's fiancée?'

'That sounds dangerous.'

'Danger, the piquant sauce! I'm a bride-to-be as well.' She mused.

He seized a silver comb and ripped at his hair with it. At least he could untangle something.

'What would happen? Speculate!'

'The fiancée would protest her innocence,' he said. 'She would swear the thing had been planted.'

'Ah, by whom? By whom but you? You with your jealous lustful motive, which was so transparent to dear, perceptive Mori. Yet how would she know your identity if she didn't already know all about the scroll, and had kept silent? Unwisely! You and her, you and her, both unwisely. I *think* that King Alexander's men don't usually have recourse to torture. They prefer to cross-examine using Aristotle's syllogisms rather than fire and rope and water and ingenious mechanical devices. But as to Marduk's men . . . well, this is an oriental city, of refinement. I have heard tales.'

Alex said cautiously, 'You wouldn't want to place *yourself* in the way of torture.'

'Perhaps my social position guards me.'

'I'm sure that dear, exquisite Moriel isn't equally protected. He was fined heavily the other day. Or so he said.'

'Or so he said,' she echoed, amused.

'You aren't seriously suggesting sabotaging the marriage of Marduk?'

Her eyes opened innocently wide. 'But that is precisely your true desire, Alex. To disrupt this marriage. To make it not take place. Correct me if I'm wrong.'

Alex swallowed. 'That would disrupt the renewal of the city; damage prosperity.'

'Oh what a loyal true patriot you are, suddenly. Admirable!'

'By the way, Moriel said you would reimburse me seven shekels I had to send him to grease our investigation. Can I have the money, please?'

'I don't carry cash. Bills are sent to my home.'

'Maybe I'd better call there.'

She laughed joyously. 'You are beautiful.'

Little more of substance occurred, except that Thessany promised to call personally at Between The Skin Shops three days later, of an afternoon, to report progress following the bribe. Moriel himself kept out of the way apart from darting in to rebuke Alex, then straight out again – after which a seemingly repentant Thessany made her promise, with which Alex had to be satisfied, and depart.

Three days. Teased and tormented, Alex wandered hither and thither. At times he felt possessed by Thessany and Moriel, by the unknown Shazar, by the fate of Deborah, by the intrigue. At other times he felt lost and adrift. He took all meals at the inn on credit, the better to harbour his resources; though his eventual bill was running up invisibly. Gupta observed his comings and goings with beady interest.

One afternoon, in the Etemenanki district, he happened upon a small marketplace. Stalls were vending linseed and sesame oil, pistachios and almonds, cumin and coriander, garlic and onions. In the midst of the little piazza an ashen man lay on a reed mat with a pillow under his head.

As Alex passed by, the man croaked, 'Halt!' He did not stick up his skinny hand for alms.

'Why?' asked Alex.

The man started to speak but instead coughed violently, which brought unwelcome temporary colour to his face. 'You must ask me what is the matter,' he sighed.

'Too true,' agreed a fat woman who was in charge of strings of onions. 'That's the law.'

'Okay. What's the matter?'

'A terrible pain, about here.' The man touched his upper chest. 'It comes and goes. It's as if I breathed in a nest of asps which sting when they're disturbed. It's worst in the early morning.'

'Have *you* been sick like that?' the fat woman demanded. 'If so, what remedies did you take?'

Alex bowed his head. This was abominable. The man was seriously ill, and here he was lying in the street asking for diagnosis and therapy from any passing stranger. Unless he was only pretending to be ill . . .

'I can't help you. I'm sorry.'

The onion woman advanced on Alex. 'Me sister-in-law got completely cured in her bowels when a Greek fellow like you told her what to take – here, on this very spot! You Greeks are hot on medicine, aren't you? Asclepius and all that?'

'I'm not a physician. Maybe that other fellow was.'

'The people are their own physicians.' The woman shrugged. 'Very well. Pass by.'

Pass by? Maybe Alex ought to sit down here in this marketplace and declare himself ill? Of heartache, turmoil, divisions within – a kind of emotional cancer as so ably diagnosed by Euripides, first dramatist of the divided heart.

Yet perversely he found himself almost relishing the prospect of a further turn of whichever screw.

That evening, which was the evening before Thessany's promised visit, Gupta remarked to Alex over dinner, 'You're looking peaky. You need perking up.' Just as though the dining room was the marketplace and Gupta was the passer-by.

'What do you prescribe?'

'I suggest a visit to a strip show.'

'What, Kamberchanian's?'

'No, no. I've heard of a much more interesting parlour. It's quite close. It specializes in, ha ha, metaphysical striptease.'

'As opposed to plain physical striptease? Do you have to *pretend* they take their clothes off?'

'The ladies' garments are shed. But their act strips the audience – to their souls. You'll see.'

'Okay, I'll see.'

So Peaky and Perky set out, with a lantern apiece, to search for enlightenment down the dark rustly streets where cats and rats were abroad scavenging the fish-heads and other offal of the day.

Lanterns outside the parlour illuminated the sign of a dancing woman shedding veils. A couple of tipsy Macedonian soldiers stumbled through the open doorway on the heels of other shady figures.

'Here we are: the House of the Veil.'

'From the sublime to the ridiculous,' said Alex.

'Sublime?'

'Not long ago I saw one of Euripides' finest tragedies.'

'Regard this as the satyr play, the caper that caps a tragedy trio. Or would do so, if modern audiences weren't so bloody lazy.'

'I didn't know Indians were experts on Greek drama.'

'Why not? King Alexander brought us many things. Take the howdah, for instance – the castle on the elephant. Alexander invented it.'

'Personally?'

'Remarkable man. Pity he's dying.'

The king had been dying for the past five years. He must be a waxwork, a dummy.

They parted with a quarter-shekel apiece to the doorkeeper, with whom they left their lanterns, and followed the soldiers to a large chamber within. A raised wooden stage, which was lamplit, was hung with an assortment of curtains dangling apparently at random. In front of the stage a female flautist sat on a stool, tootling to entertain the crowd who jostled in the rest of the room, in comparative darkness. The air was heady with incense smoke drifting from clay pots on either side of the stage.

After a while a buxom, dark-gowned woman with her hair in braids bustled onstage.

'Good evening, gentlemen and gentlemen! Staunch fellows of mature experience, and beardless striplings alike! Not to mention any dissembling lady, wearing man's attire, who appreciates the female body!'

One of the soldiers burst out laughing raucously.

The stage-madam's voice changed key to low and sombre, accompanied downward by the flute, which accomplished some unusually deep bass notes.

'Tonight my girls will dance the Dance of Death, the Descent into Hell, where all is stripped away.'

'Good!' shouted the other soldier.

'Afterwards, who knows what?'

'We do!' the soldiers chorused.

The madam withdrew; the performance commenced. A completely naked black girl of fifteen or sixteen stepped crouchingly from behind a curtain. The flute wailed like a newborn infant. Nimbly the girl began to prance about, plucking lacy black garments from behind different curtains and donning them. Expecting events in the reverse order – from dressed to nude – the surprised audience had neither cheered nor whistled. Soon black lace was dense upon the girl. By arching her feet while she danced she seemed to grow taller, to maturity. Upon her head, at last, she poised a sparkling crown.

A second naked girl leapt forth. She was white-skinned but her skin was cunningly painted with black bones so that she seemed to be merely a dancing skeleton. Her motions were awkward and angular, disjointed, yet she pursued the black girl around the stage, stripping first her crown, then each of her garments from her. With each theft, the black girl escaped more slowly. Tears – or sweat – ran down the victim's face – out of her hair – solidifying, puckering into grooves and wrinkles, just like wax hardening: and as each lace veil was pulled away and as more of the black girl's skin became visible, she no longer seemed young at all. She was as wizened as a dried-up prune. When her last garment was stolen away she was an old woman who hobbled slowly, tired and bent with withered dugs. As the skeleton-dancer seized and drew her captive behind a heavy curtain, the flute wailed weakly.

After an awkward moment of silence and shuffling,

the audience applauded. The two girls bounced back on stage ever so briefly, to bow. No longer was the black girl antique.

'Oh, very neat!' said Gupta. 'I must learn that trick with the clothes. The clingy fabric that wrinkles like old skin.'

'It was all just a trick?'

'Assisted by cunning stance and gestures.'

The madam bustled back onstage. 'Thank you, perceptive audience! Next, you will behold the journey through the five gates of hell.'

At that moment Alex himself entered the first gate of hell. He patted his purse, and it wasn't there.

Stifling his first outcry, he felt himself all over. He crouched and cast around in the gloom amidst legs and feet both bare and sandalled. 'My purse! Is anyone standing on my purse?'

He rose and clutched Gupta. 'Have you taken my purse as a joke? Tell me!'

'I did nothing of the sort. Maybe it fell at the entrance after you paid. You thought you put it back. It slipped down. That's possible.'

'Yes.' Alex elbowed his way through the audience as the flute began to play.

He quizzed the doorkeeper. He searched the ground.

'Any luck?' Gupta had followed, friendly concern written on his face.

'Nothing!' Alex grabbed the Indian and ran his hands all over him. 'This place would strip my soul, you said! And what else? What else would be stripped from me?'

'I must protest. Though I forgive you your feelings. What an awful shock.'

Alex drew back. 'Fat lot of use feeling *you*. It could be up your anus, for all I know! Please, Gupta, please, if you do have it on you – '

'I don't. Emphatically.'

Alex again confronted the doorkeeper, who had been watching with polite interest. 'Has anyone left the performance yet?'

'You two gentlemen have.'

'I mean anybody else!'

'After the very first dance? Hardly.'

'Then the thief's still in there with my money.'

'How fortunate for you, sir. You need only stand here and ask everyone in turn as they leave.'

'Ask?'

'If by any chance they picked up your purse.'

'I want the performance stopped. I want everyone searched. Thieving is against the law.'

'To be sure, but there are forty people inside tonight. Who will search them?'

'I will – if you bar the door.'

'Some might prove aggressive. They wouldn't wish to be groped intimately.'

Alex groaned. Briefly he clutched at the good Greek knife hidden inside his tunic. Ostentatiously the doorkeeper rearranged a cudgel on a nearby shelf. Alex let his hand fall limp.

'I'd like my lantern,' he said.

'You can't take a lantern inside, sir. It would spoil the lighting balance.'

'I want it because I'm going home! To bed.'

'Don't leave,' said Gupta. 'As the veils of mortality are stripped away, the thief may have a change of heart.'

'Fat chance. I'm not going to stand in the same room with someone who just destroyed me.'

'That's an extreme interpretation.'

'I haven't any money, Gupta. None at all. I'm a beggar.'

106

'Let me offer you a loan. I can spare a shekel and a half for your immediate needs.'

'Don't ruin yourself with generosity.'

'Sorry I'm not Croesus! Feel free to refuse. Be proud.'

Whose money would Gupta be lending? His own – or Alex's?

'I can't impoverish myself, Alex. That's the amount I can risk.'

'Thanks, I'll think about it.'

'I shall stay and see the show I paid for. The first dance was highly instructive! Be careful on the way home, my friend.'

'Am I going to be waylaid? Robbed again?'

'A disturbed soul treads heedlessly, thinking that nothing worse can happen. A person becomes accident-prone.'

'I have a knife – and I'll use it!'

Gupta cocked an ear to the wailing of the flute. 'Excuse me. I might miss something revealing.' He slipped away.

Alex trudged off, lantern in left hand, right hand on the hilt of his knife.

He reached Between The Skin Shops safely, but didn't sleep too well. On the bright side, he was still in good credit – unless Gupta tipped off Kamberchanian. And who knew what Thessany's visit might bring? He concentrated hard upon the image of her actually coming as promised the following afternoon. If she didn't . . .

Thessany looked demurely around his bare room. 'Haven't you anything you can sell?'

'Those seven shekels were like a loan to you and Moriel.'

'A loan? Without a tablet of receipt? No, they were an investment – in a risky enterprise.'

'In which, so far, I seem to have put everything! The little scroll included.'

'The scroll on its own is meaningless – an ugly brown ribbon. You've no idea how much effort, knowledge and cunning Mori and I have exercised. I think you're being quite unfair.'

'So what's the outcome?'

'You're also monstrously impatient. We must proceed subtly, slyly. In three more days I shall be able to amaze you. Hints would only spoil the pleasure.'

'Three days. What do I do till then? The landlord is going to present a bill. I need some money.' (Gupta's pittance – keep that in reserve.)

'You could always sell yourself.'

'Haven't I already?'

'I mean it seriously. I think I could persuade my father to acquire you for me. He might pay as much as forty shekels. The money would be yours. Your life wouldn't be harsh. You would enjoy a lot of freedom in which we could pursue our intrigue. This would be so much easier if you were under my roof.'

'And under your thumb. Sell myself to you? You must be joking.'

'There's no dishonour in being a slave. It's merely a misfortune. I could protect you.'

'I'd be a fool to fall for that. The idea's mad. Sell myself into slavery five minutes after I arrive in Babylon?'

'It can happen.'

'I'd rather leave.'

'You can't, because you can't pay the exit tax.'

With Gupta's loan, he could! She didn't know about Gupta's offer.

'Besides, you have to remain one lunar month. Money is invested in potential citizens.'

Would they let him board the hovercraft early? As

he thought of the hovercraft; it receded into invisibility inside a cloud of dust. He no longer quite believed in its existence.

Money. He could sell his knife for a few coins.

Never disarm yourself! Never go defenceless! Mitch had drummed that into him long ago. But where was Mitch now?

'Three more days? You swear it?'

She crossed her heart, then ran to the window and called to her red-headed bodyguard in the yard: 'Come up, Praxis! Escort me. I will depart.'

Alex realized that he had been fingering his knife. Perhaps he had put the wind up her. Good. Drive a fellow into a corner and his claws come out; unless he simply curls up . . .

'*Here*, in three days' time?'

'I swear I'll come back.'

Of course she would. The whiff of danger would excite her.

A fist thumped on the wooden door.

'In,' she called; and Praxis loomed, scratching the hairs on his chest.

'Think about my offer,' Thessany said sweetly. 'It's sincerely meant. You wouldn't be made into a eunuch or anything of the sort. That's against the law. You would have needed to, oh, rape the daughter of the house first!' She winked. 'Seriously, you'd do well to accept. If our venture prospers, I'm sure you'll soon buy your freedom back. Right now you only have one silly hotel bill to settle. But expenses do have a way of mounting up for a free man, don't you think? Without a quarter-shekel to your name, you're doomed.'

Alex simply looked at her.

'You'd have a period of grace,' she added encouragingly. 'You have to be a citizen before you can lose your citizenship. You'd have to go inside Babel for a week. Who wants a slave who can't speak Babylonian?'

And what games would Thessany get up to as regards the scroll and Deborah and Marduk's impending marriage while Alex was *hors de combat* learning Babylonian?

'A person,' he said, 'might be forgiven for supposing *you* want me as a slave – a lot more than I want you! Who is selling what, to whom?'

'Intriguing question,' she agreed.

So much for Thessany's visit.

Alex wandered again, with the Indian's shekel and a half, gift of Gupta, tucked in a tiny pouch, pinned to his loincloth with a bronze safety pin.

Oh yes, he had borrowed – almost as soon as Thessany had gone. It was far too dangerous to be without any money; she was right on that score. It was like being disarmed. In a sense Deborah owed him all the money he had lost. It was because of her departure – her desertion – that he had been stripped bare of funds; though this was hardly a debt he could proclaim in public should Deborah and prosperous Shazar pass by.

A shekel and a half: a breathing space. Meanwhile, forget about Kamberchanian's nebulous bill at least till tomorrow – or the next day, or the third.

Gupta hadn't asked for a receipt. Perhaps the sum was too trivial. Perhaps he was indeed a friend. Or perhaps he was laughing silently, and had no wish to scratch on clay any details about money which he himself had caused to disappear.

Failing to forget about money – since every time he tried to forget, he remembered – Alex wandered as far as the Rainbow Gardens, the Hanging Gardens.

The gardens were draped over the seven terraces of

Nebuchadnezzar's palace, on the sunward side. At street level were offices and storerooms; and tucked away at the north-east corner, the Wonder Cabinet. This time Alex approached the palace from the south side, where a broad flight of marble steps led upward into green shade away from dust and bustle. To a spectator down in the street the cedars and cypresses of the first tier, the almonds and figs, Sennacherib's cotton trees and olives half hid and half revealed the upper tiers in the way mountain terraces both hide and hint at higher terraces; except that this particular mountain was a building, a stretched-out ziggurat of seven pillared layers. The palace was longer than it was high, though its summit was no mean height.

Some Macedonian and Persian soldiers guarded the way aloft, but hindered no one. A party of fine ladies in rich array were gossiping halfway up the flight, while servants held plume-fans over their heads. A trio of magi in black robes and conical hats descended, deep in conversation: astronomers, astrologers, Marduk's men?

Alex mounted to the first terrace, strolled along some way, then climbed another marble stairway to the second tier: palm trees, ferns, ivies, and fountains. He explored one tier after another, finding himself amidst thickets of jasmine, miniature forests of conifers, a sand garden of succulents, then oranges, bays and avocados in massive terracotta urns. Watercourses ran everywhere, plashing in falls from level to level, sparkling skyward in fountains. Here was an obsidian statue of a sphinx, there of a winged bull, further on an elephant. At the rear of each terrace columned arcades gave access to the palace proper.

To be a gardener in Babylon, upon the Hanging Gardens! To forget about the 'little scroll', and about

Thessany and Marduk and money! He had passed several gardeners at their tasks. Here was another: a frail old man, sprinkling the flagstones of the fifth terrace to still any dust.

'Good day, gardener!'

'Good day to you, Greek.' The man's shoulders were bent, his hands were slow; there were liver spots upon the wrinkled skin.

('Grandad, shouldn't you be resting in a rocking chair on some back stoop with a rug over your knees, instead of labouring in Babylon?')

The gardener had emigrated to Babylon as an old, tired man! Didn't he care that he would die here all the sooner? Did Babylon represent for him a death wish? Amidst this riot of growth, here in these gardens which were the very antithesis of decay? How could that be?

'What are you looking at, Greek?' The gardener began to cough: a dangerous, wheezing noise, worse than that sick man in the marketplace.

'Are you all right? You're old.'

The gardener spat, scraped sputum with his sandal, then grinned, gap-toothed. 'Everyone dies, lad. The young king himself lies dying within, and he's just thirty-three. But that's from fever . . .

'Listen, lad. The cells in any body replace themselves only so many times – there's a limit, isn't there? A city or a kingdom is just a body writ large. What if there's some natural limit in the *polis*, the state, just as there is in any animal body? The *polis* that I left,' (and Alex took him to mean America) 'it seemed to have reached a limit. Its limits as a body . . . Think on that.'

Was that right? Was that what the gardener had learnt here in Babylon? This insight so vital to the university at Heuristics, namely that any society had an inbuilt limit to how long it could perpetuate itself?

The gardener glanced around, as if pleased at his powers of observation, half expecting applause from flowers and the clapping of leaves; and Alex remembered his suspicion that all events were being observed by tiny lenses, recorded by minuscule microphones. Had the gardener's wit and wisdom already been logged by computer, far away at Heuristics, underground?

Or was that bit of wisdom what the gardener had come here already determined to learn, so as to console himself for his own imminent departure from the world?

Many strange things were happening in this city; strange tides of consciousness were being drawn up as if by an ancient – yet younger – moon which once shone over the original Babylon.

'Alexander's dying,' mumbled the gardener, 'but that's just fever . . . Some of the common soldiers rioted yesterday. They wanted to know the truth. Whether he'll die. They fear the future without him. The king's shield-bearers and immortals were hard put to pacify them. Only when they saw him did they calm down . . .' The old fellow was fantasizing, telling an old man's maundering timeless tale – of yesterday, or of his youth, or of two thousand and more years ago.

Far away down the leaf-clad terraces beyond parapet after parapet, Alex thought he spied Deborah walking – with Shazar, the priest of Sin! He gripped the ivied balustrade. Really, the figures were too far away to be sure; now a banyan tree eclipsed them.

Still, he was about to depart in haste, to zigzag down pell-mell from tier to tier to try to intercept the walkers if he could – or to trail them, he wasn't sure which — when the gardener said, 'Why don't you visit him, then?'

'Visit whom?'

'Alexander, of course.'

'But . . . he's the king! You don't just visit a king.'

'You'd be surprised. I know a thing or two, working up here. Didn't I just tell you a delegation of troops visited him yesterday?'

'But . . .' ('But he doesn't really exist!') 'But he's dying,' said Alex, mindful of any microphones.

The gardener chuckled. 'He's been dying for long enough. Must get boring. He might appreciate a visit from a compatriot. Anyway, you Greeks are supposed to be such a democratic lot. Well, that was once upon a time . . . Now you have to grovel and prostrate yourself and make obeisances.'

'Do you mean I can really visit Alexander?'

'S'pose so. You can always ask. Me, I'm only one of his gardeners.'

This was incredible. Alexander the Great lay dying somewhere in this very building, maybe only a hundred paces distant . . . Alex knew this. Of course he knew it. Yet he had never imagined that Alexander was really here.

Did King Alexander actually exist? Or was the old man merely indulging in a joke, a piece of addled geriatric humour in which he too half believed?

Of a sudden Alex's own problems receded far off. Deborah and Shazar fled to a far corner of his mind, became distant dolls. Thessany and Kamberchanian's bill diminished.

'If you don't believe me, lad, go down to the terrace below. Ask a guard.'

'I will.'

* * *

Yes. Yes. And yes.

Alex was searched for hidden weapons – though he had surrendered his dagger voluntarily. He was clad in borrowed cloth of gold in case his tunic itself was poisonous, or lest it offend Alexander's fevered eyes. An unaccountably merry chamberlain instructed Alex how to kiss the tips of his fingers, and to bow, then to follow through by falling upon his knees, on which he must shuffle forward.

'His Majesty's in a wry old mood today,' confided the chamberlain, as Alex rehearsed how to grovel for the sixth time. 'Sometimes he feels better. He gets up. Dresses in a lion skin and brandishes a club like Herakles. Or else he's Hermes – winged sandals, caduceus, big-brimmed hat. Or Ammon – slippers and purple cloak and horns on his head. Sometimes he wears a flowered frock; and then he's the goddess Artemis. But not today.'

Flanked by two guards – one an immortal in glorious embroidery, his spear butt shaped like a pomegranate; the other a bowman in red and blue – the chamberlain led Alex deep into the palace, to left, to right, confusingly, towards the presence. Rich vases, polished ivory, and carved jade stood everywhere, lootings of India and beyond. The floors were sprinkled with scent and sweet wine. Myrrh and incense burned.

Arriving before double doors of carved teak, the chamberlain stamped his staff. The doors opened upon a spacious room, the ceiling supported by various imitation palm trunks made of mud brick. Filmy muslin curtains rippled across the windows as a light breeze blew in, but the air here too was sweet with scent, spilt wine and frankincense – so sweet that the aroma seemed more like that of sickness.

The bed where the king lay was great and golden, with claw-and-ball feet and a canopy overhead. A purple cloak lay crumpled on a silver sofa, with gold torque and armbands and scarlet ribbons perched upon the heap.

Alex prostrated himself on the Persian carpet – where some woven monarch was dropping a dead fish into a tree-shaded pool – and crawled across the wool-knotted water.

'Stand up,' a voice said wearily.

Alex beheld Alexander, plumped up on soft pillows, wearing a silken gown embroidered with dragons, jewelled rings on all his fingers.

The king didn't *look* fatally ill. But then, hadn't he been sick of this same fever for the past five yars? He didn't look thirty-three – more like forty-three – nor a dashing, muscular conqueror, either. But then, he was only an avatar of Alexander. He was stout and jowly with long ringleted hair and sad dark eyes, glinting nevertheless with a sharp intelligence; an intelligence imprisoned in pillows and sickness. Did he have rouge on his cheeks – and on his lips too? His chin was flabby and beardless.

Majolica bowls of ripe fruit and candies and flasks of wine surrounded the bed; sticks of incense fumed lazily. Alex was reminded of Nero, of Aubrey Beardsley's drawings, of some Borgia pope – phantasms from the future. Alexander, it seemed, had succumbed to Persian luxury. Scrolls lay on his bed: maps of empire? No, graphs, doodles, charts of cryptic symbols. Alchemical diagrams, astrological horoscopes. Perhaps. Or exercises in heuristic futurology.

Alex wondered whether the king was drugged, like a seer or sibyl.

He wondered whether the king would eventually be killed by his own guards – or given an overdose by his physician – and replaced with someone younger, also to be kept abed in a semi-drugged state. Allowed to rouse occasionally and caper through the corridors dressed up as Artemis or Herakles. For a moment the frightening, presumptuous thought crossed Alex's mind: what if he, Alex, was somehow to be the next Alexander?

If this king's body seemed half paralysed and comatose, what of his brain?

The king stared at Alex. His rouged lips moved: 'Few enough come to visit the maggot in the apple . . . Wine!'

A serving woman bowed, poured, sipped from the jewelled goblet, waited a while; then since she wasn't writhing on the floor in agony she held the vessel to Alexander's lips, tipping it up for him. Gulping, he drained the goblet, though dribbles ran down his chin, to be mopped up by the woman with a napkin.

'Ambassadors, petitioners, magi with their cures . . . What's yours, Greek? What's your cure for the world?'

'Babylon,' said Alex. 'Babylon is the cure.' He believed this. Even more so, paradoxically, now that he had actually set eyes on the king.

As though the wine – or whatever drugs were in it – had inflamed the sinews of his vision, the muscles of his mind, King Alexander spoke again in a singsong voice:

'We have heard tales of the morning of the earth – and of its golden afternoon, which we presume must be the twentieth century following upon some unborn Messiah, or the thirtieth or the fortieth or the hundredth. And we have heard tales of the long, long evening of decay. Perhaps with assorted rises and falls in between: new barbarisms, trips to the stars, who knows?

'But this is all nonsense. It's still the morning-time, now; and in a million years it will be the morning of the planet, still. And in a million more. Even the early afternoon will be unimaginably different – and might be inhabited gloriously by creatures which are only a few inches long nowadays: voles, shrews. Or by dogs that walk erect. Or by birds. Or by creatures we can't even imagine, because their ancestors haven't been born yet . . .

'Myself, I rather favour shrews! They're so like the tiny furry creatures scuttling and hiding on the forest floor of tree-ferns and cycads while the thunder-lizards stamped by, to their deaths. But this is mere prejudice: a wish to repeat the same old story one more time.

'Who can ever *feel* time? Who can really sense its vast arcades? Ah, but we have performed a clever conjuring trick!'

He belched and brought up some of the sea-dark wine, which the woman wiped away.

'The ancient world is obviously older than our own. It is an old man, to our brash youth – even if we live longer than anyone lived in those days. It is the evening to our morning-time, because it is ancient.

'So by re-creating it – by reviving the dawn of civilization, which is now dust – we take a giant leap into the afternoon of life, and even perhaps into the evening, in our psyche. So we reach beyond the callow early morning of time – to other, later hours of the future . . .'

A scribe took all this down, scratching quickly with a stylus. Why copy down his words, if there was a microphone listening, a hidden camera watching? Surely in the king's room, if anywhere, there ought to be. How could any team of observers cope without the latest semi-aware, fuzzy-logic computer to screen the flood of input?

Perhaps, in its supremely arbitrary yet whole-hearted adoption of ancient, alien customs, Babylon had become the first self-aware *polis* in the history of the world: self-aware beyond time and space. As nowhere else. A communal brain. Maybe Babylon itself was the computer, built of human beings. Its memory chips were clay tablets and waxed boards.

Alexander slumped further back into his pillows, exhausted, drained. He closed his eyes; Alex saw that there was kohl on his eyelids. The chamberlain plucked at Alex's sleeve; the audience was at an end.

Alex stood his ground. He had said next to nothing himself. He wanted to babble, to throw himself on his majesty's mercy.

'King Alexander!' he called; and the chamberlain's pulling became more insistent. 'Pardon, Your Majesty, but you asked me a question.'

An eyelid opened. 'And you answered it.'

'I have something else to tell you!' But which tale should he tell? The tale of the tape? The tale of Thessany? The tale of Deborah, Shazar, and Marduk? They were all really one tale but at the same time the three strands could be separated, rewoven to better effect. And Alexander's men did not use torturers to plumb the truth, only logicians ... He felt out of his depth. Yet there was nothing dishonourable about reporting his discovery. He might be rewarded. With what? With a purse of coins? With Deborah's hand? No; with the truth ...

'Your Majesty, I found a scroll made by *tekhnē* of the future.'

The eye shut again, but the rouged lips moved once more: 'Another omen book? Tell Aristander about it, not me. *I am* the omen book of Babylon; Apollo *Prophetes*.'

The chamberlain wrenched Alex down upon the carpet. 'Bad boy,' he whispered.

As Alex backed out of the room on hands and knees, cheeks hot, his brain burbled to itself.

* * *

The chamberlain snapped his fingers at the escort. 'To Aristander, at the double!'

Along another corridor they hastened, through the reek of scent and myrrh, past a dozen doors; halted at the thirteenth.

The chamberlain's knock was answered by a tall, skinny Greek with a long drooping nose like the proboscis of a tapir. He was about fifty years old, clean-shaven, his hair looping into ringlets down upon his nape. Around his brow he wore a ribbon woven of silver thread. His body was wrapped in a gown of mauve wool.

A drop of liquid appeared at the end of his nose. He wiped this on his sleeve, but another drop would well out presently. The man had a cold, or perhaps his nose was like some stalactite which grew longer over the years as liquid dripped out of him, depositing sweat-salts to dry.

The chamberlain explained; Aristander admitted him and Alex, and the guards.

Tables, couches, stools, shelves, much of the floor and half of the bed were piled deep in waxed boards and papyrus scrolls. Charts papered the walls, showing strange geometries annotated in tiny spidery red ink. A water-clock stood in one corner, a sundial by the window, and there were other contrivances of bronze and glass with toothed wheels and discs and gears.

'A scroll made by *tekhnē* of the future, eh?' Aristander wiped his nose, then tugged on his ringlets. 'Describe all the circumstances!'

'Yes . . . but who are you, sir?' asked Alex.

'Silly boy,' said the chamberlain. 'Lord Aristander is Court Futurologist.'

'I am indeed. And time runs on.'

Alex sniggered. 'I thought time stood still in Babylon.'

'*My* time runs on. As does the king's.'

'When he dies, will another Alexander be appointed?'

Aristander slapped Alex stingingly across the cheek. 'Kindly get to the point.'

Alex recoiled – and felt the point of a spear in his back. 'I . . . I'm sorry. May I speak of things which are not of Babylon?'

'You have permission.' Aristander glanced past him at the two guards. 'You men shall repeat nothing, on pain of being deafened with hot needles.'

'Well, it's like this,' began Alex; and some of his story tumbled out . . .

After astute questioning by Aristander had elicited a good deal more of his story – the man had a nose for the last drop of juice – the futurologist smiled thinly.

'I think we shall drink some wine,' he said. Sweeping papyrus scrolls aside, he found a jug and three glazed cups; filled all three.

'What do you make of this?' he asked the chamberlain.

The chamberlain slaked his thirst as though it was he who had done all the talking.

'A conspiracy,' he replied. 'That's what. On the one hand, a prankish conspiracy. And secondly, a deep conspiracy – though I hardly perceive its features yet! – with this foolish boy located in the middle: a guileful innocent, of questionable psyche.'

Alex felt himself flush. Callow, that's what he was; still as callow as the boy whom Mitch had tried to lick into shape as a survivor, none too effectively.

Yet what are men, but grown-up boys? Momentarily Alex perceived the chamberlain and Aristander simply as enlarged, time-worn boys. Briefly he saw lurking in their flesh the boys they had once been. In the absence of a mirror – other than certain polished glass discs incorporated into Aristander's futurological orrery, or whatever it was – he did not, however, see himself.

'Precisely my sentiment,' agreed Aristander. 'The deep conspiracy may be nothing else than imagination. But we must not ignore a clear omen.'

'What omen?'

'The omen of this scroll falling at the feet of a new Alexander – one who bears the name of Winter, the season of death! Our king is the ripe full sun. What could eclipse his city, but a winter of the world?'

'Ah!'

'If you'll excuse me,' said Alex, 'my name seems a flimsy reason for believing me.'

Aristander shook his head vigorously. 'It isn't a reason. It's a *pretext* for believing you – an excuse. Your story fits in with various projections I've made lately. It defines these, clarifies them. Your story allows me to choose one option out of several to test the water of the future and spy a meaningful picture reflected there. Your visit here is rather more substantive than, say, a flight of seven crows alighting on the king's windowsill and shitting there. But as an omen it is similar. The skill in reading omens lies in knowing how to *apply* them.'

'Would you have ignored my story if my name had been – let's see – Philip Spring?'

'What, when the father of our king was Philip? And when a spring rises from secret places hidden underground?'

'Can't win, can I?'

'I don't know about that. We can certainly make use of a guileful innocent. People notice the naivety rather than the guile. Alex, you will hasten to become a citizen of Babylon – now, today! Where else but in Babel is the *tekhnē* for reading such a scroll? Where else are the magi who master all means of communication? That hairdresser person will sneak the scroll into Babel to have it interpreted. You'll be shadowed by some sturdy ruffians, who'll report to me.'

The long nose drooped towards Alex as if to anoint him with the last unwiped drop of chrism.

'Tell me one thing, will you, Aristander? What happens to Mrs Marduk after her year of glory?'

'She becomes a priestess in the Underworld. In other words, she helps tend Babylon's computer.'

'Its *what*?'

'Computer. How do you suppose you learn Babylonian? By magic?'

Alex cackled hilariously. Deborah had travelled thousands of miles and thousands of years back in time to escape from being a mundane computer operator. Oh, what a fate worse than death! Death, in the guise of some ornate drugged sacrifice, she might even have accepted – come crazily to terms with. But to be a computer slave for the rest of her Babylonian career: oh, delicious nemesis! She would wish to escape *that*.

Alex hooted.

'Of questionable psyche!' The chamberlain clapped him jovially on the back.

4

In which Alex marches right up to the top of the hill, then finds poorly paid employment down at the bloody bottom

Two ruffians in mufti robes trailed discreetly behind Alex as he headed at last into the Esagila quarter, approaching Babel. Farewell to Kamberchanian's hotel bill. Farewell to life as a Greek.

Babel Tower lofted itself, expanding space, sucking him inward. Here was the tallest of all ziggurats, a skyscraper amongst ziggurats; though since the sky was a cloudless desert blue, no white scrape-marks were visible.

A single balustraded ramp wound upward, round and round. This was wide enough for several donkey carts to pass one another, as many indeed were doing. If unwound into a ribbon the spiral of the ramp would reach right across the city, perhaps far out into the countryside beyond.

The walk up to the top would take at least an hour or two; and the top was where he must present himself for initiation. He wasn't sure whether it was possible to take vertical short cuts. At ramp level, arched doorways opened into the walls of each tier. Above these arches were two further storeys of windows, so there must be internal stairways. But perhaps the stairways of one curve did not lead all the way up to the curve above . . .

A while later he decided that for him there should be no short cuts. This climb, after all, was an approach to initiation; designed as such. It seemed as necessary to tread each circuit of the ramp as, in a later age, it would be for Christ to touch base at each station of the cross. A sudden conjuring of the cross into a ladder to ascend Golgotha more rapidly wouldn't be appropriate.

He leaned on the parapet of the third tier to catch his breath. A hundred cubits down-ramp he spotted his two ruffians hunker by the inner wall and begin to roll dice.

People and produce and products flowed by. Produce, up. Products, down. The city and countryside below supplied food and raw materials. Traders conveyed these upward, exchanging goods for other goods, mediating between levels. The tower was a giant, wide Archimedean screw with many holes of doorways in it, into which goods and materials popped, out of which equivalent goods were squeezed so that a cartload of cabbages starting out from the base would have transmuted into a load of sweetmeats, scrolls, wire puzzles, perfumes, scarves by the time it reached the summit; though some cabbages had to continue all the way to the top, otherwise the Olympians up there would get scurvy.

By and large, sub-cultures obeyed their own boundaries, keeping within language frontiers. Already he had climbed through a succession of language villages comprising – benefit of hindsight! – Sumerian, Akkadian, Assyrian, Hurrian, Hittite, Phoenician, Aramaic.

As he stared down at those bustling quadrants spreading out below, a disconcerting reversal of vision occurred. It seemed as though Babel was growing fatter, not thinner, the higher he ascended. Instead of tapering inward, Babel Tower was leaning outward across Babylon, Pisa-like but much vaster, threatening to crush the city.

He staggered back, and crashed into someone. A hand steadied him.

'Oh dear me – vertigo!'

It was Gupta. (And the two ruffians had slipped quickly – though inconspicuously – closer.)

'What are you doing here, Gupta?'

'Obviously I must be chasing my shekel and a half, ha ha! No, in fact I decided my future business plans all of a sudden. So I must become a citizen. My month is two-thirds gone. Why squander more of my nest egg on hotels when I could be earning income? I suppose you had a similar idea; minus the nest egg.'

Alex thought of making a hand signal to reassure his ruffians. But Gupta would be bound to notice. In any case, to convey that the Indian wasn't about to toss him over the parapet – that Alex was actually in the man's debt, yet nevertheless Gupta ought to be viewed with caution – would have required very complicated covert waggling of the fingers. Alex compromised by scratching his head.

'What sort of business plans?' he asked.

'Ha ha, does a businessman, however humble, spill all his secrets, even to a friend? Let me merely say that it has something to do with conjuring, and with the fascinating spectacle we witnessed the other night. Ah, but you missed the best part. I'm forgetting, most crassly.'

'Don't tell me you're going into partnershhip with Kamberchanian!'

'How did you guess?'

'Well, you couldn't afford to open a strip show on your own – unless you're wealthier than you admit.'

'You have caught me. I confess. I shall be artistic director of old Kamber's other enterprise.'

'You'll copy the House of the Veil? You'll train metaphysical strippers?'

'Copy? *Transcend*, my friend. There'll be a whole new dimension. It's the naked truth, ha ha. Let's climb on upward together. If you suffer another bout of dizziness, do take my arm. I shall not misinterpret.'

As it happened, Indians resided around the next quadrant of the ramp, which was rich with smells of stewing curries and tandoori marinades.

'Time for afternoon tiffin! I spy samosas.' Gupta hauled Alex towards a food stall; gestured and gabbled in Greek.

'You don't need to speak Greek here for my benefit.'

'My dear fellow, they are speaking Sanskrit here. Whilst I am of course acquainted with our great Indian classics, I'm not exactly fluent on a daily basis!'

After a snack of spicy lamb samosas cooled with dollops of mint yoghurt they carried on, tarrying frequently out of curiosity, of which Gupta possessed an insatiable store. Thus they passed through Little Egypt, Little Armenia, Little Italia, Little Scythia, and Little China (Warring States vintage). At no stage did Alex breathe a word about his visit to the king.

It was on the seventh tier of Babel that Gupta exclaimed, 'Look! Isn't that our friend Deborah ahead?'

By now the afternoon was nearly over; evening drew close. They had tarried indeed. In the west beyond farms, beyond desert, the sun had sunk till it was a quivering bag of molten gold balancing momentarily on the horizon with a few black strings of cloud cobwebbing it. The light gilded Deborah, who was dressed in a yellow linen gown. Escorting her were two magi wearing cone hats.

'She must have come from inside,' said Gupta, 'using a faster route.'

'Deb-or-ah! Hey, Deb!'

Many Japanese faces stared at bellowing Alex;

though no one in this sector was speaking Japanese. In this endless, ever-recurring year of 323 B.C. the Kingdom of Yamato hadn't quite got its act together. The Japanese people had still been Korean immigrants amidst the hairy native Ainu. So Japan was part of China, from which its literature was yet to come. The Japanese on Babel spoke the Chinese of Confucius.

'Deb! Hey!' Alex broke into a jinking run.

'Wait for me!' Gupta dodged along behind, amidst apologies and imprecations.

'Deb!'

This time she heard, and looked. So did her magi. Deborah hesitated, waved; but the magi hustled her aside through the nearest doorway.

Arriving at the same doorway only moments later, Alex entered a tall hall where several mahjong games were in progress. A number of lamps already burned. Two further archways, curtained with silk, led onward; but neither curtain looked any more perturbed than the other. A wooden stairway climbed to a gallery — several open doors led off — and the stairs continued to a floor above. Too little time for Deborah and magi to have reached the upper floor! They had either gone through one of the curtained arches, or used a mezzanine door.

'Sirs!' he appealed. Disconcerted mahjong players stared at him. 'The woman and the magi: which way?'

No one answered, though the players twittered to one another.

He ran to one archway, parted silk, saw a further dusky hall with sleeping pallets on the floor — and two more curtained archways leading deeper into Babel.

He darted to the other arch; beyond the curtain a different hall was stacked with sacks of rice. Again, two more distant archways. No fleeing figures.

He dashed to the stairs – colliding with Gupta, spinning him round – and mounted two at a time.

The first doorway led to a sunset-lit room of screens painted with roses, herons and willows; the second, to a brightly lamplit bedroom. A naked Asian woman, astride a stool, combing waves of black hair, dropped her comb, clapped a hand to her mouth. He retreated.

The third, dingy room was empty save for the shadow of a huge vase upon a lacquer stand.

He climbed the next flight of stairs. At the top was another hall, less extensive than the halls below, amber-lit by the last of the sun. Bottles, drums and jars filled shelves and racks: powders, tinctures, ointments, pickled snakes, ginseng roots, white grass, body organs of animals. Two more archways, more stairs. He chose the stairs and ended up in a dark, hot, musty attic where he soon made out hundreds of strings of wizened mushrooms hanging from the eaves to the floor. No apparent exit, other than the door he had entered by.

He went back down to the hall of medicine. From the gallery below he heard angry singsong voices – and Gupta arguing placatingly in Greek.

Looking down, he saw that the younger mahjong players had pursued the intruders aloft. One man flourished an ornate damascened cleaver. Further below, game boards were abandoned and angry Chinese (or Japanese) milled about.

'Come down quickly, Alex!' cried Gupta.

Reluctantly Alex obeyed. As soon as he was within reach of Gupta, the Indian yanked him bodily the last few steps and began to belabour him about the head and shoulders, cuffing and smacking.

'Oh, idiot son!' the Indian shouted. 'Foolish curse of my life! Imbecile shame of my ancestors!'

Whilst vigorously punishing Alex, somehow Gupta

also managed to guide him downstairs and eventually out of the mahjong hall entirely. Since aggrieved Chinese spilled after them, Gupta frogmarched Alex up the ramp, butting and kneeing him in the behind till they were well clear.

Then Gupta stopped. 'There, I have protected you. Now you are my son. I take responsibility.'

The gathering dusk was relieved by oil lamps twinkling outside a good few doorways. The day's commercial traffic had ended – no more donkey carts ambled by – but people were starting to wander abroad to amuse themselves. Alex noticed his pair of ruffians hiding in the shadow of a nearby wall-buttress. Why the hell hadn't they intervened? Exasperatedly, he shook his head in chastisement.

'Did I not rescue you?' protested Gupta.

'Yes, *you* did.'

'Ah!' Gupta peered around. 'Was someone else suppposed to save you from the consequences?'

'Of course not,' Alex said hastily.

No doubt his frantic dash into Chinese quarters had astonished his shadows. Perhaps he had already disconcerted them by the sheer sloth of his approach to the summit. To distract Gupta, he cursed long and low at his loss of Deborah.

'I wonder why she was with two magi?' Gupta pondered.

'She's going to be Marduk's bride.'

'How do you know that?'

'Oh . . . I heard.'

'From that boy who visited our inn, and took your money?'

'Maybe.'

'Now you're jealous of Marduk? That spells danger. Speaking as someone newly responsible for your safety, ha ha, I advise discretion. Do not hare off in hot pursuit of a soon-to-be-sacred lady.'

'You're probably right.'

'Yet you mean to ignore my advice. Perhaps I should resign responsibility.'

'Do so.'

'Not yet. We must find a place to spend the night.'

'The night?'

'This dark stuff that approaches. When better to arrive at the peak than in dawn's early rays? We mustn't expect officials to deal with us any earlier. Don't worry, I shall pay for you. You are still my erring, foolish son till I deliver you safely to the summit.'

'Thanks.'

They walked on into Hunnish territory, which in 323 B.C. was still adjacent to China, and quickly found an inn. A signboard, conveniently in Greek, named the inn ominously *Edge of the Abyss*; but inside the place was hospitable, not unlike a latter-day German beer-hall, though the decorations were lugubrious stuffed horses' heads. Shortly after Alex and Gupta had sat down to eat steaks of horsemeat and drink fermented milk, the two shadows also slipped indoors.

Rising early, *Morgenlich leuchtend in rosigem Schein*, they reached the summit not quite at dawn, though not long after, without any further sighting of Deborah.

The final curve of the ramp led up on to a circular field of brick. In the centre was a stubby round brick tower, from which a spear of iron rose as lightning conductor. A wooden door stood wide. Outside at a table sat a black-robed mage sorting a heap of waxed record boards. They approached.

Gupta kissed his fingers and bowed; Alex followed suit.

In flowery vein Gupta declared, 'We present our-

131

selves here! We crave to become citizens of the greatest of cities, the Gate of God!'

Behind, the two ruffians emerged on to the brickfield and occupied themselves with the view from the balustrade.

'Hmm,' said the mage. 'Names, please. Dates of arrival.'

These they furnished; these he scratched in wax.

'Wait.' He went inside the tower – to consult a computer terminal? A guard armed with a double-headed axe appeared and lounged in the doorway. The mage soon returned, to gesture them inside.

'Don't look now,' murmured Gupta, 'but we're being followed. By two mufti men who were at the inn.'

'They probably want to become citizens too.'

'They already look Babylonian. And Alex, I have never known anyone who refrains from peeping when told not to. You didn't bat an eyelid, much less look.'

Hastily Alex addressed the mage: 'Sir, has a woman with dark hair cut in a helmet style come this way, accompanied by two magi?'

'The business of magi isn't your business, Greek.' The mage led them round the curve of an inner wall, where what they encountered relieved Alex of any remaining need to answer Gupta. On the far side of the curve was a cage door: the door of a lift. A trio of oil lamps burned on brackets within. The lift could have held twenty people.

At the summit of Babel was a shaft, plunging down to the depths.

The mage opened the cage door. Toggles protruded from an iron plate on the outside, by the door; there were no controls within.

'Descend into the Underworld! Die as Greeks; be reborn as Babylonians. Hurry up with you. We haven't got all day.'

Alex and Gupta entered and were locked inside, behind a sliding grille. The lift began to drop. Lamp flames wavered; shadows danced; a dim cliff face of brick sped upward . . .

Alex wandered the inner courts of Babel one evening (if it was really evening) during the hour of exercise. His brain buzzed with Babylonian. The new language gestated swiftly inside him, forming limbs and sense organs. Like a vigorous foetus it kicked the walls of his skull. He was drugged, dazed and dopey. For all he knew he might be dreaming while awake.

Dozens of other applicants likewise trod the floors of these vaulted, torchlit caverns and arcades deep within Babel mountain. They moved mostly like praying monks of a later age, or like somnambulistic tightrope walkers. Occasionally someone danced, pranced, pirouetted. That was when a surfeit of words suddenly fired in the person's head, jerking their nerves; it relieved the tedium of the limbs.

Apart from a half-hour on awakening and an hour before sleep, applicants spent all their time in warm, dim cells hooked to teaching terminals. The attending magi drugged their charges, hypnotized them, fed them; expelled them for recreation and ablutions.

Recreation periods weren't necessarily synchronized. Perhaps neither were 'morning' and 'evening'. Alex had encountered Gupta only once, while the Indian was being shepherded back to his cell. Deborah he hadn't seen at all. During how many days? Five?

Two more days, and Alex would be a Babylonian.

During his periods of exercise, the pair of ruffians shadowed him. They made no approaches, merely lurked in the background. No mage accosted them, so the ruffians had authority to be in these subterranean courts. Where did they eat? And sleep? What did they do for the rest of the time? Alex had no idea. One 'evening' only one ruffian was present; the next 'morning' his mate had rejoined him. During teaching hours and at 'night' perhaps they went elsewhere.

Though torchlit, the brick caverns were gloomy. Masses of shadow hung overhead, dank as thunderclouds. Black miasmas bunched between the sconces, whose fires seemed to breed darkness as much as they created light. Here was a land of the dead where souls must perambulate at morn and eve, sadly confused, their memories mumbling or gibbering half-comprehended reproaches and reminders of deeds undone, of words unsaid.

The halls and intervening arcades eventually led back to one another: some sooner, some later. After a while you paid no attention to several great brass-bound doors set in the walls of different caverns, with locked wickets in them. One, of course, gave access to the lift, but Alex had forgotten which until, on his third or fourth ghostly promenade, the wicket happened to open as he was passing and a mage ushered a group of new applicants through.

Presumably another door must lead to the computer and to its handmaidens, Marduk's former wives.

After a while the doors might as well just be decorated bits of walls.

At last, that evening (if it was evening), Alex saw Deborah.

She was walking on her own. He overtook her.

'Deb. Hullo! How are you?' What language was he speaking? Greek, Babylonian, a mixture? He wasn't sure.

She looked at him, confused. 'I am . . . well. You are here too?'

'Yes, yes. Listen to me, Deb, I know you're planning to marry a god, or at least his priest – '

'Shazar,' she said vaguely.

'No, *Marduk*'s high priest. Shazar is just the go-between.'

'Shazar,' she repeated. 'He passed by the temple of Ishtar as I entered. Overwhelmed, he turned aside and followed me. As soon as I sat down he stood before me, considering, ready to throw a coin to anticipate any other overtures; still not certain. Then the spirit of Sin came into him, and he was sure.'

If she sounded drugged and hypnotized – well, that's exactly what she was.

'Yes, but Shazar isn't the man you'll marry. Have you even *met* Marduk's priest? Was he at the Festival Temple? Do you know what happens to you after you've been married to Marduk for a year? Do you, Deb?'

'Questions, questions. He was certain. And I am certain.'

'Certain of what? Of one year as a goddess? Followed by a lifetime as . . .' – and he slipped briefly into English – '. . . as a computer operator! Yes, behind one of the doors down here. Locked away from all the light and life of Babylon!'

'After one year . . . I go to the House of Judgement.'

'Is that what they call the computer room?'

'God Marduk himself appeared in terrible glory out of thin air and told me. Then he vanished and was not there.'

'He must have been a *holographos*, Deb! That's all.'

Deborah looked scared, as though Alex himself was an apparition. She began to hurry on.

He pursued. 'Think, Deb, think!'

Distressed, she began to babble Babylonian words: 'Go away! Stop hurting me! Leave me be! You're mad.'

'Listen! Do you remember the little scroll? The *tape cassette*?'

135

'No!'

Two magi came running. They caught hold of Alex, cunningly restraining him. He couldn't struggle. They led him back towards his cell.

The two ruffians slipped like fish, like hungry pike, from pool of shadow to pool of shadow, watching.

On the seventh day Alex woke with his brain still humming and muttering, but somehow everything seemed newly coherent and connected; or perhaps more anciently coherent. He spoke Babylonian as if he had always spoken it. Babylonian was more ancient than Greek. No, it wasn't. It just seemed so.

A mage led him from his cell. Soon they came to one of the brass-bound doors. Another mage arrived, accompanying Gupta. The wicket was unlocked.

A wide brick tunnel curved upward, its goal masked by the bend of the walls.

'You are both reborn,' said one mage. 'You are citizens. Go and find your way through Babel. Discover your place within Babylon. If Babel attracts you, return in a year's time and crave admittance to the city within a city.'

The two new citizens stepped through the wicket, and set off up the brick slope. As they rounded the bend, the wicket still stood open behind, presumably so that the ruffians could follow.

Ahead, the tunnel opened into a torchlit brick cavern awash with noise.

The belly of Babel? The bowel? A hundred languages were in dispute; or at least at odds.

Persons were prattling Pentecostally, women were wailing wild words, boys were burbling a brouhaha: from marble plinths, from stone podia, from rickety wooden platforms arranged in avenues. A number of magi patrolled, heads cocked, attentive, as though they were the living recorders of these sounds.

What was this? An oratory contest? A madhouse? A bazaar where languages themselves were being traded? Or a cathedral, a temple designed to propitiate – or to delight – the God of Time who would hear all voices grow mute in the end, all poetry, all philosophy and prophecy become incomprehensible?

The acoustics of the cavern dislocated every fervent utterance into a great symphony of discord. Echoes beat down from the vault like bats frenzied by the torchlight. It seemed as though here was the melting pot of *Word* itself, the cauldron of communication where some original Ur-speech might eventually co-alesce, renaming everything in the world truly at last – and meaninglessly – in the voice of the thunder, the grind of glaciers, the sibilance of snow, the liquid vowels of flood waters which together shattered, crushed, smothered, and washed away all creations of culture.

A mage passed by; Alex grabbed at his sleeve. 'What *is* this place, sir?'

'This is the Parliament of Babel, citizen! If we are to speak with the future, we must first know what is nonsense. Most of what we say is nonsense. Yet out of this nonsense, sense is born. Out of the original random noise of the cosmos, organs are thrust. Organisms, organization, organons. Here is the voice of that organ of a hundred pipes. Here is the warbling womb of words. Here is the music of the mother of meaning in her birth pangs. Here is Mummu. Here is the hot lava welling from the bowels of being to harden into the crust upon the slopes of Babel.'

The mage swept onward, listening to left and right.

The magi who master all means of communication . . . Aristander's phrase came back into Alex's mind.

A score of separate archways led out of this parliament – to steps, to ramps, to tunnels which forked and twisted abruptly. Over each archway were different symbols in tiled relief: the sun haloed in spiky rays, the crescent moon, a bull's head, a monkey, a lozenge in the shape of lips, a bee, a lion, a cross, a dog. All the time people were entering, and people departing.

This place was more alien than anything in Babylon or crusted upon the flanks of Babel Tower. Here was a sound chamber designed to communicate with beings yet unborn, yet unconceived, beings quite different from man. A great unborn god seemed to crouch brooding in this chamber like a queen bee in her pulsing hive.

Here, thought Alex, is the subconscious of Babylon . . .

And here magi paced about, harkening to the throats of time; mastering mysteries, or maybe drowning in them.

With a hiss of breath Alex drew back behind a block of marble – upon which stood a plump, sweating, butter-skinned lad, reciting loudly.

Through the arch marked with the sign of the monkey, came Moriel, moving slyly, Thessany just behind him.

Alex plucked Gupta too behind the block, and the raving boy. 'Hush. Don't show yourself.'

'Hush? In this hubbub? It's total tohu-bohu.'

'Ssshhh! Let me watch.'

'At least tell me who I'm hiding from.'

'Over there. Small girl with brown hair. Dandy with broken nose.'

'Who are they? Why hide?'

'Never mind.'

Thessany paused by a stage on stilts where four fellows who might have been Slavs were declaiming simultaneously like some absurd barbershop quartet. The master barber himself, Moriel, sneaked onward, veering quite close to where Alex and Gupta hid but keeping his gaze fixed on the archway with the sign of the lips.

A mage emerged from that archway: hooked nose, black beard chignoned in a hairnet – a great dark goitre. The mage spotted Moriel. Moriel beckoned. Mage and Moriel met only thirty paces from the hiding place.

The two spoke softly – then the mage produced a small package which looked extremely familiar. He held it tightly while Moriel counted out coins. Exchange took place, and the man with the big ugly bun of a beard turned away.

Alex hurried from hiding to reclaim his property . . . or at least to obtain a reckoning from Moriel.

He was very close to his quarry when two skinny men wearing kilts and cloaks darted. One caught hold of Moriel's wrist, twisting so that the package fell. The cry which burst briefly from Moriel's lips wasn't on account of a sprained wrist. Already he was sagging with a knife hilt jutting from his ribs, the gift of the other assailant.

Alex thudded into the first robber, stooped, snatched the fallen package – and jumped back, not a moment early. A knife gleamed in the fellow's hand. The other robber ignored the crumpled corpse with his weapon lodged in it. Plucking a replacement blade from his cloak, he circled to trap Alex in between.

One against two! Mitch's training reflexed back into Alex as he scrabbled for his own knife.

The knife wasn't there.

He had surrendered it at Alexander's palace. The guards had taken it when he was granted audience. Then one thing happened, and another, and he forgot to claim it back. He forgot about it all the way to the summit of Babel — because he had a bodyguard dogging his heels. Thereafter he had spent a week of confusion. Only now did he realize that he was as good as naked.

As he uselessly flexed the fingers of his right hand, he could have wept. The murderer of Moriel feinted, then smiled smugly.

A mufti figure leapt in the way. It was one of the ruffians. His robe swirled free of his body, denuding him but for an undergarment. The robe was a cape swirling in the man's left hand, while a knife in his right hand slashed the air a hair's breadth from the murderer's arm. No! A line of blood welled across the killer's forearm.

At Alex's back the other ruffian danced, protecting him.

Thirty paces beyond, the mage was watching.

The fight was as fast as the dash of a cheetah which will run out of energy if it doesn't pull its prey down within the first hundred bounding steps.

A sally — and a cut across the murderer's brows dripped blood into his eyes. A moment later the ruffian stabbed his blinded opponent in the belly. A dying man jackknifed. At the same time Alex was bowled forward by the other ruffian who staggered against him, choking and burbling — clutching his own butchered throat in a self-stranglehold, in vain.

Briefly two victors faced one another; Alex between them. With a sweep of his arm the surviving ruffian knocked Alex aside. Within moments a knife was deep in the robber's belly.

The fallen ruffian soon lay still, drowned by his own blood; but the two robbers flopped like beached fish. This was the first time Alex had ever seen knives used in anger. The speedy ease of Moriel's death — result of skill, or sheer chance – had been quite misleading. As Alex looked on in horror, the robbers continued squirming their way very slowly towards death. He felt like vomiting.

He noticed the mage take alarm, begin to hurry away, beard-bun bobbing.

A slighter figure skipped through the carnage.

'I'll take that!' (Thessany's voice.) The package was snatched from his limp hand. She flitted away. He blundered in pursuit, skidded on blood and nearly fell. A glimpse of sudden movement made him turn to fend off attack – but it was the victorious ruffian, clad once more in his mufti.

'Get away from here before Babel constables come! Take the Sun exit. Be at the palace tomorrow – and recover that package if you can. Go!' The ruffian fled.

Nearby the hubbub had stilled (though elsewhere hundreds of voices competed). Many faces stared as the two brown men continued agonizing on the ground. Alex stood alone, shivering with shock.

Gupta ran to the rescue.

'I recommend a hasty departure from this revolting scene,' he said in Babylonian, gripping and shaking Alex.

'Yes, by the Sun way,' Alex answered in Greek. The ruffian – Aristander's agent – had been speaking Greek.

Together they raced to the spiky Sun sign. A level brick corridor zigged and zagged, then spilled them into a market-hall mostly crowded with jolly, round-faced Sumerians. Stalls were piled with fruit. Arched doorways at the end of the hall framed dazzling white sunshine, and city buildings not far distant. Gaining one of those doorways, they found themselves at the very bottom of the great road-ramp. A quick sprint, and they would be safe in the Esagila quarter. Alex squinted tearfully into the flood of light.

'No one pursues us yet,' said Gupta. 'Let's wait till our eyes accustom. Meantime, maybe you can illuminate me? What was in that package? Who is the young woman? Who were the fighters who saved you? What did the survivor say? These little details puzzle me. I do have to safeguard my shekel and a half, ha ha!'

'Um, well.'

'A bargain! I'll tell you what I observed, and you can comment. The mage who handed the packet to the foppish fellow wanted big money. He also yearned to keep the packet, enough to hire thugs to murder the said popinjay immediately afterwards. So the packet wasn't originally the mage's property; he wasn't selling it. It belonged to the woman, with the fop acting as her accomplice. She was wild to recover it. If she had possessed the packet previously, why entrust it to such a venal mage? She must have needed to know what the packet *signified* – how it could be interpreted. *This* was the service which the mage performed. Did he not use the arch marked with lips? A route which must lead towards certain items of *tekhnē*, with which we have spent a dazed week, and no doubt other hidden *tekhnē* too! If the enigmatic contents of the packet were merely scribed in a strange tongue, I feel sure she could have had it interpreted more easily somewhere up on the flanks of Babel. The contents must have demanded high *tekhnē* to unravel them.

'I assume, by the way, that the packet which she snatched from you *does* contain what it contained originally. As the intention was to murder, the cloth wrapping may have concealed no more than a block of wood!

'Another point: did the mage know that the woman would be a witness? If so, was the intention to warn her off brutally? The plan couldn't have been to murder both of them, otherwise the mage would have contrived that fop and woman were closer together. Perhaps that young woman is of too much consequence to murder idly . . .'

Alex felt that he was being spun into a tight cocoon. No doubt Thessany would have twitched a few strands loose and darted clear.

Maybe challenge was the best defence? 'Do you seriously pretend you don't know what's in the packet?'

Gupta's dark eyes twinkled. 'Just because I come from an elder civilization, please don't assume that I'm omniscient or telepathic! Your response casts a sad light on your attitude to me. I am wounded. You probably imagine that *I* stole your shekels to play a game of hide-and-seek. Much more likely, in retrospect, is another explanation. Your impoverishment wasn't due to some opportunistic pickpocket who haunts parlours where men's attention is compulsively distracted; nor was it due to mischievous me. It was deliberately engineered, by someone you have intrigued with unbeknownst to Uncle Gupta. By the fop who died? Perhaps he played a part in it. By the young woman who robbed you *once again*, as easily as snatching barley-cake from a baby? Undoubtedly!'

'I meant,' lied Alex, 'that you likely knew at a glance what was in the packet because you're so damn clever.'

'Oh, forgive yourself! You meant nothing of the sort. Why ignore what I just said? That young woman robbed you a few minutes ago. She probably robbed you at the inn, using that boy messenger – and again at the strip show by proxy. But what has *she* to do with the real object of your obsession: namely Deborah, soon to be the bride of Marduk? How did you and she become acquainted if she occupies some exalted social position, way out of reach of a newly arrived Greek?'

'You tell me.'

Gupta thumped his forehead. 'How slow I am. Of course! That morning when you followed Deborah to the temple of Ishtar . . . *that's* where.'

Alex groaned. 'Her name's Thessany. The dead man's name was Moriel.'

But Gupta gripped Alex's elbow, sending a shaft of pain shooting up arm and shoulder, paralysing his tongue. 'That same mage – and three brown persons. Let's go!'

The two hastened across unduly bright flagstones, heading for the nearest donkey-clogged gateway into Esagila. Which they reached, unpursued.

At the far side of the gate, a burly red-headed man stepped forward: bare-chested, kilted, wearing a short sword. It was Thessany's chauffeur and bodyguard. Another armed man accompanied him.

Praxis; that was the chauffeur's name. Thessany must have left him here to wait for her. Therefore she hadn't yet emerged. Had she been hiding in the Sumerian market? Had she rushed up the ramp to lose herself for a while in Little Akkadia or Little Assyria?

Wrong.

'Greetings!' said Praxis. He produced a clay tablet; his companion stroked the hilt of his own sword meaningfully. 'Alex, you have been acquired as a slave by my mistress.'

'*What?*'

'Innkeeper Kamberchanian sued for default on your unpaid bill before a magistrate three days ago. My mistress generously settled your debt, reasoning that you would hardly wish to become a slave at a second-rate inn, emptying slops and paid a pittance which might only cover the interest on your debt. The magistrate consigned you to her. Here is the notarized transaction.'

Alex seized the clay tablet and scanned the cuneiform signs, understanding them now.

Gupta peered over his shoulder. 'Oh, Alex, this is why you were robbed. I should have foreseen it.'

'You told me that Kamberchanian is your partner!'

'So he is. So he will be soon. This occurred while you and I were both becoming citizens. Obviously old Kamber was persuaded to take this action, and now it's out of the good fellow's hands, so my influence would be in vain.'

Praxis grinned. 'Come along, slave. The tattoo artist awaits.'

Alex drew his arm back to hurl the offending tablet at the gatepost to smash it into shards. Praxis made no move to stop him, but Gupta snatched the tablet away.

'No, Alex. Foolish! At least this shows exactly how much you owe, with a magistrate's seal on it.' Gupta thrust the tablet at the chauffeur, who pocketed it grudgingly in his kilt.

'Gupta! You have money – enough to redeem me.'

Gupta seemed to suffer a few moments of inner conflict. 'I rather wish you had not said that, Alex. My money is pledged to partnership with Kamber. Believe me, I will help in every other way possible. Excuse me now, excuse me.' And away he went.

'We go the other way,' said Praxis.

'With no fuss,' added his companion. 'Nice and obedient.'

At least now, thought Alex sourly, he would find out where Thessany lived and who her father was.

Then he thought: surely he had told Aristander of his pressing money problems? He had, hadn't he? Why the hell didn't Aristander warn him that his debt could result in enslavement? Why didn't Aristander offer to settle the hotel bill?

Had Aristander hoped for some such outcome – with a potential informer, Alex, planted in Thessany's home? If so, why had the ruffian told Alex to present himself at the palace?

Because the more likely option was that Alex would remain free? But at the same time there was that other wild card up Aristander's sleeve . . .

Unfortunately Alex hadn't got round to telling *Gupta* about the visit to Aristander. Ignorant of all that palace business, how could Gupta help?

Another possibility occurred: if Aristander hadn't in fact dreamed of any such wild card, how would he take the news that Alex had gone straight from Babel to Thessany's home, to stay there? (If he *did* learn of this!) Might he suspect that Alex's tale of the tape was all part of an intricate prank designed by Thessany?

Hardly, when there had been four bloody deaths! Not unless knifings of the minor actors were an acceptable part of a good Babylonian intrigue.

Moriel hadn't been minor, had he? Certainly not to himself. To Thessany, maybe; Thessany, whom Moriel had described as a snake pit . . .

'Clever lad!' said Praxis's sidekick. 'Be demure. Come to terms. No use protesting. Curse not the gods. Save and be diligent. Keep your nose clean. Don't pick your teeth in public.'

The two servants hustled Alex along.

It was only a fifteen-minute walk to the house at the north end of Scribe Street, close by the compound wall of Marduk's temple – Scribe Street being the noble avenue which led to the Borsippa Gate. If there were numbers on houses, this house would be number one.

Its great notched windowless walls rose up three or four storeys high. Several subsequent houses on both sides of Scribe Street were also huge but then sizes diminished, with the street gradually tapering roof by roof down to smaller business residences in the distance. This produced a curious perspective effect, as though the street was very much longer than it actually was. The Borsippa Gate at the end of the avenue dwarfed the most distant buildings, yet seemed also to be set at a vanishing point somewhere near to infinity.

An imposing residence indeed was number one.

'Who *is* Thessany's father?' Alex asked.

'Who is "my mistress's father",' Praxis corrected him. 'Go on: get used to saying "mistress".'

'All right. Who is my mistress's father?'

They passed inside, nodded through the portal by a black doorkeeper.

'He doesn't live here in the flesh,' Praxis said. 'You needn't concern yourself.'

'Doesn't live here? In the flesh? Is he dead?'

The two men laughed.

As usual there was a courtyard, overlooked on all sides by windows. Whereas curtains of loose reeds had hung in windows at the inn, here the wood-framed holes in the walls were screened by Babylonian blinds of waxed reeds strung together so that they could concertina up and down. The sizable yard contained a fish pond, three date palms and a fig tree; also an espaliered quince and many pots of red and damask roses, which a servant was busy watering. At this hour, since the house stood on the west side of the street, the nearer right-hand portion of the yard was sun-drenched but most was still in shade; and in the shade, on a stone bench, an elderly man sat snoozing, with an open box beside him.

The servants led Alex over to this man, whom Praxis nudged awake. The box contained little rolls of papyrus, pens, bottles of coloured dyes, and a range of needles.

Alex grew aware of spectators at windows. A couple of whispering women who giggled when he stared at them. A girl on her own, peeping out. Maids, servants. And Thessany – watching intently from a third-storey window. Alex waved urgently to her, and Praxis slapped his hand. Thessany merely continued looking down at him.

'Uh? What? Ah,' said the elderly man. 'Here at last. Kneel down, fellow.' Reluctantly Alex did so. 'Shuffle a bit closer! I've no wish to stretch.'

'What are you going to do?'

'Tattoo you; what else? With a fine lion's head in red and blue, the sign of this house. Upon your left cheek.'

'My cheek?'

'Mistress Thessany wishes it put there. To enhance your abrasive skin! The cheek may hurt trivially more than the forehead, but I shall do my best to avoid the main nerves. When you buy your freedom back, come to me to have the pigments pricked out. Only a faint ghost of a lion will remain. Unless you run away, of course, in which case when you're caught you get branded there. No blacksmith can unburn a branding.'

The tattooist sorted through his papyrus patterns till he found the lion's head he was seeking. Holding this by Alex's cheek, he took up a charcoal stick.

'An hour, no more, to do a fine job.'

'Mind you hold still now,' growled Praxis. 'I've other business, but Anshar here will be keeping an eye on you.'

'The pot obeys the potter,' said the lanky, dark companion. 'You don't want a needle in the eyeball.'

The sketch was finished in a few minutes, but then Alex had to kneel for a further hour while the tattoo artist patiently dug little holes in his flesh with different needles and rubbed in flecks of what looked frighteningly like cobalt and cadmium. He tried not to flinch too often or otherwise betray pain. Blood and sweat dribbled down his chin, to be mopped periodically with a dirty rag. He had no idea whether Thessany observed the whole of the process. He felt as if the needles were tapping into the nervous system of his head, as though to extract his mind and make a copy of it.

Eventually the tattooist rubbed his needles clean on the same rag, packed them away, and left the bench, humming to himself.

Alex tried to rise, on creaking knees, but Anshar thrust him down again. 'Now it's time for your slave's haircut.'

A fat cook-like woman brought a bowl of water, bar of soap, scissors, iron razor, and thumped herself down where the tattooist had sat. She snipped his locks, stropped the razor on stone, sending sparks flying, soaped his head and carved till only a crest of hair remained.

'I'll do you once a month,' she said, 'unless your hair grows fast, in which case it's barbering once a fortnight.'

At last he was able to rise. He had been allowed to keep his scrubby growth of beard.

Anshar pointed to a reed door. 'Strip and clean up. I'll kit you out in a kilt.'

It was a different Alex who was led into Thessany's room an hour later. A bare-to-the-waist, shaven-skulled, kilted, lion-tattooed Alex. There seemed to be a permanent cold numb spot on his cheek.

Thessany clapped her hands in delight. 'What a Babylonian you've become! You may go, Anshar. I shall explain this slave's duties to him.'

As soon as they were alone, Alex observed, 'You don't seem unduly sad about Moriel's murder.'

'An awful upset, I agree. At least the man trained his staff properly. The lovely wig I ordered for my wedding will not disappoint.'

'Your wedding?'

She toyed with a silver comb. 'Yes, let us speak of that, rather than of dead hairdressers. Especially considering the circumstances of his . . . his . . . hmm . . .'

'His squalid betrayal by a mage? To whom you paid *my* money – to discover the contents of *my* little scroll.'

'Yours! When you simply found it in the street?' She laughed. 'Anyway, if it's yours, who owns *you*?' She did not, however, deny that she knew the contents of the scroll, even though Moriel had been killed before he could report back to her. Alex noted this omission.

'Since I'm able to buy my freedom, I presume there are laws governing the property of slaves.'

'Oh yes. But one never knows how a law will be interpreted.'

'I don't suppose you'd want me to complain to a magistrate about this matter. Or to your father.'

She tossed the comb down. 'Wedding dates need to be fixed, so I suspect you'll see my father at prayers this evening. A genuine personal appearance! Much will become clear to you, Mori.'

'What did you call me?'

She stared out of the window.

'You called me Mori. Pet name for our departed friend. I'm not a new Moriel for you.'

She turned. 'No, you know so much less than him.' She walked to him, cold fire in her eyes, and fingered the lion mark on his cheek. 'I shall have to make do with second best, and educate you in the ways of intrigue. Delicious intrigue.' She let her hand sink.

'Won't Praxis run sly errands for you?'

'Praxis, at heart, is a bit of a puritan. A moralist. Even more so than Anshar, who utters morals out of mere unoriginality. Praxis will dislike you, without fully knowing why. If you seem obedient he won't punish you arbitrarily.'

Alex swallowed. Her touch had made his numbness smart painfully. 'So I'm not moral enough to suit Praxis, am I?'

'You're a mixture of distrust and treachery and ambition. *Would-be* clever treachery; frustrated lustful ambition. You also share with . . . you-know-who . . . a certain streak of masochism, the desire to have people punish and betray you, in your case because you have failed to live up to expectations. Those, for instance, of your clan, who expected something else from you . . . Yet you also imagine that these self-inflicted punishments of fate free you from your personal obligations, thus giving amoral rein to your own smothered desires, which this city might fulfil.'

'Is that all?'

'No. You also protect yourself with a species of wit – cold irony – so as to appear strong when in fact you are callow, lacking real experience. One of the prime reasons why you distrust people, why you cannot give yourself, is that no one else really exists for you in your egotism. Other people are objects. You are the only subject, the only "I". Other people are merely inventions, though often admittedly unco-operative ones.'

'Am I by any chance your *mirror*, Thessany?'

'You shall address me as "Mistress". For now you are my subject. You may not be able to give yourself, but I have taken you. I told you once in Ishtar's temple that I prayed for you. Now I *have you*.'

'On the subject of giving oneself, this husband – '

'Wit. Bankrupt wit.'

'Who is he?'

She smiled. 'I suppose we are two of a kind.'

'You and him?'

She tutted. 'You, slave, and me. So be my mirror; and I will polish you. My future husband is Muzi, son of Lord Gibil the financier. Gibil is rich, through crude cunning. Muzi is a bit brainless, but he makes up for it with bravado. His passion is hunting wild beasts. He is athletic, a handsome young stallion ideal for taming and training; and when he gets too pent up I shall always let him have his head. What he cannot conquer in me he can compensate for by slaughtering lionesses.'

'Risky business. A lion might bite his head off, leaving a rich widow.'

'You're being impertinent.'

'Sorry. Please continue polishing me. Tell me what's in the scroll that was worth killing for.'

'Wait till after you've seen my father. An event is better than a thousand words. That's why I had you tattooed like a temple slave. Otherwise you wouldn't have properly experienced your change in circumstances. That tattoo is the seal on our private contract.'

'A lion tattoo,' said Alex. 'And Muzi is a lion-killer.'

'Yes, isn't that appropriate? I suppose he thinks of me as the trophy he has won thanks to his own gallantry.'

Alex asked on impulse, 'Do you know the story of Andromeda? The *Andromeda* of Euripides?'

'No. Why?'

As well as he could, Alex recited the speech of Andromeda in bondage about gallantry of the heroic kind, and gallantry towards women.

When he had done, Thessany clapped. '*Excellent* and deserving slave! I ought really to give you a lute so that you can sing such speeches to me. Of course,' she went on, 'lesser egotists always feel the need to ingratiate themselves. Admiration is important to them; so that they can justifiably admire themselves. You may go now, slave.'

Alex was allocated a roll of bedding and told that he could sleep in the courtyard at nights, or in the kitchen doorway. He had no room of his own, though undoubtedly there were rooms to spare. Mama Zabala the cook slept in the kitchen itself, on the floor, always near to her bread oven and brick range with its elevated troughs for charcoal braziers where meat was cooked.

Following a light lunch of lentil broth, a barley-cake and a plate of awkward undesirable parts of several river-crabs – then a brief siesta under the shade of the fig tree – he spent the afternoon fetching water, scouring copper frying pans, peeling, and grinding corn in a handmill of volcanic stone. Mama Zabala's intermittent chatter built up his picture of the household – as regards menservants, maids, the slightly lame but doughty doorkeeper, the horse stabled round the back, and the two cats.

Mention by Alex of his new mistress produced respectful discretion rather than the intimate domestic outpouring of affectionate anecdote which he had rather been hoping for from a motherly cook in a house lacking any other matron.

Mention of Thessany's father seemed to fill Mama Zabala instantly with superstitious awe and anxiety. She kneaded her amulet, a clay blob, by now barely identifiable any longer as an elephant, thanks to several years of rubbing and squeezing.

That evening Alex found out why.

A gong boomed.

'Time for chapel,' announced Mama Zabala. 'Come! Afterwards we eat.'

She led him across the courtyard to a wide door of dangling reeds. Several oil lamps failed adequately to light a large, windowless, corbel-vaulted room. Maids and doorkeeper and Anshar were already kneeling on hassocks, facing a wall with a heavy black door-size curtain hung midway. A circular, jet-black rug at the foot of this curtain made it look as though a dark shaft opened down into the earth. There were no statues, no images of any god, no offerings of roast lamb or wine or barley-cake; just the curtain, the rug, and a single incense bowl.

Mama Zabala urged Alex to kneel; and knelt herself, somewhat more cumbersomely than an elephant. A groom hastened in, followed by Praxis; both knelt down. A couple of minutes later Thessany arrived, dressed in a white silk gown. She walked around the little congregation and knelt in front, a few cubits from the dark shaft. Alex looked for her father, but no one else had come.

Then Thessany cried out: 'Come, Lord Marduk, Mage of Magi, Father of us all! Lugalugga, Dumuduku, Bel Matati, Shazu, Tutu, Suhrim, Zahrim! Hear us, bless us, tell us.'

The black curtain flew aside; Mama Zabala moaned softly. Behind was empty, clotted darkness. The next moment a dazzling figure stood on the black rug. He hadn't stepped out from the darkness. He had appeared instantaneously, blindingly. His most disconcerting feature was his beard, which was plaited tightly thrice. Three furry auburn tentacles sprouted downward from his chin to the middle of his chest, making him seem not a human being at all but some other species of creature — something ancient and horrid who fed himself by means of those hairy appendages. He wore a triple-horned crown which matched, aslant, the horns of his beard. His eyes were watery blue, his nose squat, his lips fleshy and sensual. Silver lions embroidered his cloak. He stood motionless, staring into the chapel.

The figure just had to be a *holographos*, such as had appeared to Deborah. A piece of future *tekhnē* here in the chapel of a Babylonian house! What's more, the figure could be none other than Thessany's father. It must also be the god Marduk in the guise of his high priest!

This was the man who was going to marry Deborah; just as he married a beautiful new woman every year.

All at once a number of puzzles resolved themselves. Thessany was virtual mistress of her father's house. Marduk didn't – or couldn't – make it his home. Each year when he remarried gloriously he spurned the memory of Thessany's mother, whoever she had been. Symbolically he rejected his plain daughter. Still, he dominated Thessany – he was power incarnate.

How it would delight Thessany to upset her father's wedding! She would be jealous of the new bride: the woman whom Alex happened to adore, as had easily become evident to his mistress in spite of his dissemblings. By humiliating Alex, Thessany struck out at Deborah (at least in the equation of her own emotions).

In the midst of her capers Thessany had, however, collided with a deeper, bloodier plot connected with *tekhnē* and with power politics . . .

Thessany clasped her hands. 'Kinma, Tuku, Aranunna, Irkingu, Lugaldurmah! Hear us, bless us, tell us!'

Marduk shifted his phantom weight from one foot to the other. He flexed his arms, as though gathering the world in and crushing it against himself.

'I will wed ten days from now. The city will be

renewed.' His voice – a deep if hollow baritone – came from some way behind him. 'You, my earthly daughter Thessany, will wed Muzi, son of Gibil, one week afterwards; and dwell in this house with your husband. He is of good stock. Vigorous! You shall bear a son who will be reared in my temple to inherit the mantle of Marduk when I die.'

Even in the pearly backwash of light from her father's image, Alex saw Thessany blanch with shock and anger.

She stood up to face Marduk.

'Sir,' she said – and all the servants hid their heads – 'while it amuses me to be wed so soon after my father's annual bout of concupiscence with beauty, am I suddenly to be a breeding cow? And am I not to be allowed the stall of my own choice, to dwell in with my new bull? And is my first-born boy – if any – to be taken away from me? Just as I was once taken away from my own mother!'

'Your mother was unsuitable,' said Marduk. 'She drank, she took drugs.'

'Living with you, Great Lord of the World, who would blame her?'

'Silence! She stunted your growth. Great was my love for you. So I rescued you.'

'Kidnapped me! Brought me somewhere without laws!'

'I am the law, by and large. Your early memories mislead you. They are fantasies; concoctions. Your mother was almost a mad criminal.'

'Why then, so am I! Almost! Being her offspring.'

'And mine too. Mine is the strength in you, hers the weakness.'

'I certainly inherited your beauty, sir.'

'You know what you inherited. You have brains. Muzi, son of Gibil, has body, comely and muscular. Do not pretend that the arrangement will not suit you. I know you. And these arrangements are necessary.'

'Are they? What a shame that all your wives have been barren, except for one, my mother! One might almost suppose you impotent through guilt, Great Lord. Or have your wives given birth in secret to useless daughters?' Thessany slapped her narrow hips derisively. 'I will die in childbirth, producing a dead daughter.'

'You will produce a son. A Greek physician from the palace will ensure this, thanks to a cunning elixir. When your time approaches he will deliver you, unconscious, of your son directly through your belly without danger to the child; or you. As Lugaldurmah, navel of the world — by which title you invoked me — I assure you of that.'

Thessany's mood seemed to change. She sank back down on to her knees.

'Great Marduk, how could I disobey? It shall be exactly as you command. I shall even prepare a delightful present for your newest bride. I love you, Marduk. I honour and obey you. Needless to say.'

'Good. Let Praxis notify Lord Gibil.' Marduk's image vanished, plunging the chapel into darkness. By the time eyes adjusted to the dim lamplight, the black curtain was back in place.

Thessany strode from the chamber. Alex jumped up and pursued her. He had begun to feel a great pity for her welling up in him. He overtook her in the dusken courtyard, constellations of diamonds already glinting overhead.

She swung round. 'How dare you follow me! I will have you whipped.'

'No, please listen, I beg you! I *understand*.'

'Understand me? How little you understand! Each lash will make your poverty of wisdom plainly visible.'

'I understand the political plot. I know why Moriel was murdered – and what's happening in the House of Judgement!'

She hesitated. 'Go on.'

'Why are we all here, but to discover the best way to survive? How this city shall survive. How a culture – how history itself – shall survive. Different civilizations have tried different ways; and all have failed in the end, and the dust has covered them because they didn't understand the processes, they weren't sufficiently alert. The Egyptians had the will and the energy. They poured so much wealth and work into the future. Their dynasties endured the longest. But it was a future *after death* which obsessed them. So in the end they crumbled too.'

'I'm not interested in a lecture. Get to the point. Failing which, you will be whipped repeatedly day after day.'

Alex swallowed. 'Marduk and some of his men have decided that a hereditary god is the key to survival. A god with a human blood line. A son of Marduk himself and his year-wife would only become a priest. The boy wouldn't inherit the mantle. But a grandson from his family *can*.'

'So my father wants to perpetuate his power even after he's dead?'

'Yes, but that isn't the whole of it – though the proposed increase in Marduk's power is causing violent, covert opposition. A hereditary supreme god, plus mundane military administration: that's the new formula. A king and a court – plus a boss god, descending son to grandson in a single family line. At the moment the various gods – the different interest groups – are fairly well balanced. Each god takes it in turn to present a woman to Marduk as his wife. Even so, I

don't think Marduk's aiming to be a monotheist god –
the way Pharaoh Akhenaten tried to fix the system.'

'The other gods will still figure, but rather less so?'

'They must. See how Shazar, priest of Sin, supports
your father.'

'Does he?'

'He must. I'll tell you why. Each year-bride is chosen
by a rival god who has all the time in the world to
train her and make her loyal to him, rather than to
Marduk. Afterwards she goes to the House of Judgement – where fates are decided, I suppose. Where the
city's horoscope is plotted; where plan and reality are
compared, where formula and experiment are matched
– that's my guess. Where she's dead to the world, but
can still push buttons. Perhaps!

'Why should Shazar choose Deborah as this year's
bride? Apart from her attractiveness! Why her, rather
than someone he had trained and prepared for ages?
In this, the first year of Marduk's enhancement?

'The answer has to be that she was a new arrival.
An innocent – in a sense! Shazar didn't trust other
possible candidates. They might have been subverted
by magi hostile to the plan, who knew in advance that
this year it was the turn of the temple of Sin. Shazar
suspected this; Shazar feared it. So he must be co-
operating with Marduk.'

'Who else is co-operating in this amazing intrigue?'
she asked.

'Offhand, I'd say: mundane finance – in the person
of Lord Gibil. And how about the palace futurologist?
One day the ever-dying king will be replaced – not by
his bloodline, but by a copy of himself. The secular
ruler dies and dies, but the god is reborn and reborn.
That's the pattern.

'I think the palace must support your father – at
least in a qualified, heuristic way, for the sake of

experiment – because Aristander seemed to have made projections that fitted in with . . . yes, I see it now! . . . with what your father's trying to do. The palace was giving him the nod; but the hint of a deep conspiracy was news to Aristander. So the magi who oppose the plan haven't approached the palace.'

Thessany stared at Alex tensely as he rushed on, intoxicated. 'Who does support those magi? Some other temple? Foreigners on Babel? Or even foreigners from outside? Thessany, Mistress, I must know what was in the scroll – which was smuggled in from outside!'

Thessany caught hold of Alex, nearly dragging him off his feet. '*What*,' she whispered fiercely, 'do you know of the palace? *How* do you know about Aristander?'

The other servants had bunched in the chapel doorway. They were keeping clear of trouble, and perhaps striving to eavesdrop.

'How do you know?' Her lips hardly moved; the words were growled softly in her throat.

'Um . . . before I went to Babel I visited the Hanging Gardens. One thing led to another. I met the king and Aristander. Aristander found out about the scroll, and – '

'So *that's* who the two fighters were, who intervened! I thought they were constables of the babble parliament in plain clothes. Instead they were men from the palace. Oh, damn it. I never thought that *you* . . .' She regarded Alex with more admiration than anger.

'Well, we both got things wrong. *I* thought Praxis was waiting for you, not for me. How did he time it so neatly?'

She answered distractedly: 'I had a beggar keeping an eye on the temple of Sin. When Shazar's magi took that Deborah woman off to Babel, my beggar raced back to report. I nipped along there on impulse, spotted you ascending on your own. I guessed you'd defaulted at the inn. Your language lessons wouldn't start till the day after; and pumping Babylonian into applicants always takes the same length of time.'

'I see. So Deborah was ahead of me. She must have taken the ascent as easily as we did; or else she stopped for a long siesta.'

'*We?*' queried Thessany.

'Gupta and me. Gupta caught up with me while I was climbing.'

'Do you mean that Indian who was with you when Praxis and Anshar nabbed you? Praxis said you had an Indian friend who wouldn't lend you his worldly wealth.' Her eyes narrowed. 'Who is he?'

'Oh, of course – you didn't spot the two of us together in the parliament, did you?'

They had begun to converse like fellow-conspirators. Thessany must have recollected that she and Alex weren't actually accomplices, even if their relationship had nominally begun under that guise. She drew back a pace.

'Who is this Gupta? What does he know?'

'I . . . I got to know him at Kamberchanian's inn. I had no chance to tell him about the palace, thanks to Praxis.'

'Why should you be wanting to tell your Gupta about the palace at *that* particular point, when you had ample opportunity earlier on?'

'I . . . um, one of the fighters told me to turn up at the palace tomorrow.'

'So you hoped Gupta would go there instead – to explain your current predicament and beg Aristander to bail you out?'

'Something like that. I wasn't thinking too coherently.'

'Bail you out?' Brusquely Thessany shook her head. 'He would love to have an agent placed here, if I'm mixed up in this, as I obviously am. His men will come seeking you, fishing for information.'

'No, they won't. Aristander doesn't know I've become your slave. Gupta knows – but he doesn't know anything about Aristander.'

'I think a court futurologist might manage to deduce your presence here, given the limited number of possibilities. And here's where you'll stay – indoors.' As though she had only now noticed the servants still loitering in the chapel doorway, she screamed at them: 'Get about your work, you lot! Aren't we ever going to eat tonight?'

Praxis shoved at the cook, the maidservants. They fled across the courtyard, giving Thessany a wide berth.

'You, Praxis: come and see me later!'

The change from whisper to scream almost deafened Alex so that he hardly heard what she murmured next.

'What?'

'I said: so, thanks to you, Aristander knows I have the scroll.'

'He doesn't know what's in it.'

'No.'

'Neither do I. Has it occurred to you that the mage might have given Moriel back a blank scroll, if he could lay his hands on such a thing?'

'Why kill someone to steal a blank scroll?'

'To eliminate a potential nuisance. To scare you off.'

'Same scroll. I put secret marks on it. Good thinking, though.'

'Thanks. What's in the scroll?'

'So that you can try and tell the palace, given half a chance? Not likely.' Thessany did a double take. 'What makes you think *I* know what's in the scroll? Mori was knifed before he could report back to me.'

'You wouldn't have gone there in person for the handover unless you had swallowed a big chunk of bait already. Up in your room earlier on – that's before you heard about the palace – you didn't deny that you knew.'

'True.'

'Let's hope you were told the truth about the scroll.'

'Oh, I believe so! No one would have concocted . . .' She shook her head. 'How could I feel safe telling you?'

'I've no wish to tell the palace. It's for *me* that I want to know! Don't you see, I've been . . . in bondage to that scroll ever since I arrived in Babylon? It's been controlling me, making me do this and that.' He laughed giddily. 'It almost seems appropriate, with the damn thing in your charge, that now you should be controlling me!'

A smile hesitated on her lips. 'A scroll that controls . . . What a fine description.'

'Yes? In what way?'

She wouldn't explain. Nevertheless, she seemed to soften. 'I never dreamed you'd managed to meet the king . . .' She spoke gently. 'Tell me about him.'

Sensing that this was bait of a kind, Alex related every detail about the dying king in his bedchamber. She listened attentively, as though he were a favoured factotum telling a bedtime story to a little girl.

At the end of his tale she said, 'It's music for the wild dance of this city; that's what our little scroll is. It's the score.'

'You said "our" scroll,' he remarked gently.

'Ours. Yours and mine. Everyone's. Babylon is a great big brothel – and we are whores, all of us.

Dressed-up, painted, performing whores. It isn't just at Ishtar's temple or in one of those striptease parlours that one's a whore. You are. The king is. I am. All the time. So will my father be, if he has to dance to someone else's tune.'

Smells of lamb were now drifting across the court-yard from the kitchen. Mama Zabala appeared in her doorway and called out into the darkness impatiently: 'Alex the slave! Hurry up!'

'You'd better go and do some slaving,' Thessany said. 'I must talk to Praxis about making sure you don't sneak out; and that nobody sneaks in to bother you.'

She said this, however, as though taking Alex into her confidence.

5

In which a whipped dog wishes he were invisible

Beneath the fig tree Alex tossed and turned on his straw pallet amidst loosening blankets. As dawn began to dim the stars he woke shivering, rolled the warmth of wool tighter around him; and worried. He told himself that it was rarely a good idea to worry about anything whatever in the small hours of night or early in the morning, when the body is sluggish and the mind a prey to pessimism. But his mind preferred to fret about what Thessany had said in connection with the scroll, though she may have spoken fancifully.

In what sense were the denizens of Babylon all whores? In what way was the city a brothel?

What is a whore? A person exploited by others. Sexually. But not always. A person used. Allowing herself to be used; or himself. Often with little choice in the matter. Forced into it. Then accepting the situation, coming perhaps to relish it.

People came gladly to Babylon. Did they come principally – had Alex? – so that they could live out fantasy roles in a conceptual brothel given massive shape and substance? Here in a zone where future laws and morals and customs had been abolished?

Was Babylon his own brain-brothel where he submitted himself – willingly? – to impoverishment, slavery, entrapment, humiliation? Where he sought to initiate himself into ancient wisdom by suffering traumas which stripped away the unfunctional modern self, the self which could not survive? What was the real logic of the events which had happened to him? Were they accidental, or did they happen according to some invisible design? Some program? A program which matched the city with his psyche?

Did that scroll from the future, in some strange way, really control him? Like some precious dream talisman which forever slips through your fingers, like some dream book which you can never manage to open and read, did it exist not as a key to his situation but as a tangible symbol of that situation? Did the scroll *represent* some program which was operating his Babylonian delirium?

He stared through the dark branches of the fig tree at the fading stars in the sky, then at the dimly windowed walls around the courtyard, gradually emerging from obscurity and becoming visible again; and this thought came to him:

What if I'm not a person of flesh and blood at all? Not a being of nerve and saliva and semen, but a ghost – a copy of a person called Alex Winter?

The idea seemed oddly familiar, like a long-lost memory, as though he had known this once and then been forced to forget it.

Why build a whole city of Babylon in the Arizona desert at such enormous expense when you could simulate it instead? When you could program a fuzzy-logic, self-steering computer capable of carrying out billions of operations per second?

Where would such a computer be located?

Under Babel? No, because Babel would be part of the pretence.

At Heuristics. At the University of the Future, tucked away underground in some dust-free, steady-temperature, protected environment.

What if such a computer did not merely monitor Babylon, but actually generated Babylon and its inhabitants within its circuits?

Perhaps there was a city of Babylon in the desert miles from Heuristics — but it was a *holographos* of a city, a complex interacting evolving *holographos* projected there so that the experimenters would not have to rely merely on print-outs or animated graphics but could stroll around inside the *holographos* observing events, unobserved themselves, the unseen yet solid haunters of a ghost city, a city of dreadful light, which was ghostly except to those ghost citizens within it who were of the same frail substance.

How far had computers advanced? Could they simulate human consciousness? And if one consciousness, why not many?

What year had he really left Oregon and come to Babylon? Had several years been edited away? Was it later than he thought — and he the volunteer or victim of some fascist government think-tank? Was the question meaningless, because he had *never* existed outside of Babylonia, or the university? Not this particular version of Alex.

Could Deborah somehow discover the answer when she went to the Underworld after her year as Marduk's holy whore? Trying to contact her then might be like a living person trying to contact the dead to enquire about an afterlife!

Maybe Alex could never lay his hands on the secret of the scroll. Never, by definition, if the scroll was no more than a symbol, an internalized symbol, of the program which governed him.

And maybe Babylon wasn't concerned with survival at all! Maybe Babylon was all about consciousness instead. Maybe Babylon was a computer programmed to achieve consciousness — to become a living being by intuitive symbolic leaps, using as its data its internal persons, its whores of the mind who were copies of real persons, models.

Shivers racked him, and he rose.

Everything he had just thought about was insane. How chilling to imagine that things weren't real; yet in a stupid way, how comforting! Lunatics must feel both frozen and consoled by their rejection of reality. Yet eventually all richness, all depth would leach away till their lives were a diagram, a sketch of life.

To warm up, Alex jogged round the courtyard half a dozen times; then, recalling Nabu, he did some press-ups. The exercise invigorated him. Soon there was colour, and warmth.

Mama Zabala popped her head out of the kitchen door. 'Slave!' she bellowed amiably. 'Fetch water!'

He ran to oblige, glad to be occupied; purged of anxiety.

The scroll? It might prove a key to gaining his freedom from Thessany; but he wasn't sure that he wanted to be free from her yet.

As if to confirm Alex's new mood, while he was heaving his second bucket of water from the butt, the doorkeeper limped into the yard and gave him the once-over, nodding significantly to let him know that he was guardian of the exit. That's one white slave who's going no place on his ownsome. No, Missee Thessanee!

Then Alex remembered the curtain in the chapel. What was there in the blackness behind it? A niche to accommodate a *holographos* projector, linked by magic cord to the temple over the way? Or more? An actual hidden route into the lion's den . . . ?

Alex's day was full of domestic circumstances, none of which amounted to an event. In chapel that evening the black curtain remained closed. Eventually Alex dossed down under the fig tree, telling himself, mantra-like: *till midnight till midnight till midnight . . .*

He slept.

He awoke at an hour which certainly felt like midnight – the sparkling constellations overhead were no clock for him, no timepiece of a thousand jewels. Creeping from the comfort of his blankets he bunched these to resemble a sleeping figure, then trod softly to the chapel door.

Just inside, as he recalled, there was an oil lamp on a shelf. His fingers searched; he struck a stinking brimstone match and lit the wick. The chapel became feebly visible.

More lights? No. But he took several spare matches in case a sudden draught extinguished his lamp.

He wasted no time examining the mechanism which had tugged the curtain aside, simply lifted the fabric and stepped behind. He was in a deep alcove, with a flight of stone steps at the back leading steeply down. A glint of glass in the wall suggested part of the *holographos* system. Ignoring this, he descended twenty steps, counting each one. He found himself in a round-arched tunnel disappearing into darkness on a downhill gradient. The floor was hard earth.

Now let's see. The south wall of Marduk's ziggurat must be a thousand or so cubits from where he was standing; though maybe crypts or catacombs extended outward under the temple grounds. Hard to be sure, but this tunnel seemed to be heading somewhat in the wrong direction.

After walking a while he came to a door of solid iron blocking the way. This door had a curious lock, like a combination lock for the yet uninvented bicycle, built into it. Four little inset iron wheels were embossed with the letters of the Greek alphabet. The wheels rotated easily enough, not needing oiling from the spout of his lamp.

So what was the right combination?

He tried bits of the name Marduk and bits of the name Thessany; without result.

Did Thessany know the combination? Maybe she knew it without knowing that she knew. At evening prayers she would chant a whole string of names. Marduk had at least fifty names cataloguing his various virtues. Why not one of those? A short one. A four-letter one. After all, Marduk had to be able to remember the magic word.

He held the lamp up and stared into the flame, to put himself into a responsive state of mind. The flame danced as he breathed, blanking out the iron door, taking him back to the chapel where this same flame had burned amidst its frail friends. The tunnel walls were the chapel walls. Keeping the lamp at eye level, he knelt down and mumbled till fragments of the hymns emerged, and names.

'The charm which lulls ... sweet life restored ... *Tutu* is life renewed!'

Casually, so as not to break the charm, he dialled tau upsilon twice; in vain.

Wasn't there another name just like that? Damn it. Oh yes.

'Mutter curses ... power of words ... spellbinding ... this is Tu, Tu, Tu ... This is *Tuku*!'

Alter the second tau to kappa.

Click.

The door yielded to his push.

His lamp did little to light a much larger arched brick tunnel. Marduk's corridor joined this at an acute angle. Alex's nose and ears told him of the rustle of dirty water, and soon he stood at the brink of a stream

170

running down a channel in the centre. The effluent, or canal spillage, might be any depth, but it was a trivial jump across. From the other side he considered angles and directions. If the large tunnel ran on in a straight line it would eventually reach the river about where the river left the city; and it would *come* from under the grounds of Marduk's temple. He walked that way, shielding the lamp flame, and soon came to an iron door just like the other one, even to the combination lock. The tunnel still continued, presumably towards the bowels of Babel.

Setting the lettered wheels to spell TUKU, he tugged the door open.

A corridor led him to a black curtain of heavy wool, which he shifted slightly to peep round.

He was looking into an immense rectangular hall patchily lit by torches; most was in gloom. The walls sloped inward, with the upper halves cantilevered further inward. Trace their line upward in imagination and they would meet at the lopped-off peak of the ziggurat. Fat mud-brick pillars disguised as the trunks of palm trees rose to a ceiling where corbels jutted. A gallery ran the length of one wall, slung under the cantilevered upper portion.

This wasn't the chamber of eerie music and red lighting and stalagmite pillars into which he had looked during his climb to the temple summit. This hall must be below, or below again, and was proportionately vaster.

A few black-robed figures with cone hats – magi of the night – moved in the distance before a bulky statue of a bull seated on an altar slab. Even with its legs tucked under it, the baroque bronze beast was a monster twice the height of any mage. A fire flickered beneath, and maybe within, the body of the idol. Shadows and tongues of firelight darted ominously.

171

As he watched, the magi finished whatever they were about and departed up a grand flight of stairs, leaving the hall deserted. He waited a good many minutes, but no one returned. He set his lamp down, extinguished it, and stepped out of hiding.

Other black woollen banners hung here and there, maybe hiding other exits and entrances. Quickly he soft-footed to the wall overhung by the gallery where there was only one such curtain, which must conceal steps or a ladder leading aloft. He was sure the gallery was empty, but it might easily be a cul-de-sac. Stupid to climb up there.

However, he might be able to sneak up the grand stairway, slip through the temple unnoticed at this hour of night, and escape into the city . . .

With what aim? To seek refuge at the palace?

This bottom hall had to be the hugest in the building. It was perfect for a lavish wedding celebration. Here was where Marduk would wed Deborah.

He recalled what Laurel or Hardy, one of the two, had said about the climax to the marriage feast when the bride would be stripped naked and ogled by everyone present before Marduk finally claimed her. Alex couldn't quite stomach the prospect. Yet the way things had worked out, that was the only way he might ever behold Deborah nude. Supposing a slave was invited to the feast! Maybe Thessany might *ensure* that he attended, either to rub salt into his wounds or to burnish the mirror of his soul.

What did Deborah really signify to him – compared with Thessany?

He tried to visualize brighter lights, wild music and dancing, tables heaped with wine and viands, the throng of guests, the naked bride before the altar of the bull. He felt excited and horrified.

Oh what whores we all are here! Thessany was right.

Yet why shouldn't we give free rein to our desires and fantasies? Otherwise we stifle ourselves; as Alex had been stifled by that commune in the Cascade Range, with all its prohibitions. Do not skinny-dip with thy sister; thou shalt not commit incest and inbreed. Do not horse around homosexually with handsome youths; we must maintain our population. And no random exogamy with foreign boys and girls; the stranger to the clan is a potential enemy, looter of food stocks, bringer of sickness, rapist, murderer, communist, Judas. Armed survivalist morality.

Yet if people weren't stifled, how would fierce desire ever arise? It was desire which created history. A society which simply enjoyed itself made no mark. The lotus-eaters of Polynesia had survived only by default.

Babylon wrote out a different equation: the fulfilment of desire plus the peril of punishment, enslavement, death.

And all this while, as he was imagining the frolics of the feast — with its tough underlying theocratic motive — he approached ever closer to the massive ornamented bull. Two unlit candlesticks, each the height of a man, flanked the brazen beast. It drew him mesmerizingly towards it, just as Babel had drawn him.

A shout from behind: 'Stop, slave!'

The words echoed. He spun. A mage! The mage stood by one of the black banners; he must have stepped out from another corridor or room.

'Slave!' The shout rebounded.

Alex began sprinting back towards the curtain which hid his exit. Robes aswirl, the mage moved to block his path. Now other footsteps were clattering down the grand stairway, but Alex didn't waste time looking back. The mage darted and feinted; his cone hat fell off. Racing, Alex got ready to dodge should the man try to grab him.

Instead, the mage hurled himself in a full football tackle, crashing into Alex's knees and flooring him.

Before he could scramble away, the mage tackled again, sending him sprawling. Scant moments later, two other magi were pinning him.

Held in a painful armlock, he was dragged to his feet. He couldn't help crying out.

'Silence!' hissed a captor. 'Let Lord Marduk not be woken!'

'Stop breaking my arm, then – '

The agony subsided to discomfort.

'He isn't one of our slaves.'

'No, he isn't.'

'He wears the lion mark, though.'

'Yes, indeed.'

Hours later Alex was hauled out of the black cell where he had been dumped. He was marched before the altar.

Up on the basalt slab, Thessany's father stood leaning against the bull's rump, thoughtfully stroking the bronze. By now the fire within and below had burned out. In the light of newly lit torches Alex could see by virtue of several slits and openings, located where the metal hide rumpled, that part of the idol was hollow. Marduk wore a nightgown, though he had donned his triple-horned crown. His curiosity ws piqued, as well it might be.

Alex answered humbly, blending truth with lies. He was unable to forget Thessany's hints that Marduk's men might use torture. She had heard tales. Who better than her to hear tales? Maybe she just said so to scare him.

174

'Lord God,' whimpered Alex, 'I beg forgiveness. I'm your daughter's slave. Mistress Thessany's! That's why I wear this mark. Curiosity possessed me. I couldn't sleep last night. I went into the chapel and looked behind the curtain. I went down the steps and found the tunnel – '

'*How* did you open the locked door?'

Alex told Marduk, and the god's watery eyes became blue ice. The priest's eyes; the god's – he was one and the same.

'Mistress Thessany never told me, Lord. I just guessed.'

'Of course she didn't tell you; since she doesn't know! Why should I even suppose that she might tell a slave such a secret?'

Alex hung his head. 'I don't know.'

'And maybe you came from the other direction! From Babel. Only an imbecile would attempt to escape from my house by breaking into my temple!'

'I wasn't trying to escape, Lord. Not really. I was just looking.'

'Maybe you are an imbecile; a mischievous one. And maybe you're an assassin.'

'I wear your mark, Lord.'

'Anyone can have themselves tattooed with any sign, if they have sufficient reason.' To one of his magi, Marduk said, 'Go and request my daughter's attendance upstairs to identify this person.' The mage hastened away.

'I'm often a merciful god,' said Marduk to Alex. 'Especially now while I am jocund with the prospect of my wedding. I must also be just and terrible to defend this city from disorder. If my daughter fails to identify you, the truth will be wrung from you – and then the truth behind the truth. After a while you will cease to be the same person. Eventually your separate parts will swim away down that gutter to the river, with your trunk wallowing in their wake. If my daughter does identify you – you who were consumed with curiosity – then you will be consumed by fire, within my bull.' Marduk slammed the idol and it rang a hollow bell-note. 'Your screams will bellow from its nostrils. By comparison, this will be quite a quick death.'

'Lord,' murmured a mage doubtfully.

Marduk glared at the man, then smiled. 'I'm joking, of course. Human sacrifice shall be carried out as compassionately as possible. You will probably be given drugs, naughty slave, to dull all sensation. We have been pondering the identity of the first sacrifice.'

Alex's heart thundered. 'Sacri . . .'

'Yes, sacrifice! To affirm Marduk – just as Marduk affirms this city. It is needed. A god slain in substitute! Then the eternal Marduk weds once more.'

Madness.

Or was it?

Maybe the awe and terror of this event – and the sense of salvation felt by everyone who wasn't himself the victim – would be a psychic bulwark to the state. Maybe that was part of Marduk's scheme.

Fuck his schemes, thought Alex. Fuck psychic salvation. Fuck everything except surviving; except for not being slaughtered in such a mad, vicious, ancient way!

Would Deborah intercede? Could she beg for his life as a wedding gift?

'I had thought,' continued Marduk, 'of obtaining an unwanted child. A bastard brat, a beggar baby. Now a slave has presented himself. Maybe, my magi, this is a sign? *If* he's a genuine slave. We shall see.'

* * *

Two hours later Alex was taken upstairs through the hall of stalagmite pillars and fearsome statues, then further aloft to a private suite – to the décor of which, in the circumstances, he paid scant attention. Thessany was seated, sipping a cordial. Marduk, draped in a rich robe, stood toying with a glass of wine.

'Ah,' said the god, 'do you happen to know this slave?'

Alex gazed at Thessany, begging her with his eyes to acknowledge him, trying desperately to communicate that he hadn't really been attempting to escape from her, and also that he hadn't betrayed her. Too many things for two silent eyes to say?

Thessany hesitated, then said firmly, 'Of course I know him. He's my slave.'

'Ah. In that case he will remain here. Thank you, Thessany. I'm sure you have much else to occupy you.'

'Was he running away?' she asked idly. 'Praxis waits outside. We'll take the slave back with us. He merits a whipping and a branding.'

'No, he stays.'

'Why does he stay?'

'They're going to kill me, Mistress!' Alex burst out. A mage backhanded him across the mouth, squashing lips and jarring teeth.

'Do not spoil his looks,' said Marduk.

Thessany stood as if to go: and Alex despaired. But she didn't go. Instead, she amazed Alex.

Calmly she said, 'Father, if you keep my slave here I shall certainly – out of sheer pique – stab Muzi to death on his wedding night, while he lies snoring after ravishing me.'

'If you kill your husband, you'll be publicly impaled.'

'Oh, no; for I shall kill myself too. Indeed, why wait to be violated by Lord Gibil's son? If I don't take that slave home with me, perhaps I shall poison myself before the wedding.'

'Praxis!' bellowed Marduk. 'Fetch him! He will watch you like a hawk, or suffer terribly.'

'Even hawks close their eyes, Father.'

'You'll be confined to one room, which will be rendered very safe indeed. Someone from this temple will sit with you permanently.'

She shrugged. 'Supposing my suicide is delayed until the wedding, then Muzi will definitely die; followed closely by me. And if Muzi doesn't die on the first night – say because an official supervisor attends our copulation, which might well hamper my husband's performance – then he will die on some subsequent night. In view of Lord Gibil's high esteem for you, Great Marduk, I think that when he claims the corpse he will discover his son's virile member cut off and rammed down the throat . . .

'Alternatively, if I can take my slave – my wilful kitten, my songbird – home with me right now, I promise you that Muzi will enjoy himself lustfully. Or lustily, as the case may be. On that first night; and on many nights. And that,' she concluded, 'is that.'

Marduk stared expressionlessly at his daughter.

'Take him,' he said finally. 'Make sure you whip and brand him.' And he strode from the room; just as Praxis was ushered in by a different door.

Thessany snapped her fingers. 'Come, Alex. Come home.'

Gladly, though trying to look hangdog, he joined her; and together they went out by various turns and doorways to the ramp, with Praxis at their backs.

'Walk well behind,' she told the servant. 'I want some privacy.' Praxis dropped back.

'I can't thank you enough,' said Alex. 'They were

going to burn me alive in the bronze bull. Now they'll burn a child. Maybe a baby.'

'Say that again!'

'They're going to start having human sacrifices. An unwanted child was going to be burnt to death during the wedding. Then I blundered in. It's part of Marduk's plan to increase his power.'

'I see,' she said. 'But aren't I just as lovely, threatening to stuff my beloved husband's equipment down his throat!'

'No, you aren't. You said that to save me.'

'I meant it.'

'At the time you meant it.'

'True. A threat is no use unless you mean it with your whole being – at least temporarily. Though once a threat is uttered, one's pride is involved.'

'Do you intend to keep your other promise, to delight Muzi? I'm very sorry – '

'That you involved me in that promise?' She smiled. 'Did *I* use the word delight? Why should you think me an expert in delight, all of a sudden? Ah well, tomorrow night you can turn your own expert eye upon Muzi and advise me. He and Lord Gibil are coming to dinner. Incidentally, *were* you trying to escape?'

'Not from you. I know that now.'

'I believe you, Alex. Tell me everything that happened: especially how you got through the iron door. That was a neat exploit.'

'I guessed the combination. I suppose Marduk can change it.'

By now they had reached the base of the ziggurat; they headed across the courtyard towards the southern gate.

'Tell me everything from the beginning. Come on; we haven't got all day. Remember, you have to be whipped and branded.'

'What . . . ?'

'Yes. My father will enquire. He can observe you in the chapel, through his glass eye, from afar. We can't pretend a punishment. But the whipping will agonize me too! I'll order Anshar to perform. He's more flab than muscle, more doughy than doughty. I'll make it quite clear to him how peeved I'd be if he really damaged you.'

'Thanks.' He dared to be intimate. 'Thess, why don't you give me my freedom; quit me my debt? That would be one in the glass eye for your dad.'

A shake of the head. 'My conduct would seem bizarre. Marduk might grow suspicious. Besides, you would have to leave. That doesn't suit me at all.'

Yes, she wanted to keep him with her. Yet Alex sensed that the quality of her wanting had changed.

'So much is involved,' she said. 'His marriage; my marriage. Power and the palace – I believe you. Now the slaughter of children too. Tell, tell!'

He told; and carried on telling for another half-hour after they reached the house, closeted up in her room.

The household was marshalled in the courtyard. A straw pallet was laid across the stone bench so that Alex would not break his ribs by bucking. Grunting, Anshar roped Alex's knees to his elbows beneath the bench. And stepped back.

Praxis proffered a horsewhip: a long snake of leather a thumbnail wide with no knots or cutting edges.

'Right!' said Anshar. 'Slaves don't run away. Slaves obey.' The whip descended.

After the fourth stroke Alex decided that it was best to bellow his lungs out, not try to keep quiet. This also drowned some of Anshar's sententious adages, delivered in an ever more huffing voice.

Fifteen strokes in all – from the feel of them they

were distributed widely; some inevitably crossed each other. Alex's final three screams were involuntary.

Then the whipping was over. Mama Zabala bustled to spread a cool salve on his back. Snorting and puffing, Anshar untied the rope. Alex sagged. Tears blinded him. Anshar and Praxis hauled him to his feet, and the cook wiped his face with a rag.

Alex's gaze met Thessany's. Her lips pouted one slight kiss-you-better. She went away quickly.

He lay all afternoon on his whipping pallet upon the chapel floor as if doing penance, benefiting from the cool and dimness and relative absence of flies. When he next got up, to kneel humbly for evening prayers, his back felt as though it had been basted and half cooked. He moved carefully in case he tore his skin open.

Prayers commenced. The black curtain flew aside. The image of Marduk stood there.

'The slave has been soundly whipped,' declared Thessany. 'Show your spine, slave!'

Alex shuffled round, though the dim lighting must make the extent of his weals ambiguous.

'His screams were terrible. A sparrow died of shock.' This was surely going rather whimsically far! 'The cook will confirm. Zabala!'

Shocked not so much by the whipping she'd witnessed as by being forced to address Marduk personally, Mama Zabala's voice quavered, sounding truly appalled.

'Awful, Lord, awful . . . yes, awful, indeed.'

'Tomorrow the cattle-marker comes,' promised Thessany.

Marduk vanished without comment.

* * *

That night as Alex lay flat on his belly beneath the fig tree, prevented from sleeping by feverish hurt, he thought he heard footseps, but ignored them. They faded. The courtyard was very dark. The moon was new and low.

Much later the footsteps returned, came close.

'Hush.' Thessany squatted down. She had come to him in the courtyard by night! 'I went to the iron door, Alex. He has already changed the combination. I tried bits of all the fifty names of God. It took ages.'

Alex faced her. 'The new code could be anything.'

'No. If it's anything, he might forget. It has to be something associated with Marduk.'

'It could be the name of someone you've never heard of.'

'Will you rack your brains? You cracked the other combination.'

'I was lucky.'

'And subsequently not so lucky.' Her hand brushed his back. He shuddered, but her hand stayed in contact. 'I went tonight because he might have chosen another god-name in haste, meaning to reconsider later. Also, it occurs to me that he might have left the temple lock unchanged for the moment. If he has agents in Babel they'll still need to regain the temple secretly. You said that the stream in the tunnel probably flows into the Euphrates?'

'Underwater, I bet! Otherwise any busybody could wander up that tunnel.'

'Hmm. Can you dive and hold your breath?'

'Not just at the moment.'

'When you're feeling better we could take a trip in a coracle.'

'Thessany . . .'

'Yes?'

182

'I don't specally want to mention her, but do you suppose his bride-to-be – '

'Goodness, call the woman by her name. I don't mind.'

'Do you suppose Deborah's aware that her wedding is to be solemnized with a human sacrifice? I can't imagine it! If she doesn't know, how would the news affect her attitude?'

Thessany chuckled. 'So I should send you on a sly trip to the temple of Sin? Ah, any excuse to see the woman – particularly with you in such a pitiful state!'

'I don't think I want to see her. You could go yourself.'

'An intriguer, run errands in person? What are go-betweens for?'

'This is much more than an intrigue.'

'But it must be treated as such! Or one may lose all sense of proportion; begin killing babies.'

'He'll steal yours away.'

'After making sure I have a boy. I know, I know. Listen, Alex, I'm going to tell you about the scroll. I believe what Mori found out is accurate. Swine such as that greedy mage are essentially unimaginative.'

'You called it a scroll that controls.'

'Mm, sort of. You understand how Marduk manifests himself in the chapel, do you?'

'He's a *holographos*, beamed from the temple along glass wires. A creation of future *tekhnē*.'

'And of course we Babylonians tend to forget the origin of such things. Supposing we ever knew about them in the first place! Look at Mama Zabala's attitude; it's real magic to her. So such an image easily becomes awesome. Bold religious effects can be arranged. Gods can suddenly put in a personal appearance, popping out of nowhere. Okay, so a high priest embodies a god – but if the image flashes itself at people mysteriously and inexplicably on some street corner, that's the veritable god. You know the role of omens in Babylon.'

'Omens are what you make of them,' he said, remembering Aristander.

'Exactly. What people make of them. Marduk's no great mystery to me, and even I can get caught up in the mood. Right here in his own back yard, where he tests his image out. Most people hardly ever see such an image. If they do, it's powerful stuff. You haven't been in Babylon long: but one hears wild tales occasionally. Gods show themselves unexpectedly, miraculously. Gods are watching and listening. Prayers can be heard. Sometimes a god will command something: it would be dangerous not to obey. This doesn't happen too often.'

Alex remembered speculating whether tiny lenses were planted all over the city, recording events. Not only that, it seemed! Images could be projected through those lenses.

'Is it safe to plot anything in this city? Is anywhere safe?' he whispered.

'Oh yes! Not every wall has ears. Not every window has eyes. Else you'd need a whole second city the same size as this one to keep an eye on us all.'

'Would you? What if there are artificial brains built by *tekhnē* which can decide things for themselves, and which think so fast that we can't imagine how fast?'

'Alex dear, you're betraying symptoms of what the Greeks call *para-noia*. There will only be a few glass eyes here and there. Apart from that, we're free as the birds are to conspire.'

'We can't escape from *tekhnē*, Thess; even if we use oil lamps and worship Marduk and whip slaves.'

All this while her palm had remained on his flesh.

Now she squeezed, and the nearest whip-ridge pulsed. He gasped. Her lips brushed his ear.

'Listen. The scroll is an image of Marduk. It's a Marduk who cries woe on his own temple. A Marduk who repents of too much power. Apparently it's very cleverly made – the spitting image of my dad. That's what I was assured for my money; and yours.' Her fingers relaxed. 'Put that scroll inside a certain piece of *tekhnē* in his temple, during his wedding feast . . . do you see? I played in that temple a bit when he and I first arrived, before our lives really got under way. That piece of *tekhnē* was up in the gallery, above the altar where the bull is. Use the scroll – and he won't dare sacrifice a child.'

'What about his wedding?'

'It'll be disrupted, but not cancelled. My dad isn't going to let himself be chopped as high priest. Oh, he can cope. His big ambition will simply be aborted.'

'And *your* wedding?'

'I think this may cast new light on where Mr and Mrs Muzi take up residence.' She kissed him. Briefly her tongue quested inside his ear, tickling him; then she drew away. 'Tomorrow Mama Zabala will give you something to drink to help you. Be brave; don't flinch. It'll be over in a moment. There's no avoiding it.'

Oh God. The branding.

But God was Marduk, and God would look in to see that his instructions had been carried out – before his household greeted their guests, Muzi and Lord Gibil.

As promised, once the porridge bowls were cleared away the cook gave Alex a beakerful of some brew.

'What a nuisance!' she said in falsely jolly vein. 'What with such guests coming tonight, and all! Every *manner* of work to see to. Can't have you laid low.'

'I can hardly move as it is,' Alex said truthfully.

'Oh, but you must keep on the go – like a mountain stream in winter – or else you'll lock up, and it'll be spring before you're flowing about again.'

He drained the beaker. In the mixture he tasted strong beer, a lot of spirits, and the tang of powerful herbs. He became giddy almost at once. He felt he was floating. His eyes wandered, doubling his vision. His head had turned into a cabbage, a numb vegetable. The rest of his body tingled, mildly on fire, and his back ached worse than ever. Maybe the prophylactic was as bad as the impending pain; it certainly wouldn't have helped out with the whipping the day before.

Mama scrutinized. 'How d'you feel?'

'Ghastly. Poisoned.'

'Oh. I do hope as it hasn't taken hold the wrong way. Drugs mixed in drink sometimes do.'

'Where's my head? It just fell off.'

'Why, that's *fine*. You'll be right as rain by noon.'

Presently Anshar arrived to escort Alex to his favourite bench, where a muscular rosy-complexioned man in kilt and long leather apron waited, with tools of his trade: portable charcoal brazier, bellows, stone jar of water, branding iron. The stamping end of the iron was wrought as a little lion's head, identical to the tattoo Alex already wore.

A silent audience had gathered. Thessany was nibbling at her lip. Alex sat, and the smith checked the fit of the iron lion, cold. Anshar tied a rag round Alex's head to hide his eyes. 'In case the brand slips, if you jerk . . .'

Anshar gripped blind Alex tightly by the ear lobes. The pressure of knuckles caused a noise like rumbling wind in a deep cave so that Alex hardly heard the brand crunch into charcoal and the bellows puff.

Heat surged at his numbed cheek. A momentary

awful pang, as if a rat was savaging him; and he smelled burned meat. It was over. Anshar released his ears. The blindfold was whisked away. Snakes hissed as the brand plunged into the water-jar. Mama was patting salve or mud on his cheek.

By the evening Alex's whip-weals bothered him more than the brand mark. He could keep his cheek still, but not his back. Every time he moved an arm his back stung like a hive of bees. The cabbage condition of his head had resolved into a low-grade hangover.

He had attended prayers to show his naked scar to Marduk's image. Now, with salve restored and with an early meal in his belly, he knelt servilely (though not serving) at one side of the dining room while other servants bustled, and the honoured guests dined with Thessany; with Thessany's aunt as chaperone.

This woman, Ningal-Damekin, had ridden in from her country estate that afternoon to orchestrate arrangements for her niece's wedding. Alex hated the look of her. Ningal-Damekin was tall and scraggy, with an axe of a face. Her jaw jutted assertively; her voice was a harsh if cultivated bray; she strode about the house angularly as if she had no knees. Her complexion, ruddy from hours in the sun, was adorned with sparkling purple and gold paint as though she was a beauty as well as a great, if rural, lady. Or perhaps as though her face had gangrene. Her passion was hunting foxes and other furry beasts and seeing them torn to pieces. Obviously she had much conversational interest in common with Muzi, hunter of larger game.

Muzi was built like a quarterback and wore his blond hair shoulder-length and well shampooed (that night, at least) with a rainbow-hued sweatband. Round his wrist was a bracelet of what looked like stiff grey wire. 'For luck!' he confided to the aunt. 'Elephant's ass-hairs! Begging your pardon, Ma'am.'

Muzi's father was a tubby tough with a veneer of lordly courtesy; his wife was a slight, precious, wistful sort whose bunned-up hair was silky and milk-white. She only picked at the banquet – of suckling pig, crabmeat in little baked crusts looking exactly like crabs, sheep's brains, ostrich eggs, spiced bread, spotted partridges stuffed with baby mice, and a roast peacock, its tail reconstructed in boiled split leeks with mushrooms for the eyes. The floor had been drenched with scent. Many lamps burned aromatically. A hired quartet of musicians played softly on lute and flute.

Gibil ate steadily; his son with gusto; and Ningal-Damekin greedily, though only so as to provide an encouraging example.

Thessany, dressed in cloth of silver for the occasion, did justice to the various dishes; and to the wines – though she did not betray much tipsiness, unlike Muzi.

'Hey,' Muzi said to her, jerking a thumb. 'Been meaning to ask. That slave over there. What did he do, huh? Run away from a doll like you?'

'No, he went for a walk without permission.'

'So you had him whipped and branded?'

'Naturally.'

'Wow, what a lioness! Why's he here? He ain't doin' nothing.'

'Does he put you off your food?'

'Me? Naw. Last week I saw a wild bull elephant's trunk lopped off with a double axe.'

'How unfortunate for that elephant.'

'Thessany!' exclaimed Ningal-Damekin. 'It must have been a bold man who did that deed.'

'Yeah,' agreed Muzi. 'Let me tell you all about it.'

'In just a moment . . . Thessany, does that slave

really have to be in the dining room when he looks so unsightly?'

'Of course. He's my personal slave.'

Lord Gibil winked. 'I think the little lady's trying to show she's woman enough to handle my son. No offence intended, Mistress! I admire it.' He burped, and recollected his lordly manner. 'By the by,' he drawled, 'your repast is exceptional! The board positively groans. Is that not so, Lady Gibil?'

'Indeed it is,' said his wife. With her fork she hooked a baby mouse out from a partridge and placed it nearby.

'We need have no fear of our son starving when he returns from the hunt, once the nuptials and the moons of honey are over.'

'Aw, dad, do I really have to knock off hunting – '

'Until conception, my son.'

'That could take for ever!'

'Muzi, are you not a full man?'

'He is a lion,' said Thessany promptly. 'He is an elephant.'

'Yeah, I was gonna tell Lady Damekin here about the elephant's trunk.'

Thessany leaned over to address Gibil: 'Does the arrangement that we shall live here entirely suit you, sir?'

'Suit me? There are reasons, my dear.'

'I'm sure there are! They'll be beyond my silly little head. But I fancy it's cruel to deny such an active young man his sport for very long. Wouldn't you agree, Aunt Damekin? Inactivity might sap his vigour; produce results contrary to those required. His buddies might mock him; this could hamstring his virility.'

Muzi flushed. 'Hamstring, yeah. We got on to that after we'd axed the trunk.'

'I wonder if you may have a point there?' said Lord Gibil.

'Wow, its tusks were something else!'

'I should feel like a positive invalid,' said Aunty, 'if I couldn't ride to hounds for months – to compare small things with large. Indeed, it's a considerable sacrifice on my part to be stuck here in town so long; though the two events merit it – Marduk's marriage and my niece's – so I submit to duty without murmur.'

'Maybe I could just lay off hunting for a week, Dad?'

Lady Gibil sighed. 'Son . . . how shall I put this? . . . Even the most virile buck can't perform miracles. The doe must be receptive within; in her womb. Even then, nothing is guaranteed. It's a fact of nature.'

'Dad told me there was gonna be drugs to help her along. The astrologer fixed the wedding night, didn't he? She's supposed to be on heat.'

'Perhaps,' suggested Ningal-Damekin, with a rare display of diplomacy (or maybe she was only itching to hear hunting tales), 'Muzi might tell us about the elephant?'

Muzi launched into a long, tall tale of derring-do out in the wild-game reservations to the south-east, where Indian elephants roamed free, where prides of lions roared amid herds of deer and goats.

Thessany hung on his every word.

Four days later over breakfast, to Ningal-Damekin's displeasure, Thessany announced that she was going for a coracle ride on the Euphrates that morning, accompanied by her personal slave. She had dreamt a dream, she declared, of flowing water and round boats and a baby boy nestling in her arms; then she had found herself in a desert, and the boy in her arms had become a girl. Obviously a jaunt on the river would help irrigate her fertility.

'A dream?' sneered her aunt. 'Who cares about dreams? You might drown.'

'My slave swims strongly.'

'Huh. Would he rescue you – or himself?'

Alex, now much recovered thanks to the cook's back-salve, was serving at table; he felt moved to say, 'Madam, I would rescue Mistress Thessany if it cost me my life.'

Thessany glanced at him with an eyebrow raised, then said to her aunt, 'You see?'

'Trust the word of a slave, who recently was whipped? Somebody else should accompany you. That slave is also a *man,* Thessany, not a eunuch.'

'How dare you imply . . .'

'I imply nothing. I merely point out.'

'At the moment I am having my period, Aunt.'

'Ah!'

'Ah, indeed. In another week Marduk is wed. A week later, I'm to be wed, in the middle of my month. Are you quite satisfied? Or do you wish to inspect me?'

'Nothing was further from my mind. But maybe that's the reason why you dream of flowing liquid?'

'The point of the dream was whether I should bear a boy or a girl. To do my very best for husband, father, and God, I shall take a nauseating spin on the river.'

'You must have a proper bodyguard.'

'The slave will carry a knife.'

'The slave? What incredible folly!'

'Not at all. I'm sure the slave doesn't wish to be impaled for treachery. Besides, Aunt, I'm quite accustomed to finding my own way round the city. You, from the country, are not. The city probably seems more dangerous to you than it is. It isn't really risky at all.'

* * *

'Are you really having your period?' asked Alex as they walked riverwards; which was hardly any distance at all from Scribe Street.

Thessany nodded. 'Father checked up on my cycle months ago.'

'Why did you insist I have a knife?'

'Who knows what scrapes we might get into? You can always scrape better with a blade.'

They soon reached and crossed the river road, and descended a flight of steps to the quay. A few coracles were tied up, unloading food and wine. A gloomy tunnel led in under the road towards some bazaar.

Thessany explained: 'This is the southernmost tunnel. It leads up to Giguna Street. The trade tunnels are all quite short and I've pried into each one. None connects with our tunnel. Ah, there's our boat.'

A single-donkey coracle, bobbing by a bollard. The moke's master, and the boat's, was swarthy with droopy moustaches; Hispanic. He dragged the craft tight against the quay so that they could board.

'You have the anchor?' asked Thessany. The owner shifted a sack aside. 'Right, I want you to keep as close to this bank as you can.'

The boatman cast off. The coracle began to drift along, bumping against the quayside, trying to whirl about. The man heaved on a steering oar, put his vessel a few cubits into the stream, and hauled to control its urge to rotate. The donkey observed phlegmatically, shifting its hooves from time to time. Maybe the straw boat seemed like a mobile stable, and it was totally indifferent to the river.

The waters weren't as murky as Alex had expected; or hoped. Visibility was about four cubits. A few sizable fish – maybe tench – idled along, gulping little snacks of sewage.

Soon they were approaching the riverside tower

which served as exclamation mark to the city wall. Shading the water with her hand, Thessany peered keenly down; Alex less keenly. Something loomed below.

'Anchor!'

The boatmen tossed the drag-anchor over the side, which was currently the stern. Shuddering to a halt, the boat tried to pirouette; held steady.

'Down there! It's the top of a brick arch. Can't see the bottom of it. Can you?'

'It's deep,' said Alex.

'Yes; the first hundred cubits of the tunnel might be flooded.'

'Unless the opening slopes steeply.' Alex preferred to suggest so, and have her refute him, rather than the other way about.

'No reason why it should! There it is; but you'd be a drowned rat. Up anchor, boatman! Onward. Land us at the Borsippa Ferry.'

The donkey brayed deafeningly. A guard glared down from the tower, then saluted derisively. Hastily the boatman poked the beast in the chest with a stick. The moke jerked backwards against the edge of the coracle. It arched its tail; a torrent of amber piss descended into the Euphrates.

Some distance past Nebuchadnezzar's outer wall and the great New Canal which left the river just beyond, they landed at the ferry stage. The Borsippa Road ran right to the water's edge, then continued on the far bank. Bridging the intervening flood was a rope along which a ferry was hauled by hand.

Thessany paid the boatman. Alex handed her ashore, and the coracle spun away southwards. They strolled back along the road which would turn into Scribe Street once it passed through the inner wall,

Thessany humming to herself light-heartedly amidst the fields of beans. When they reached the wooden bridge which spanned the New Canal, she leaned on the rail. A coracle laden with baskets of excrement was being poled inland.

After a while she spoke: 'As a slave with the sign of the lion on you, you ought to be able to sneak up into that gallery without undue bother. Musicians will be playing; they'll provide cover. You slip the scroll into the *tekhnē* contraption, press a button at the appropriate moment, and lo! *Mene mene tekel upharsin.*'

'Who?'

'Old Hebrew curse; often chanted by a rabbi on the quayside. "God hath thy number, and thy game is up. You're more of a lightweight than you think, Daddy-o. Thy power will be spread around." Free translation. It's a nuisance you had to be branded as well as tattooed. That marks you out from other slaves.'

'That's funny. I thought it was a nuisance too.'

Laughing, she slipped a hand into his. 'Try to be invisible. Afterwards just abandon the scroll and skedaddle. Nobody will enquire too strenuously how it got there; not right away. Everyone will be too busy covering their asses.' Her hand squeezed his. 'Alex, I do wish it was your baby that I'd be blessed with, instead of that oaf's. I wonder, I do wonder! I'll probably be as fertile on the night *before* my wedding. You've already had some practice, unlike the mighty hunter.'

Spectres of dire danger flitted through Alex's mind. 'But . . .'

'Don't worry about Aunt Damekin. I'll make sure she's snoozing drunkenly. I promise I won't cry out and alert the house. If you like, you can gag me. Though I'd prefer not. And I won't claw your back. You can tie my hands; though I'd rather you didn't.'

'We don't want this to look like a rape, do we?'

'It won't look like anything to anybody. It'll be our secret, yours and mine.'

'How about when the baby's born with my face?'

'Oh, I'm sure it won't have a lion tattoo on its cheek! Joking apart, the baby isn't likely to resemble you strikingly. Babies are all squashed and blurry and blobby for ages.'

'Not if the baby is cut from you.'

'I want your child, Alex.' She removed her hand; a gang of peasants were approaching from the ferry. 'I want you as my lover, Alex, my only real lover. I'm not playing a game; not now. Well, I *am* playing a game – but I want you to play it with me! Will you?'

'I'm surprised you can like me well enough after your analysis of my character, first time I visited your room.'

'Oh, that. I was grooming you. I wanted you to respond to me. Probably I was mostly talking about myself. One says all sort of things at times. Words become a story, a fable. I'm saying none of this now just to enthuse you about the scroll scheme. I fear for you. I hurt for you. Ishtar has wed us to one another. Oh, there I go again! But I mean it.'

'Maybe you do, as well. I . . . I want you too.'

'Good, that's settled. We'll do it. And Alex, we'll *love* doing it. I think you'd better walk a pace or two behind me, for appearance's sake. We must still look like mistress and slave. But I'll be a different sort of mistress to you, come my wedding eve. And thereafter, whenever Muzi's busy mutilating elephants.'

They walked on, with Alex lagging behind watching her hips move, till they came to the Borsippa Gate and passed through into the throng of Babylon beyond. Rather to his surprise Alex felt radiant, sane, and happy. Some kind of cloud had lifted from his life.

At the junction of Scribe Street with Zababa Street, he spied Gupta walking through the crowd.

Gupta spotted him. 'Alex!'

Thessany turned her head. 'Is that the Indian who climbed Babel with you?'

'Yes. He's one fellow who *could* make himself invisible!'

'Do you mean that seriously?'

'Well . . . yes. I do.'

Gupta had observed that Alex was accompanied; or accompanying. He stared in disgust from the brand mark on Alex's cheek, to the portions of whip-marks he could see, to Thessany.

'Pardon me, good madam!' Gupta sounded virulently sardonic. 'May I have your gracious leave to speak with an old friend?'

'Yes, but calm down,' she said. 'All is not as it seems. Your friend here made the mistake of breaking into the temple of Marduk.'

'And they whipped him and branded him? Ah.' Gupta looked puzzled. 'Is that true, Alex?'

'Not precisely. But – '

'I thought not!'

'Any other great lady,' said Thessany, 'might be sorely offended by your scepticism, Indian. Please don't leap to the wrong conclusions.'

'My name is Gupta, not Indian.'

'Mr Gupta. My apologies. Alex, in view of . . . you-know-what . . . I want to ask: how much do you trust this person?'

'I trust him quite a lot.' Alex grinned sloppily. 'He lent me some money.'

'Oh *did* he? You never mentioned that. How much was it.'

'Shekel and a half.'

Fumbling in a hidden purse, Thessany produced two

silver coins. 'I don't normally burden myself with cash, but today I had to pay a boatman. Here you are, Mr Gupta. Your debt is quit. With thanks.' She thrust the coins into Gupta's hand.

Gupta promptly tossed the silver on the ground. 'I am not being bought off!'

The money didn't stay long on the ground; an urchin darted, snatched, and scampered away.

'You have just contributed to the poor,' said Thessany. 'Congratulations.'

'Not I! You have.'

'Proud Mr Gupta, let me ask you: can you become invisible?'

'Oh, you wish me to vanish! Disappear! Never offend your eyes again! Amidst my other business concerns I have been making enquiries about you, let me tell you.'

'What sort of enquiries? With whom?'

'General enquiries; on Alex's account. I promised my assistance.'

'You *can* assist him, Mr Gupta. Teach him to become invisible.'

'You are japing me!'

'No she isn't,' said Alex.

'When we saw you just now, Alex said to me, "There's a fellow who can make himself invisible." I ask in all seriousness, can you do it? If you can, and will tell Alex how, you'll make a perilous exploit much less risky.'

'What exploit?'

It was Alex who shook his head. 'No, we can't tell you. Even knowing is dangerous.'

'Seriously, this is how you wish me to assist you, Alex?'

'You'll have kept your promise,' said Thessany.

'Your conscience will be clear. You'll have a light heart.'

'And I shall not turn into a weasel in the next life, ha ha! You're quite sure, Alex?'

'Absolutely.'

'So be it.'

'Shall we share some refreshments?' suggested Thessany. 'I know a little place up Zababa Street, with the sweetest roof garden.'

The roof was shaded by crowns of palms; you could reach and pluck fresh sticky dates. Hibiscus bloomed in tubs; the furled pink parasols of fallen flowers lay scattered like cocktail ornaments. And there was a brick pot of fox-tailed lilies. Alex and Thessany drank cold beer; Gupta, lemonade.

'It's an odd fact,' expounded Gupta, 'that it's quite impossible to keep your eyes open during a sneeze. Now sneezing is sometimes caused by sexual excitement. That's why many women close their eyes while kissing, out of secret fear of sneezing in their partner's face! So a vision of bodily beauty excites – but it can also cause momentary blindness. Hence the myth about naked goddesses blinding men who spy on them.'

'All eyes will be on Deborah for a while, blinded to everything else . . .'

'That's too late in the proceedings, Alex,' said Thessany.

'Equally, certain polluting sights may be unseeable. Would you stare closely at someone excreting or drooling phlegm?'

Thessany giggled. 'I must bear that in mind, if Aunt Damekin pesters me.'

'More importantly, people can recognize only what they already know. If the eye sees nonsense, the mind concocts a plausible alternative; something else is seen instead. To avoid observation you can dress shape-lessly, in contradictory colours which cancel out. But this is only the start. The body, you see, has a language of its own consisting of a finite number of fixed phrases. The body doesn't flow smoothly; though our mind perceives smooth movement. The body actually jerks about, jumping from one state of posture to the next. Gestures and expressions are rituals, to which we respond ritually without realizing. If your body can learn to glide through the gaps between these discrete states of posture, carrying out its true actions therein, then these acts often go unnoticed by other people. Or, if you dislocate the seeming connectedness of your behaviour so that your body engages in contradictory manoeuvres, then the mind of the observer applies the Blade of Simplicity and cuts away what it can't recon-cile. If you continually break step while walking and destroy all regularity, it quickly becomes unpleasant for an onlooker to watch you, though he doesn't know why. Contrariwise, extreme monotony of motion drugs the observing eye.

'Watch me. I'll demonstrate a few tricks of posture and movement . . .'

Half an hour later, Alex was sure he would need to spend a whole year (or five) as the Indian's disciple in order to master these indisciplines. These dislocations of the expected; these ruptures of normality into which a person might, effectively, vanish.

Gupta reassured him: 'We were both hypnotized deeply in Babel not so long ago. So you are still very receptive; and in any case I can hypnotize, albeit not as deeply as *tekhnē* can. At the moment I'm busy training Kamberchanian's strippers, using my own light touch of hypnosis. What's more, given the proper stimuli of circumstances, a hypnotic trance state may return spontaneously, just as a drug fugue may. Everyone in this city has been hypnotized before, so everyone is potentially suggestible; which helps.

'What I suggest is that I train you under light hypnosis for a couple of days. Obviously I can't transfer years of knowledge and experience in so short a time. But I *can* write down a word which I will hide in your mind. When the moment of peril comes, look and read aloud. Your body will remember. At that moment you must not oppose your body. You must believe that you are truly invisible; you must have no doubts. For example, you should walk as though no one else can see you; and thus would bump into you, ha ha!'

'Under hypnosis,' observed Thessany, 'Alex might well tell you his mission.'

'Only if I ask him. I promise I shall not. I swear by my friendship for him.'

She nodded. 'Okay. Alex will go with you for two days. And I'd like to say that I'm quite impressed by your demonstrations, Gupta guru. I'm a bit busy for the next few weeks, but later I'd like to study with you – deeply and obediently, till I learn. I shall of course pay lavishly; on the understanding that I am your only serious pupil.'

'One or two of the strippers may become serious.'

'And one or two thieves? And one or two assassins?'

'Ha ha! Invisible assassins might stab me without my noticing. Invisible thieves might steal your lavish money from me.'

She leaned forward intently. 'Doesn't a Master truly succeed in his teachings only when his pupil masters him; bewilders him?'

'For that insight alone, lady, I would accept you as a pupil. However, I must continue to perfect the strippers.'

'All right. But no gentry or nobles, priests or politicians.'

'Agreed; since I prefer to practise my art in the gutters.'

'So as to avoid becoming a courtly charlatan; a performing monkey? So that mud may be made into gold rather than gold into mud?'

'Ah, you do understand. I definitely accept you.'

'I'll pay you lavishly; but you can keep the money – better still, jewels – in an old rag stuffed in a dungheap for ever, if you like.'

'Alex, my friend,' said Gupta, 'you are fortunate to have found such a mistress.'

'Yes. Yes, I am.'

'And now,' said Thessany, 'let us visit a scrivener so that Alex has a tablet with him granting leave of absence. Otherwise, before he learns to become invisible, constables may notice how recently he was whipped and branded, and arrest him on suspicion.'

Gupta took Alex back with him, not to the inn, but to the adjoining strip parlour.

Yet here, where the topic is the intriguing one of the art of invisibility, the events of these twenty-four double hours which Alex spent at the skin shop, now renamed The Eye of Horus, must needs also be invisible; for Alex was in a hypnotic trance during that time, unaware consciously of what Gupta was training him to do. One hastens forward to the hour of his return to Thessany's house, with a sealed scrap of paper tucked in his kilt at which he mustn't yet look.

His body ached in odd ways which seemed to bear no relation to his whipping. He felt as if he had been extensively massaged without actually being touched. Several new muscles might have been invented, or grown suddenly from threads, especially in his legs and hips.

As he was approaching the house he noticed a raggy beggar sitting crossed-legged at the mouth of an alley.

That was no beggar! It was the ruffian – Aristander's agent.

Alex glanced twice – which was perhaps one glance too many – then ignored the man. '*I'm* a slave,' he told himself. 'Been a slave for years. I slave and slave slavishly. That's all there is in my life: slavery. Nothing else.'

However, the ruffian stirred. 'Hey, you! What's the hurry?' Two shakes of a lamb's tail later, the man was confronting Alex. 'Look at me!'

'Buzz off, beggar. I haven't a bean for you.'

'There's something wrong here. You remind me of . . . Why were you walking along so jaunty-like, when you've obviously been whipped within the week? Run away again, have you?'

'Certainly not. I have permission from my mistress.' Alex fumbled for the tablet; encountered the knife, which Thessany hadn't taken back. His hand froze. 'It's here somewhere.'

'Why should you show a beggar your permission?'

'To save you a whipping for making a stupid mistake. Whippings hurt.'

'Naw, you know who I am all right. You've disguised yourself as a slave. Hell, you've been branded. What happened to you? Why didn't you come to the palace? Why are you pretending?' There was still a note of doubt.

'I'm not whoever you suppose. But *that's* my mistress's mansion which you're spying on! I think you're a thief; I'll raise hue and cry.'

'Don't waste your time and mine.' The ruffian delved in his rags and produced – not a knife, but his own tiny clay tablet inscribed in Greek and cuneiform, stamped with the royal seal of Alexander. 'See this? Palace police.'

'Stolen, no doubt.'

'You're a rum one. It *is* you, isn't it? If it weren't for that damn brand!'

'I am *not* – '

'What about the scroll?'

'What scroll?'

'You know very well.'

'Some play by Sophocles, perhaps?'

'*You* know what's in it.' The ruffian's emphasis suggested that *he* didn't know. Whatever subsequent enquiries had been conducted in the bowels of Babel must have run into a brick wall.

'This is quite absurd. I shall report you.' Alex walked on, his back naked to any knife; however, he reached the doorway safely.

'Doorkeeper!'

The lame black man stomped out from his cubby-hole. 'Well, I don' know. The brazen cheek of it!'

'I was . . .'

Accosted.

The ruffian had vanished; doubtless up the alley.

'Summ'ning me out as if you're some fine gen'l'man! You get your ass in here and no nonsense.'

6

In which Belle and Shazar feast, though the writing is on the wall

Since Marduk's wedding celebrated the annual spiritual renewal of the city, festivity spilled from the temple as from a fountain. The whole of the huge courtyard was filled up with dancing devotees of the god, drunks suckling on free wine and beer, family parties picnicking, the roasting of oxen and pigs, barbecuing of pheasants and peacocks, many bands of musicians, marquees of Ishtar, tents of Sin, booths of Shamash, satyr players and off-duty soldiers, as well as with a mini-exodus from Babel: of tipsy Chinese poets, lithe yogic Indians, Phoenicians who worshipped Marduk as Baal, Hittites, Egyptians, Italians, Huns. The ramps of the ziggurat were so crowded that the edifice resembled a sports stadium of the distant future. By tradition only the Jews of Babylon stayed away, conducting a day-long anti-celebration of their own on the quayside.

Thessany's group arrived a full double hour before the noontime start of ceremonies. (This was to be a day of no siesta; good Babylonians should not sleep through the period of renewal.) Thessany herself walked arm in arm with Ningal-Damekin, both robed in pink silk and painted up to the nines. Praxis and a groom preceded, armed with sword and club. Anshar and Alex brought up the rear. The abuse done to Alex's back had faded by now. Concealed under his kilt were: the little scroll, and Gupta's magic word of invisibility.

Progress was slow. When they reached the first level of the ziggurat, guards scrutinized the tablet of invitation carried by Praxis and admitted three to the balefully lit red cavern: Thessany, her aunt, and Alex. Praxis, Anshar, and the groom would amuse themselves elsewhere. Together with other guests and retainers, Thessany, Ningal-Damekin, and Alex descended to the vast chamber below, the Hall of the Bull.

Today hundreds of torches and lamps were lit; and in the man-size holders on either side of the bull two leg-size candles flamed steadily. No fire yet burned below and inside the bull, but kindling and sandalwood logs were in evidence, as were pots of oil to speed combustion.

Trestle tables bowed under cheeses and cold joints of venison, bowls of dates and figs, whole fishes in aspic, wine and sweetmeats, hills of bread. Many stools were already claimed. No one was eating as yet, but drinking had commenced. Great was the rumour of conversations, though not noisy enough to drown the beat of the kettledrums from the gallery, the ripple of harps, the whistling of ocarinas.

On a throne before the bull sat a red-headed woman, glamorous and shapely in a green gown. Her cheeks were painted silver; the bush of fire which was her hair supported a diamond coronet. A twin throne beside hers stood empty. Most of the time she gazed radiantly at the assembling guests; occasionally a sour, mournful expression crossed her face. She was last year's bride, Mrs Marduk of the past twelve months, the goddess Zarpanit enjoying the final hour of her reign.

It was she, at the height of the feast, who would rip

all the veils from the new Zarpanit, stripping her naked — briefly — before the eyes of all beholders. Marduk would snatch the coronet from his ex-consort; immediately she would hasten off, bound for the Underworld. The god-priest would crown his new queen and goddess and throw a cloak around her. The feast would continue.

Below the altar slab a small laden table awaited, with two carved chairs as yet unoccupied but reserved for Shazar, priest of Sin, and for the bride-to-be.

'If only there were ushers to assure us a place of honour!' Ningal-Damekin complained.

Thessany said distractedly, 'Everywhere's a place of honour today, Aunt. Even my slave could sit with us, if I gave leave.'

'I want him to. Very wise! Otherwise we might have greedy neighbours. I think . . . over there! By the baron of beef. Come along.'

Thessany resisted. 'Slave,' she told Alex, putting a peevish malice into her voice, 'you may *not* sit with us. Go and stand by the wall.'

'How perverse!' exclaimed Aunty.

Alex bowed and filtered away through the crowd.

Magi were strutting about making final arrangements. Temple slaves with the lion tattoo on their foreheads were conveying more wine and last-minute dishes, aided by slaves who must be Shazar's since their tattoo was a crescent moon.

With a polite, 'Pardon me, Lord,' Alex lifted a plate of candied quince and carried it off so as to look busy.

For what seemed an undue hollow volume of time he loitered at various points along the wall beneath the gallery, mingling whenever possible; till at last he saw the black-bearded, beehive-turbaned Shazar emerge from behind a far banner, leading a figure heavily veiled from head to foot. For a while now no more guests had been descending the grand stairway. Alex sidled to the nearest trestle-top and deposited his plate. As the priest of Sin and the hidden Deborah seated themselves in the carved chairs, a gong boomed from the gallery.

Hoping he wasn't acting precipitately, Alex burrowed for Gupta's bit of paper, broke the seal, and read aloud:

> 'Ziggy-Zaggy-Zu,
> No sight of you!'

His body twitched electrically. His flesh squirmed as though hairy caterpillars were crawling all over him. Wriggling and shimmying, he scaled the steep stairs leading to the gallery. He writhed his way past harpists, drummers and ocarina players. How odd that no one batted an eyelid, when he felt like a victim of Saint Vitus's dance. *That's because I'm invisible. Nobody can see me. I must have faith.*

Next to the gong-percussionist stood a mage, his attention on events below. Just beyond was a decorative wall-boss which Thessany had assured Alex would conceal the piece of *tekhnē*. He twitched past and examined the boss. Three holes burrowed into it. He stuck his fingers into these and twisted. The boss came loose.

Then the gong boomed – BOONG! – and his heart thumped like a drumskin. The din was so close! *Boong, boong, boong,* went the gong as if striking the hour. *Boong, boong.*

He risked a glance. Marduk was striding towards his throne.

The last gong-beat died slowly. The whole hall was quiet.

Alex heard Marduk's voice hailing his guests, but

he no longer looked. In the hollow behind the boss was *tekhnē* familiar from some misty future age. He fingered a black plastic surface, a cassette slot. He delved for the little scroll, thrust it into the mouth within. And crouched, harking to Marduk. His whole body continued wobbling.

'. . . shall be a holy sacrifice!'

A gasp rose from the audience; and chatter, quickly stilled.

'. . . child of Babylon shall burn within my bull . . .' No, Alex was none too soon! He jabbed a button and a little red eye glowed.

Hastily he replaced the boss. Mage and gongman were even more intent on the spectacle below. Alex let his body jiggle him away.

He missed much of the apparition; he was still shivering his way past musicians, then squirming downstairs. He heard a much greater gasp, then a louder, thunderous voice crying woe.

As he slunk away from the curtain which hid the stairs, all backs were turned to him. Everyone was staring transfixed at a radiant, giant Marduk who stood by the bull, dwarfing his human counterpart by a head and shoulders.

'. . . without abuse of power!' proclaimed the godhead. Did the voice issue from inside the bull close by? 'Bear this sad victim away unburnt, and let there be joy!'

A cowering mage was holding a slumped child in his arms; a boy of four or five. The boy must have been drugged, but he wasn't unconscious; his head lolled from side to side. By now Alex's own palsy was abating.

'No one god shall dominate the council of the gods by blood! I am but the first amongst equals! Rejoice! Renew our city.'

Thessany's father had adopted a bland, attentive look. Deducing that the harangue was finished, he bowed to the apparition. At the same moment the *holographos* vanished so that he was left bowing to thin air.

Gossip and rumour welled in a flood tide. Quickly Marduk spoke to the mage, who hurried the floppy boy away; then he gestured up at the gallery. The gong *boong*ed, silencing most guests.

'Our god has shown himself to me,' Thessany's dad cried out. 'This sacrifice was ordered by the god to test obedience to his will. Now the god has interceded mercifully. Marduk is the stern ruler, but he is also generous. Did he not just tell you to rejoice? Begin the feasting! This next year will be fruitful!'

The guests, who had been working up an appetite with wine for ages, needed little encouragement to commence gorging themselves; though they talked as they ate. How they talked, chewing over the scandalous mystery!

Marduk took to his throne beside his consort, soon to be deposed. He drank; he consulted with magi – suddenly a kerfuffle occurred in the gallery, though harps and ocarinas carried on playing. He waved Shazar over; they whispered together. Then Shazar returned to his table and ate lustily. Deborah's veils – and perhaps nervousness – prevented her from partaking. Soon Marduk perked up.

Alex kept an eye on the whereabouts of magi and temple slaves so as to avoid encounters if he could. Hardly anyone was using the grand stairway, otherwise he might have tried to sneak up it, and out. Lose himself in the crowds.

What, leave before the main scene of the wedding? He had almost forgotten about it . . .

The wood under the bull was drenched with oil and

lit. Furnace light blazed from within; smoke issued from the nostrils – but no screams of agony from anyone penned in the bronze beast's back.

Dancers cavorted, snaking rainbow ribbons and white veils behind them.

Within fifteen minutes the tables had been stripped as by locusts. Lack of a stool at table deterred none of the stand-up spectators from raiding the boards – Alex spied Ningal-Damekin in hot altercation with one hungry wolf who had descended on her fold. But it might attract attention if a branded slave began snatching food. It took only one Aunt Damekin to kick up a fuss. So Alex merely moved his empty mouth from time to time as if munching. He lurked by one or other of the massive pillars, though never for too long. He mingled whenever a sizable knot of people gathered. He noticed Lord and Lady Gibil and Muzi seated nearby, and avoided them.

A mage carried a black cloak to the altar. Marduk rose. The gong boomed. Shazar stood and ushered his veiled companion forward. The red-headed woman rose from her throne, one hand caressing it lingeringly in farewell.

'I relinquish Zarpanit,' cried Marduk, 'and I regain Zarpanit.'

'I proudly present the gift of Sin,' declared Shazar.

As if in a rage, the redhead began to rip the veils from her rival and successor. Deborah was stripped naked very rapidly. 'Ah!' breathed voices here and there. Mostly the assembly was silent and intent.

Alex had looked to see if Thessany had spotted where he stood; and whether she was watching him watch Deborah. She wasn't; she was watching Deborah herself. But thus it was that Alex missed the majority of the spectacle; for already the coronet was on Deborah's head, already Marduk was swirling the

210

black cloak open. All too briefly Alex saw naked womanhood, but he had no time to refine his impressions, to spy details, to see a naked *Deborah* – before Marduk wrapped the cloak around her and led her to the vacant throne.

Alex sighed deeply.

A neighbour nudged him in the ribs. 'Superb, eh?'

'I don't know,' said Alex. 'I don't damn well know.'

'Oh. You been castrated?'

'No,' he said sarcastically, 'I'm short-sighted.'

Where was the redhead? She had already fled.

Deborah looked pleased with herself now that her crisis was over. She smiled dreamily at Marduk. He stooped to kiss her, and the tentacles of his beard quested at her bosom like furry fingers. He resumed his seat and the couple chatted a while till Marduk fell into a brooding silence. Presently the gong boomed again, and amidst Saturnalian cheers he led his queen away.

As soon as Mr and Mrs Marduk were gone, the party broke up. Alex rejoined Thessany, who paid him no special attention; the three of them joined the crush heading up and out.

Ningal-Damekin was full of the amazing interruption earlier on. 'Still don't know what to think! What a to-do! Fear fair clutched at my heart for that poor child; though he was likely only a beggar's boy.'

'Like a fox cub to the slaughter,' said Thessany. 'Ah, there's Lord Gibil. I must have a word . . .'

Thessany's father, to no one's surprise, did not put in an appearance at prayers that evening. Afterwards, in the dusky courtyard, Thessany called her slave aside.

'Nice one, Alex! Lord Gibil will be sending a note to the temple tomorrow. I foresee a change in arrange-

211

ments as to where us newlyweds dwell, come the great day.'

'Good. But I've been thinking. This could all have happened irrespective.'

'If the scroll had reached its original destination, you mean? If it hadn't fallen into our hands?'

'Exactly.'

'Ah, but then I shouldn't have been able to take advantage. In any case, the recipients might have bungled the job. I bet they don't know the secret of invisibility.'

'Nor did they know *we* intended to use the scroll! The mage whom Moriel bribed can't have been an accomplice, or he wouldn't have given the goods back even for a moment.'

'What a surprise for the conspirators! They'll be wondering how their dream came true.'

'Hmm!'

'What's the matter?'

'If *I'd* been pinning my hopes on a certain scroll and it went astray – I'd have laid alternative plans.'

'What sort of plans? Nothing else weird happened.'

'That's what's puzzling me. The crucial event today was to be the sacrifice, right? Now supposing I hadn't used the scroll when I did, how would they have sabotaged the sacrifice?'

'Ah. The fire blazed fiercely enough. The oil jars weren't full of water.'

'The bull! Something to do with the bull! The mage was going to climb up the bull and put the boy into the cooking compartment.'

'Yes?'

'As things turned out, he never did climb up there. But if he *had* done, what would he have found when he opened the bull's back? He would have found . . . something which stopped him from putting the child

212

inside! Something which would have made him shriek with fear. Something that would have been a terrible omen.'

'What kind of thing?'

'I don't know. Something dangerous, like cobras. Something horrible and polluting. I bet you they sneaked a surprise into the bull's back. We didn't need to use the scroll, Thess!'

'Hmm. And the palace might tell my dad what they think we did . . . Just as well if there *is* a heap of cooked cobras to be found! Though I guess hot snakes would have tried to get out through the nostrils.'

The following evening, Marduk's image did appear in chapel.

'I've received a message from Lord Gibil,' he said without more ado, 'sent, I believe, at my daughter's instigation. He informs me politely that Muzi will take his bride elsewhere to live.'

'Oh no!' cried Ningal-Damekin. 'After all I've done in this house for dear Muzi's comfort. And at the last moment. It's really too bad.'

'Be quiet,' said Marduk. 'There's no choice in the matter; not after the . . . instance of divine intervention at my own nuptials.'

'Wasn't *that* a surprise!' exclaimed Thessany. 'Marduk would appear to have cunning enemies. Was he really intending to kill a child?'

Thessany's father made a gesture of disgust. 'Abomination; at my own wedding.'

'Divine intervention can't be an abomination, Daddy.'

'If only that was all!'

'Did something else disturb the wedding? I can't say I noticed.'

In two minds, Marduk struggled with himself. 'Thessany . . . you have a keen mind. My idol was violated.'

'Ah. By the same hands that arranged the intervention.'

Marduk did not disagree. 'How could it have happened? After your slave broke into my temple –'

'He was scourged for his naughtiness.'

'I don't point the finger at him. In a way I'm grateful. On his account I changed the word which opens the door to the temple, as well as the door downstairs. Anyone coming from Babel or the palace by the tunnel route, burdened with the abomination and expecting entrance, would have found their way blocked. That's the enigma.'

'One of your magi must be a traitor, Daddy.'

'No. I hadn't told anyone else the new word yet. I'm sure I hadn't.'

Thessany thought briefly. 'But you must have repeated the word to *yourself* so that you didn't forget it.'

'What do you mean? That I walked in my sleep and polluted my own altar?'

'Polluted it with what, Daddy? That may be a clue.'

Ningal-Damekin was so agog that she held her hand clamped tightly over her mouth so as to avoid interrupting.

'With the corpse of a leper – to judge by its scorched meat! With its stumpy hands reaching up to seize whoever opened my bull!'

'How do you know it was a real leper? I expect the fire didn't improve its appearance. It might have been any corpse artfully made up to look like a leper. Fingers mutilated, and such.'

'Oh, it was a leper, and no mistake! Are there not several lepers in Babel? One of those wretches must have murdered him.'

'*Who* would have manhandled the body of a leper? I

214

suggest that the corpse of an ordinary man was worked over. Amputated, decorated; that's more likely.'

'Oh my God,' growled Marduk. 'Of course.'

'So how did the traitor discover the word to gain entry for the corpse? The answer has to be that you told the traitor.'

'I didn't tell anyone.'

'You told *yourself* the new word. Many times. The word would have been high on your mind – high enough for you to mutter it in your sleep. Did the previous Zarpanit share your bed during her last days?'

'Yes . . .'

'How did she feel about being banished to the Underworld?'

'She accepted the inevitable.'

'And wished for revenge? And hoped to buy favour with the Underworld, if the Underworld was conspiring against you? Or had she simply been biding her time all along, as a sleeping enemy?'

'I uttered the word in my sleep . . . and she heard me? Yes, you do have a good mind. It all hangs together. It's plausible.'

'Perhaps Marduk should confide in his daughter more often?'

'Perhaps. My plans are delayed, not destroyed. You shall still give birth to a boy.' So saying, Marduk vanished.

'That was a fine piece of concoction, Thess, blaming the last Zarpanit.'

'I think it's probably true. True of the leper's corpse and the locked door! So now Daddy believes that the same persons were responsible for both the corpse *and* the scroll; double indemnity. That's excellent. The palace haven't told him about the scroll; which means they've withdrawn their tentative support, because he failed. Aristander has lost faith in the scheme.'

'The palace haven't told him *yet*.'

'Maybe they never will. Maybe they'd rather keep the news of his daughter's deceit as a horrid surprise to spring; a potential lever. Maybe now they won't even supply Greek medicine to fix the sex of my baby. Or they might supply dud medicine; something innocuous – though one can't rely on that!'

'And we've learnt that the tunnel runs all the way to the palace.'

'Doesn't it just? Daddy said that the abomination came from Babel *or* the palace. He must suspect the palace too.'

'When you first opened your mouth, I thought you were going to blow everything wide open.'

'Ah, but I've known him longer than you. To me he looked perturbed. He didn't quite know what was what.' She clapped her hands gleefully. 'I've solved the puzzle for him. Zarpanit was the fly in the ointment, the bug in his bed.'

'Which god gave *her* to Marduk last year?'

Thessany laughed. 'It was Ishtar. I think, Alex, we shall begin Operation Conception tonight. I feel in the mood. Creep to my bed at midnight; ravish me.'

To Thessany's bower, at some hour approximating midnight, Alex duty crept; feeling his way up dim stairs, then along a dark corridor.

He slipped through the door without rustling the reeds, and immediately met a heavy inner curtain which Thessany must have hung to baffle any sounds that might leak out. Once beyond, he could see clearly enough: the bedding laid upon the floor, the shape beneath the blanket. The blind was up, and a gibbous moon approaching full painted the part of the room near the window ivory, the rest as a grisaille.

'I'm here,' he whispered.

No response. She was asleep.

But it was Thessany, right enough. (The suspicion had faintly occurred to Alex that Thessany might instruct one of the maids to use her mistress's bed, while the mistress herself slept up on the roof bathed by moonbeams . . .)

What to do next? He dropped his kilt and undid his loincloth. Naked, he knelt and pressed one hand over her mouth.

Her body squirmed beneath the blanket. He pulled this aside and pressed his body against hers. Her hands roved over him, though avoiding his back. She made no effort to free her mouth. Releasing his hold, he replaced the pressure of his palm with the pressure of his lips. She kissed, deeply.

To his surprise (considering that she was being ravished) she contrived to roll over and straddle him. He lay beneath while she held his cock and, with some fumbling, mounted it; and sank down wriggling, enclosing him. She panted as though in childbirth already – until soon she drew up into her the quick, hot fountain of his seed. She slumped upon him and they played softly for a while, she humming at him, he throbbing throatily, two cats purring.

He felt wetness. 'It runs out,' he whispered.

'On to you. My bed won't betray me. Now that you aren't so full of juice, take me from behind like a beast.'

So he did. He stayed with her for an hour, by which time she was dozing. As he disengaged himself she held on to him, mumbling protests. He kissed her ear. 'I must go, or I'll sleep. Moonlight will fool me. I'll not know when it's dawning.'

He dressed and tiptoed through darkness back to his own pallet beneath the fig tree in the pearly courtyard.

The next night he visited her; and the night after. By then he knew without doubt that they were not merely having sex together; they were making love.

By day the house wasn't quite as hectic as it might have been had Muzi still been due to take up residence there with his own little entourage; not forgetting his black hunter-stallion Galla, named for those devils which pursue their prey relentlessly.

Even so, Ningal-Damekin was forever scratching lists on beeswax and striding hither and thither as stiffly as if saddle-sore. Tradespeople called to deliver food and wine and to decorate and stack trestles and boards in the yard – the dining room couldn't possibly accommodate all the guests. Wedding gifts began to arrive and were displayed in the dining room: a Chinese dragon vase, a jade figurine of an imperious lady, twelve cubits of silk, two amphoras of Chian wine, a handsome leather saddle, a throwing spear; and so on. Gupta sent two mirrors hinged so that they could look at one another for ever, like the happy couple. From the temple of Marduk came a bag of gold as dowry.

The courtyard and entry had to be swept repeatedly; the chapel must be spruced. In the kitchen Mama Zabala laboured amidst steam and smoke, generating a mound of refuse to be hauled away and spread along the street.

Meanwhile Mistress Thessany mostly sat in her room, ignoring the fuss and bother, conceiving – so she told her fraught aunt – a poem.

The night before the wedding, as they lay in bed together, Alex asked Thessany, 'Are you really composing a poem?'

'Yes. But in my head. It's to be called *The Whores of Babylon*.'

'Will you recite it to me?'

'It isn't finished, Alix Phallix. It'll take nine months.'

'Oh, I see. You can't know *yet*.'

'If I believe strongly enough, that'll encourage my womb not to shake the true fruit loose. Incidentally, I ordered Aunt Damekin to invite Gupta to the wedding. If Gupta's to be my guru of invisibility, Muzi had better get used to the sight of him.'

'Will your father attend in person?'

'After all the useful tips I gave him? I should be offended if he didn't. And Lord Gibil would feel insulted. Are you wondering, by any chance, whether the new Zarpanit will be acompanying her spouse?'

'Quite honestly, I'd rather she didn't.'

'She probably will.'

She did.

Marduk and Deborah-Zarpanit arrived at the front door last of all, riding in triumph in a four-wheeled carriage escorted by three magi and a small squad of soldiers. Courtyard and dining room were already crowded. The bridegroom and his father were circulating, with Ningal-Damekin angularly at the latter's elbow. Thessany was still upstairs, having her wedding wig bouffanted. In the chapel the magistrate who would marry the couple was holding court; city gentry were ingratiating themselves, if they happened to be involved in lawsuits. Alex had been busy replenishing wine-cups but was now only pretending to, while Gupta chatted to him.

'Since I've been honoured by this invitation, I presume that your mission was crowned with success? But do not tell me what it was!'

'I shan't, great guru.'

'Ha ha. A very private guru, to one noble lady alone who wishes to slip from her house unseen. I must take care I don't become a plaything to a lively lady: someone on the fringe of society, who will perform dubious missions which no wise man would stick his neck into – errands which ensure that he must perform more of the same in future!' The Indian scrutinized Alex. 'Have I just hit a nail on the head?'

Gupta as the new Moriel – if he wasn't careful? Was that the real deep reason why Thessany wanted him as private visiting guru? With lessons in the art of invisibility as a mere pretext, a front? Lately Thessany seemed to have reformed emotionally, but old tricks die hard. Maybe such tricks were vital to survival – or at least success – in such a milieu as this.

Gupta chuckled. 'Alex, even branded with a lion to distract attention your face is the least secretive of faces! Don't worry for my sake. Once you have truly charmed a cobra of the animal kingdom you can charm most human snakes, even the most insinuating. We're all potential cobras down at the base of our spine – but that's a long way from the brain, which often fuddles rather than sharpens instinct by trying to be too clever. The Lady Thessany will learn *more* than invisibility. She will need to learn clarity. That's the first essential of invisibility: to become a transparent pane of glass without blemish. When that happens, you who love her may also learn clarity.'

'Be quiet! What do you mean?'

'If I'm silent, how can I tell you? Not that I need to! Nor need I be any Pandarus of your love . . . not when you dwell in her house, and I only visit.'

At that moment the god-priest himself strode into the courtyard, arm in arm with Deborah-Zarpanit, cloaked but not veiled. Three magi followed; two soldiers stationed themselves at the entrance. From the street you could hear the neigh of horses and voices of other soldiers.

Deborah's gaze did cross Alex as she accompanied her husband towards the chapel; she obviously had no notion who he was other than simply a slave. Even if Alex got close enough to whisper, later, he did not intend to open her eyes to the truth. To her, he thought, I am invisible. He felt a surge of joy. In that moment he felt her image vanish from his heart, becoming that of a stranger.

Thessany, dolled in white satin and puffed pompadoured wig, her face painted silver and gold, descended into the courtyard.

When the festivities came to an end, a procession set out. The home which Lord Gibil had purchased for the newlyweds – a home unseen as yet by Thessany – was in the new city over the water.

Thessany and Muzi rode in one slow chariot, the Gibil parents in another. Anshar, Mama Zabala, Alex, and a couple of maids followed on foot. Behind trundled carts and sledges loaded with personal possessions and wedding gifts, pushed or pulled by hired porters; while an escort of soldiers brought up the rear to guard such rich pickings from robbers. The soldiers were those who had come with Marduk; he and Zarpanit had driven back to their temple, accompanied only by magi.

Praxis would stay behind in Scribe Street as majordomo of the empty house, and would hire a few extra staff to keep it ticking over. Lord Gibil had appointed his own choice, Muzi's valet, to Praxis's position at the new residence. Gibil had also selected a doorkeeper, since Lady Gibil feared that daily sight of a lame black man might cast some fatal shadow over Thessany's womb. The exact future of the old house was still undecided, though with its secret passage it must obviously remain Marduk's. Ningal-Damekin (also remaining behind) declared that she would use the place as her town house, should she ever reluctantly feel compelled to tear herself away from country sports.

Also in the procession was a Greek doctor, Cassander. He had come to the wedding as Marduk's guest, leather medicine satchel slung over his shoulder, along with the libation jar and censer of his calling. Cassander was silvery-locked, clean-shaven, benign, avuncular. But he had a hook of a nose like some tool for carving maggots out of people's feet. During the reception Thessany had engaged Dr Cassander in flattering banter, to which he seemed amenable, becoming quite garrulous with wise anecdotes. Propitiation by prospective patients obviously softened him — so long as his own diagnoses were not doubted; opposition might bring his stern hook into play. This, then, was the dispenser of the male-child potion. This was the surgeon who would cut Thessany open to remove her baby boy, and sew her back together again. He was paying his first house-call, to be sure where the new house was.

The procession made its way to the river road and along past the Euphrates Gate of Marduk's temple to the bridge. On the way, from his chariot Muzi tossed occasional coins to beggar boys who scrambled and scrummaged while their benefactor shouted, 'Go to it! Block, and tackle! Down! Dead coin!'

Once over the river they made their way along the Adad Road which would lead eventually to the westerly Adad Gate, the gate of storms. At the crossroads with Larsa Street the procession turned south. Unlike central city properties which were crowded together directly abutting on to streets, with garden courtyards inside, here in the suburbs gardens – with high spike-tipped walls – surrounded homes. (Beyond the west wall of the new city were poor relations of these suburbs, with mere picket fences of sharpened stakes or thorn hedges protecting vegetable gardens and mud shanties.)

The new house, on a lane some way off Larsa Street, compromised between suburban living, passable proximity to the heart of the metropolis, and a convenient exit from the city for Muzi when he would ride out a-hunting – by way of southerly Larsa Gate, and then the Borsippa Ferry.

Eventually the head of the procession arrived at a gateway set in a tall, long garden wall. The tiny clay-brick porter's lodge adjoining was just large enough for one well-built fellow to stretch out full-length on the floor to sleep. A squat, bulky gatekeeper stood expectantly, holding a short sword across his big bare slab of a chest by way of salute. His head thrust up out of his shoulders without much benefit of neck. His tight black hair might have been trimmed with a scythe in one fierce sweep across his skull. A red nose suggested a flaw; he might be a drunkard, though perhaps the kind of drunkard who rouses quickly, becoming a wrathful automaton.

Thessany refused to let her chariot proceed through the portal; she pointed accusingly down the lane.

'What is that ugly omen yonder?'

Everyone peered, including the gatekeeper. Near, but not very near the gateway, half hidden by weeds, lay the rigid corpse of a cat gathering flies.

'What is that abomination doing there?'

Lord Gibil intervened: 'Clear that thing away immediately, Nettychin. Burn it. You'll have a shekel docked from your pay for negligence.'

How to make friends with your local gatekeeper, thought Alex.

'No,' said Thessany. 'He is in my employ, and I choose not to dock his pay. Today is my wedding day, and I am full of bliss. Perhaps his eyes are not what they used to be?'

'Madam,' stated Nettychin emphatically, 'I see well; but your eyes are keener than mine. Just as your kindness is greater than anyone else's.' He spoke as if stamping each utterance upon the fabric of eternity. He shifted his weight from one elephant foot to the other. 'Madam, maybe it crawled there recently. The spikes are fresh-tipped with poison.'

'By you?'

'Aye, madam. The cat must have been stupid clumsy.'

'Unlike you. How did you reach those spikes?'

'With a ladder I keep behind my home. I think to myself: no intruders allowed!'

Thessany favoured him with a smile. 'Thou good and faithful servant.'

As Nettychin stomped up the lane to collect the dead cat, the procession entered the walled garden, which was a somewhat desolate pleasance. The house beyond must have stood empty for a while — it was of two sprawling storeys with a tower at the south end rising one storey higher. The top floor of the tower had windows; otherwise only the main doorway broke the blank zigzag of the front wall.

Plain to see that no one had watered or pruned the roses or trimmed the tamarisk bushes or hoed out choking weeds and coarse grasses till recently, when a hasty effort had been made. A bonfire of torn-up vegetation still smoked lazily. Roses sprawled in thorny tangles with scant blooms and black-spotted, mildewed leaves. The sandy soil still supported much tussocky grass and invasive coarse green things, with petty blossoms, as though the clearer-up had realized halfway through his task that completing it would just produce an acre of desert. The garden may have been more charming before the effort was undertaken.

Heaps of horse droppings lay on the ground. Thessany wrinkled her nose.

'I do apologize for the condition of this,' Lord Gibil said to her. 'All was arranged in haste. In a few months this garden will be as splendid as the house already is.'

'That manure'll help,' observed Muzi.

'By lying around attracting flies?' asked Thessany.

'Manure feeds flowers.'

'It doesn't contain flowers, lord and husband. It likely contains thousands of wild grass seeds. Alex,' she said to her slave, 'please clear all the mess away. Trim and tidy; put in order. Especially water the poor roses. They're suffering neglect.'

'Something which won't afflict you, my rose!' declared gallant Muzi; though his gaze drifted nostalgically to the horse dung.

With a terrible yapping and baying a great brown hound bounded from behind the house, dragging a leash behind it.

'Tikki-Tikki-Tikki!' Muzi jumped from the chariot. He intercepted the animal before it could cause mayhem, such as knocking people over or upsetting carts. Heedless of his embroidered wedding cloak, he wrestled the hound over on to its back and tickled its belly.

The dog's minder followed apace: a dapper, sandy, middle-aged man with the look of an ex-soldier. Muzi continued rough play with the beast till this other man had reattached the leash to its studded collar.

Muzi scrambled up, his fine attire dusty and hairy.

'Tikki sure missed me!' he told his bride. 'I didn't think I oughta bring him to the wedding.'

'Who's that person who let him loose?'

'That's my man, Irra. Irra, this is your new mistress.'

'Madam.' Irra inclined his head sharply to one side. The leaping hound prevented any more obsequious or straighter bow; if indeed Irra had contemplated such.

Alex saw Thessany speedily sum up Irra.

'Chain that creature,' she said sharply. 'And keep it well chained. Use metal, not leather, to control it.'

'Tikki's just affectionate,' protested Muzi.

'I'm not having it soil my gown or nip my slave while he's putting this wilderness to rights. As for you, Irra, did you suppose I wished to be greeted by that lolloping, slobbering monster? I loathe dogs. I am the daughter of the lion.'

Irra stood to attention; however, his attention was directed at Muzi.

'Yeah, chain Tikki up.'

The major-domo began to haul the hound away.

'Irra!' Thessany's voice was pitched to halt a man in his tracks.

'Madam?'

'When I bid, Irra, you do *my* bidding.'

'Yes, madam. But what if – suppose – you were to bid me to slit Tikki's throat? Begging your pardon, I merely enquire.'

Lord Gibil hastily abandoned his chariot, strode at Irra, and slapped him hard across the cheek.

'You dare enquire, before servants and menials, as to the extent of your mistress's authority? You shall lose ...' He turned apologetically to Thessany. 'Dearest Daughter-in-law, I overreach myself.'

'He shall lose *three* shekels from his salary ... to be

restored in nine months' time – with interest – if he has carried out his duties to my satisfaction.'

'A judgement of wisdom!' declared Lord Gibil. 'A wise wife is a treasure,' he told his son, in case his son was unaware. Lady Gibil nodded vaguely.

7

In which, after a pregnant pause, we encounter ingots, ergot, and apricots

After hectic activity there is often a long moratorium; as in war, so in life. A quick campaign is followed by ages in camp. Or since most Babylonians cared a lot more about money than they cared about war, you might say: initial investment of capital is followed by slow accrual of profit.

You might, except that the banker Lord Gibil had been known to lend out money at extortionate interest rates; and his financial probity will soon play a part in our tale. Metaphors fall apart. Suffice it to say that the tempo changed from allegro to adagio; a long slow movement set in.

By day Alex mostly laboured in the garden or brought water by bucket-barrow from the nearest canal for kitchen, toilet, and stable use, and to pour around the roots of roses.

In the neighbourhood many gardens were orcharded, with plum and pear, apple and crabby medlar. Bees hummed from hives nearby. On the way to the canal he would pass a school for rich kids and hear young voices chanting answers about the jargon of jewellers, the categories of songs, how fields are best divided, secret meanings of words and other useful information. Down the lane to the west was a dairy where gallons of milk hung from the walls in the bags of calves' stomachs, turning into ghee-like cheese by contact with the rennet. Mama Zabala sent him there twice a week.

And at home? (Where he now had an out-of-the-way cubbyhole all to himself indoors.)

The reeded windows along the rear of the house looked upon stables and kennels and a spiked back wall masked by a line of weeping willows, two of which were dead and wept dry sticks. The prospect was not of roses but of horse and hound, which to Muzi's way of thinking must have made the house ideal. Within ten or so days of his marriage he had ridden forth upon black Galla, accompanied by Irra on a mare, several mounted young cronies, and a dog pack, bound for a spot of hunting and three nights away from home; which was the first occasion for adultery in the tower room which Thessany had made her own.

Alex and she lay together sated in the darkness of the night.

'I must be pregnant,' she murmured, 'else it would be time for my period by now, and I'm not puffed up, and not at all twitchy.'

Alex nibbled on her ear lobe. 'Bit early to be sure. Such upset! A new home – '

'A new husband in my bed. Or me in his.'

'Just how did you persuade him that you needed separate rooms?'

She chuckled. 'I said, "Muzi, are my circumstances to be diminished to one half of what they were – so that I must share like a poor lodger? No, my lord and husband, my life is doubled by you. We need two bedrooms of love." I also disconcerted him a bit about miscarriages and morning sickness and menstrual flows and other mysteries.'

'What happened between you and Dr Cassander?'

'Oh, him. He gave Muzi liquids to make me take on the first and subsequent nights, so that I could drink a toast to our son and heir before each swiving. Naturally, when Muzi's back was turned I poured the liquids through the window and refilled the phials with water.'

The house contained its own private chapel where Muzi's new house-god had been set on a pedestal with a curse inscribed on its back, as on a boundary stone, to prevent removal. Following Muzi's instructions the image-maker had crafted a baked-clay warrior with the head of a dog, modelled after Tikki. The chapel at the north end of the house was half roofed and half open to the sky. Unlike at the house in Scribe Street, where Marduk could appear magically and wouldn't have brooked a rival house-god, a solid image was essential here. A few days after the wedding a thaumaturge had visited the chapel, of an afternoon, to consecrate the domestic god before the assembled, kneeling household.

Muzi and Thessany had knelt foremost, with their hands joined upon the clay dog's head. The thaumaturge – whose bland moon-face bore the scars of acne or pox – swung a censer and chanted formulae to chase away any lurking imps.

He poured crushed, dried thyme over their linked hands and the head.

'Now your god comes to life,' he told his little congregation. 'The senior lady of the house must feed him every morning so that he doesn't wish to run away. If an alive god runs away he becomes dangerous and degenerate because he has no proper home any more. Everyone must look after their own gods, otherwise there's robbery and murder and rape caused by vagrant gods who resent the happy households they observe; but can't enter except deceitfully or violently.'

Thessany cocked her head. 'Do a lot of gods run away from home through neglect?'

'It can happen, lady. How else can people be inspired to burglary and other foul crimes?'

'Supposing the entire family dies of disease; what then?'

'Why, the god must be broken quickly by a thaumaturge – just as the family has been broken. But your god will guard you against disease; to the best of his ability.'

'Are bones a suitable diet for him?'

Moon-face looked disconcerted.

'Since he's a dog,' added Thessany.

'A barley-cake is most suitable, madam. With a saucer of water for him to wash his fingers. How do you not know of this?'

'Well, you see,' drawled Thessany, 'I'm the daughter of Marduk; so we worshipped a bit differently at home. Okay, no bones or dead cats on the altar.'

Muzi chortled at his wife's wit.

A few days after that, Gupta had made the first of what were to be many regular weekly trips across town to train Thessany for an hour or two in esoteric discipline. Thessany explained to Muzi – so she later told Alex – that Gupta was her dancing instructor, and she wished to learn Eastern dances. All the best married ladies ought to pursue a graceful hobby, a proposition at which Muzi could hardly demur since he meant to amuse himself, too, by chasing wild beasts. She did not mention that Gupta taught dance in a striptease parlour.

So as not to arouse suspicions in Muzi's breast – though really his breast harboured few suspicions of any sort, perhaps to the chagrin of Lord Gibil, whose banking business he would inherit – Thessany and

Gupta exercised downstairs in the dining room; and indeed the manoeuvres, often in slow motion, through which the Indian put Thessany did bear superficial resemblances to exotic dances, albeit dances not of display but of ultimate disappearance.

Time flowed by, like the Euphrates, which Alex never saw these days; no more did he notice time elapsing. He fetched water. Mama Zabala cooked. Nettychin guarded the gate. Muzi went out drinking – moderately – with his cronies. The god, assisted by sparrows darting in through the open roof, devoured a barley-cake a day.

Away at the palace, reportedly, King Alexander was even closer to death. The king's favourite, Hēphaestion, was alternately drowning his sorrows and sprinting around outside the city, naked, fit to burst his heart like some mad Philippides bearing news of death's imminent victory. Some crack troops, disgruntled at the prospect of no Alexander, had brawled with magi in the old city, knocking off cone hats and busting heads.

Then Thessany announced her pregnancy. A delighted Lord Gibil arrived, followed shortly after by Dr Cassander, who presented Thessany with herbal potions designed to 'fix the foetus' and ward off miscarriage (substances which she no doubt poured away).

Charmingly, Nettychin presented his mistress with a simple clay amulet of a hen perching on an egg.

'It cost a shekel, madam, but it's a pleasure. You know which shekel.' Amulets always cost more than they were worth, since their value might prove immeasurable.

'I shall wear it and treasure it,' declared Thessany, 'as if it were gold.'

* * *

Surprisingly soon, six months had passed since the wedding; and with the advance of the pregnancy, despite Gupta's guruship, Thessany became somewhat more rather than less visible.

For a good while now, she had fretted to Muzi about the pressure of his organ perhaps displacing their heir. Whenever he absented himself from the house, riding away for a night or two under the rural stars, she would have Alex visit her tower room, and no such objections occurred; though nowadays Thessany always rode upon him, rocking her way to climax.

'I've found a delightful way to satisfy my consort,' she confided one night. 'You know that skin of a lioness in his room, mounted on a frame? Well, I creep beneath. I kneel growling, facing the backside where I enlarged a certain hole under the tail and sewed smooth satin. He mounts. I use my hands with unguent smeared on them. Or my mouth, if it amuses me. He likes that. It's hotter and wetter. He once pierced the lioness dead with his spear. Now he pierces her once again with his weapon.

'Not that I scorn him, you understand?' she went on, when Alex said nothing. 'He seems to enjoy himself more this way. With a horse between his legs he's a warrior. With a lioness to mount he's the King of Beasts. Almost a god . . .' She sighed with satisfaction. 'I'm stretching his imagination. I'm training him.'

'To be a better banker?'

'I'm sure Gibil notices a change.'

'He'd be rather surprised by the method.'

'Are you jealous, lover? He *is* my husband, you know.' She nuzzled into him. 'And how lavishly could you support me, dearest slave? This way, Alex, he supports us.'

'Until he realizes, and sticks a spear through me.'

'If I could protect you from Marduk, I can easily protect you from Muzi.'

'Luckily I don't feel like a gigolo – with all the water I have to haul.'

'I assure you it's harder work trying to become invisible.'

'Ah yes, the struggle for insight! Does Gupta think you're filling with transparent clarity?'

'I'm transparent to you, dear. This is, you realize, my way of apologizing – about the lioness.'

'I rather gathered you enjoyed it.'

'I do, quite. One gets excited. Why not have fun? It's like a visit to a top-notch brothel must be for you men.'

'I wouldn't know.'

'But here, Alex dear, in this bed with us, is love. And the baby is *ours*; together. Besides,' she went on after a moment, 'I didn't *need* to tell you about our frolics. I told you because you're part of me; I'm part of you.'

'And honesty leads to clarity, which leads to invisibility.'

'Right. Though honesty isn't the same thing as virtue; as Gupta proves by running a striptease parlour, albeit with metaphysical nuances. Virtue is the vice of those without insight, those lacking in imagination. That's why virtue is often evil at heart. Not that there's too much virtue in Babylon – and consequently little deep evil, though many serious peccadillos.'

'Sacrificing children seems rather evil.'

'Yes, Daddy always lacked imagination. You heard how he denounced my mother that night in the chapel? He never could imagine what it was to be her; or me. He could certainly imagine being himself, ten times over. Here's a city where, with luck, you can become what you imagine; unless your associates have livelier

234

imaginations. I think I shall now imagine that I'm invisible; and you can discover my hidden form.'

He chuckled. 'It *is* black dark at the moment.'

'So? Maybe once I learn how to be invisible in daylight, I can learn how to be visible in darkness.'

'Are you really serious about Gupta's teachings, Thess?'

'Alex, if we can't joke – ha ha! – about serious matters then we'll never master them; don't you see?'

'No. But I feel.' And he felt.

She moaned to herself.

Late the following morning Alex parted the reed door to Muzi's room and regarded the skin of the lioness mounted there on its hidden framework in a semblance of the life which Muzi had destroyed, presumably at peril to himself.

Alex stood there some while, imagining himself creeping closer, visualizing resting a hand upon the tawny rump, then lifting her tail – yes, he spotted an edge of satin and stitching. He fantasized that he was Muzi by night, knowing Thessany in a way that he never himself knew her – yet not knowing her at all, since to the invisibility of darkness she added the extra incognito of a false coat of skin.

Should he tiptoe closer? Should he pretend at first hand, rather than from the doorway?

He recalled imagining a number of things about Deborah; and realized his folly. He went downstairs, intending to work in the garden.

When he opened the front door, Nettychin was stomping at speed towards it, clutching a message tablet.

'Notify the Mistress! Tell everybody! Lord Gibil sends word: Lord Hēphaestion is dead! The king has ordered the biggest funeral ever in the history of the world!'

Hēphaestion: the king's favourite. The Patroclus to the Achilles of Alexander . . .

Alex had never set eyes on Hēphaestion (so far as he knew). All those months ago when he visited the palace and the king, and later as weddings loomed, Hēphaestion hadn't seemed to play any role in the affairs of the court. He might easily have been absent from the city. Of late, as the king's illness worsened, the name Hēphaestion had been bandied about increasingly. Hēphaestion, getting drunk in sorrowful anticipation. Hēphaestion, performing absurd athletic feats.

How ironic that the young stalwart who could sprint the whole circuit of the city walls in record time should now lie dead, while the gross, decadent, terminally sick Alexander survived him. Unless, of course, Hēphaestion had quite literally broken his heart through overexertion.

By late afternoon more information – perhaps of dubious quality – had arrived, courtesy of Mama Zabala, who had hastened to the nearest suburban market. (The letter received that morning had been a palace announcement despatched to Lord Gibil, and sped onward to his son. Thessany had scratched a message of acknowledgement, regretting that Master Muzi was out of town hunting. Since Gibil's messenger hadn't lingered, having other urgent letters to deliver, she had sent her tablet to Lord Gibil's house in the care of Anshar.) By now word of mouth had spread the news almost as swiftly from street to street, from bazaar to bazaar.

In chapel that evening Thessany said a prayer for

the soul of Hēphaestion, then asked the cook to rise and repeat what she had heard – lucidly, now that some time had gone by.

'Oh, the whole city's buzzing,' announced Mama Zabala. 'Well, it must be buzzing for the buzz to reach all the way here, from over the river! Poor Lord Hēphaestion, who was surely the most handsome man alive, and one of the most vigorous. He wrestled yesterday evening as if he was wrestling with Death for the life of the king himself, defeating five champions in turn. Then in a boiling lather, hot as an oven, he rushed directly to the king's bed to warm Alexander with his own body – to try to sweat the fever out of the king. And he sweated the life out of himself. In the morning, still lying in King Alexander's bed, Lord Hēphaestion was dead. I think his heart had stopped.

'The king has ordered last rites such as no one has ever seen. He wants thousands of cubits' length of the city wall pulled down for bricks to build the inside of the pyre. The outside will be so gorgeous it'll likely consume a year's revenue. That's all to go up in smoke – fumes rich enough for Hēphaestion's shade to smell in the afterlife. Then the hulk will be cladded with marble as a monument.'

Later that night Alex crept to Thessany's tower to warm her in bed; though wrestling would be inappropriate.

'Hēphaestion's death seems to have caught the public imagination as much as the king's would have done,' he whispered after the first soft bout.

'More so,' she replied. 'Much more. The king's death would have scared and saddened people. Hēphaestion's exhilarates them.'

'He died instead of Alexander, didn't he? He's a substitute.'

237

'Yes, I think so. Alexander will perk up now. He'll throw off his blankets and hurl himself into the business of the funeral, I bet.'

'This is a new survival strategy designed by Aristander, hmm?'

'It's better than murdering babes. But there still has to be a death; a fine exemplary death.'

'It's a different variation on the sacrifice theme?'

'Apparently.'

'The secular option . . . I once thought the king might be snuffed by his own court, and a new man appointed as Alexander.'

She laughed quietly. 'You thought the new man might be yourself! A secret prince, breezing into Babylon from exile . . . oh dear me.'

'You don't suppose the king might actually have died – been stifled by a pillow – and that Hēphaestion is taking his place?'

'Hence their spending the night together? Not in a hot sweat of homosexual health therapy! – but one of them smothering the other, then slipping into his royal purple nightdress? It's a thought. It's years since *I* last saw the king. If it's the wrong king who attends the funeral, do tell me!'

'Will we get a chance to see Hēphaestion's body?'

'Maybe not close up. And it'll be embalmed; has to be. It could take a whole month to build that pyre. Oh, what a business.'

Oh, what a business indeed. That the funeral was business became obvious when Lord Gibil called at the house the next day, fussing to know exactly when his son would return.

Gibil didn't even enter the house. While his chariot waited outside he strode about the garden impatiently, then once his daughter-in-law had come out he marched her around with him (less rapidly). Alex was busy planting and staking a young poplar. Lord Gibil and Thessany circled him as focal point, like horse and gravid jockey exercising before some prize race.

'Six storeys high the pyre will be, around the brick core, each tier supported by trunks of palm. Along the base there'll be golden quinquereme prows with scarlet felt draped between 'em. Giant torches on the next level, with eagles rising from the flames. Further up, hunting scenes – a battle of gold centaurs – golden bulls and lions; all hollow-cast, of course. Next, a row of weaponry. Up top there'll be a squad of sirens. Choristers will squeeze inside 'em and sing laments through their golden lips. The choir'll need an escape chute out back for when the caboodle goes up in flames.

'Oh, there's money to be made supplying that lot! And there's money to be *lent* to buy it all. Palace'll need to raise a bit of a loan, I shouldn't wonder. Don't you credit that silly yarn about demolishing some of the city wall for the core. You can't build smoothly with smashed-up rubble. I've already cornered the spare capacity in the brick market. Then after the fire, it'll take masses of marble to cover the burnt core.'

He puffed. 'I need my boy going round with me from stage one, seeing how you handle a big deal like this.'

'He'll be back sometime tomorrow; so he said.'

'Where is he exactly? Oh, what's the use!'

Thessany spoke brightly: 'Let's see: you're hoping to lend the palace money to buy goods from you, which they'll then destroy? Same principle as war, but less harmful. Also, you're hoping to tender for the job at a price which is attractive enough – yet does require a bit of national debt, which swells when the palace get behind on interest payments?'

'Yeah, that's it. You got it.'

'Why don't *I* come round with you?'

'But my boy . . .'

'Is missing at the moment. *You* missed something, yourself.'

'What did I miss?'

'This oh-so-complicated pyre – what detailed specifications! It can't all have been dreamed up in a quick frenzy of inspiration.'

'Could have been.'

'Unlikely. I'd say it required forethought. Forethought implies foreknowledge of the event. With respect, Father-in-law, you could have seen this coming – if you had a proper paid informer at court, instead of desultory cronies. Frankly, you could have forecast something along these lines when my own dad's bid to become a hereditary god ran into a spot of bother.'

Gibil goggled. 'You mean you suspected, and you didn't warn me?'

'I was never asked. I was wed to breed an heir. Your signal ought to have been when the palace started to boost Hēphaestion.'

Gibil pulled out a cloth and mopped his brow. 'Yeah, I see it. That's pretty perceptive.'

'Thanks. Now let me perceive something else. Marduk wanted to sacrifice a child, which is highly emotive. Hēphaestion was a grown man, so what makes his death equally emotive? Why, the size and cost of the cremation. How many talents of gold will be consumed?'

'Ten, twelve.'

'What happens to all that gold when the pyre goes up in flames? Some gets lost as hot particles whisked into the air. Most of it melts down.'

'And gets mixed up in the core; then covered with marble.'

'Suppose the pyre is cleverly constructed with channels or pipes running through the core . . .'

'My God.'

'You can lend the palace money to burn gold – which ends up back in your hands as neat little ingots. You'll have doubled your profit, Daddy-in-law. Why should the gold benefit some monument robbers in five hundred years' time? Or even sooner if we get a greedy king, worried by interest payments.'

'Oh my God, yes. Pipes, channels, ingots ready to be hooked out. I can see it all. You're a genius.'

Alex was agog. Thessany would have a marvellous hold over Lord Gibil for ever after: the knowledge that he had swindled the palace and robbed Hēphaestion's grave.

Gibil halted suddenly. 'Hey, is that slave snooping on us?'

'No,' said Thessany hastily. 'He often looks like that. The beauty of living things overwhelms him.'

'Uh? Okay. Thessany, soon as you're ready we'll go together. Just us two. I'll take the reins; my driver can trot home.'

'I'm ready right now, Dad-in-law. I'll drive, if you like. I know how. Of course,' she added, 'sneaking the cooled ingots away will be a delicate operation, what with soldiers on honour guard. You need someone who's virtually invisible . . .'

'When are you going to break the news to Gibil that *you're* the invisible one?' Alex asked her that night; which might be their last together for some while. 'Especially as you'll be at least seven months pregnant, come the day?'

'Pregnant women can still move, you know.'

'I've noticed. Gold bars are heavy, Thess. There'll be a lot of to-ing and fro-ing.'

'Actually, I don't know that I'm quite ready to be invisible myself. I didn't say that I was going to be the one.'

'The magic-word method doesn't last long enough. The effect fades.'

'True. That lets you off the hook.'

'Gupta? Surely not?'

'The escapade might amuse him. It injures no one; and it does have a kind of fabulous significance. There are only three matters that most humans really care about: gold, sex and death. The robbery would be emblematic, almost metaphysical.'

'Apart from scheming to rob a grave, how did you get on with Lord Moneybags today?'

'Excellently well. He's calling for me tomorrow too. My heroic husband will have to accept a note of apology on his return.'

So it was that Muzi arrived home from the chase midway through the afternoon, more caked with dust than with blood, to be met – in lieu of a wife – by Anshar, with a waxed board.

Anshar volunteered assorted gnomic information about the sad death of Hēphaestion and the forthcoming obsequies, earning a meed of gratitude from Muzi who, by consulting with Irra, soon put two and two together and hastened to the bathhouse, thence to his room, to become clean, well dressed and diligent-looking. Irra called Alex to help him stable the horses, rub them down, and feed them; then replenish the household water.

A couple of hours later Lord Gibil dropped Thessany off at the house, to be met by a spruced, conciliatory son who invited him in for wine.

'No time, boy. There's a mound of things to see to. I

could have used you with me these last two days. Thank your stars your wife's a wonder.'

'It isn't Muzi's fault that Lord H died unexpectedly,' Thessany sweetly intervened. 'Who could have fore-guessed it?'

'Hmm,' said Gibil.

'Also, I think Muzi's right about your taking a glass of wine. Lord H seems to have died from overexertion. Business is a race too. Pace thyself.'

'You won't die of overwork, will you, Son?'

'I'm sure Muzi has been exerting himself like a lion these last few days. And who knows how influential his cronies will become?'

'Yeah, there's that.'

Muzi flashed Thessany a look of gratitude, but then became puzzled; and finally burst out laughing. 'Like a lion! Like a lion. I like it.'

'What's the joke?'

'Nothing, Dad. Nothing at all. Come on in for half an hour and relax.'

Gibil did so.

Alex thought he had understood the joke – a bit of supposedly private erotic banter between wife and husband – till Anshar murmured in his ear, 'It's *Mrs* Lion who does the hunting. Lazy Mr Lion only lies around.' Then Alex wondered which joke Muzi had been laughing at, and which Thessany.

Ten days later Alex was shoving a barrow of water-buckets back from the local canal when he met Gupta heading away from the house.

It was Gupta's tutorial afternoon, and on this occa-sion Lord Gibil had arrived to observe, so Thessany must have confided the nature of the skill which the Indian was actually teaching her. In the intervening days Alex had had no opportunity to talk to Thessany alone. Gibil had won the contract to build the pyre outside the walls at the north-east corner of the city; thus Thessany was often absent on business. In company with her father-in-law she was visiting architects, builders, brick-makers, timberers, carvers, goldsmiths, felt-makers, choirmasters, fuel-oil vendors; as well as inspecting the chosen site and liaising with the palace. Muzi was usually a third member of the team since he was, on an emergency basis, trying to be as useful as his wife.

'Aha, Alex! I have had a *plot* presented to me, which I gather you may have overheard.' Gupta grinned. 'Don't worry! Lord Gibil has been assured that you are slavishly loyal; rather like Tikki the hound. What's more, you like nothing better than to help transport heavy little articles from place to place.' His fingers drummed on the side of a water-bucket. 'Muzi, of course, is brawnier than you; but he must know nothing.'

'Not know? But he and Thess and Gibil are driving all over together, fixing things up.'

'Muzi remains in the dark concerning the crucial arrangement. He might get drunk in some hunting tent one day, and blab. Gibil concurs; I presume Thessany put this very delicately to him. Which is a neat little trick from your point of view, if Muzi should ever suspect about you and Thessany.'

'Hush!'

Gupta inspected his reflection in the water, then stirred it with his finger. 'If he consults Daddy, Daddy will send him packing. "Don't be daft, Son! The slave is faithful. So is your wife."'

'Maybe that's the whole point of this escapade?'

'What, Gibil shall not smell a rat so long as his nose smells gold? I think that's a dodgy proposition. The man had no interest in you before.'

'Afterwards Thess could destroy Gibil publicly, if he caused unpleasantness. With me as witness.'

'Rubbish. She would ruin herself at the same time.'

'Bluff, Gupta. Bluff.'

'Speaking of bluffs, Alex my friend, you haven't explicitly said what the plot is. Do please remind me! Just for reassurance.'

'In case I'm merely fishing for information?'

Gupta dabbled in another bucket. 'No fish in these waters, ha ha!'

'The idea is to rob Hēphaestion's funeral pyre.'

'Quite right. Top marks.'

'And you'll be the invisible man who sneaks the ingots away after the brick core cools.'

'Wearing a special coat with strong pockets inside. A coat which bores and baffles the eye . . . I estimate a dozen trips to and fro. I shall need to be on tiptop form. Quite a challenge, eh?' Gupta giggled. 'What if afterwards I waved a wand and showed Lord Gibil that by running so much risk I had stolen naught but gilded bricks? What a lovely lesson that would teach about bravery and folly. I'd really be the philosophic thief of Babylon; if not of Baghdad! Why, such a shock might be the salient slap upon the skull which suddenly enlightens Thessany.'

'Why are you making a jape of this? To worry me?'

'Maybe . . . it's to preserve my self-respect.'

'You don't really want to steal? But you're prepared to because – because you feel that Thessany is on the brink of clarity?'

'Of sainthood,' said Gupta. 'As patron saint of sinners.'

'That lot are a corvée gang, aren't they, Dad?'

Lord Gibil nodded. 'Bright of you to spot it, Son.'

They stood surveying the ascending structure. Many

men in loincloths swarmed upon it like some species of ant building a nest with bricks scavenged from the great pile nearby. A double line of ants traced a crooked path between the supply dump and the core of the pyre-to-be, carrying bricks one way, returning empty-handed for more. As with ants which follow the scent-marks of their fellows even if the consequent route has kinks in it, so the sweaty labourers seemed locked into their initial, less than totally efficient route. Those returning to the dump at a jog trot held their empty hands out ahead of them, twitching like ants' feelers.

The brick core was already three-quarters formed, a thing of simple art by contrast with the natural chaos of the hill of bricks nearby, though there was a generic similarity between the two heaps. Donkey carts delivered bricks to the dump; the ants strove to reduce this heap and rear a geometric copy, stepped and rectangular, two hundred cubits long by a hundred wide, with – so far – four distinct zigguratic tiers.

Lord Gibil sat with Muzi in one chariot; Thessany with Gupta in a second, drawn up alongside. Alex the slave had clung on to the second chariot precariously; fortunately traffic jams had slowed the vehicles down.

The sun beat down upon the work and upon the great city wall behind, which would be backdrop first to an artistic masterpiece of friezes and statues, then to an inferno, and finally to a serene, enormous marble tomb, honourably guarded for ever.

'I guess a corvée gang's cheaper, Dad. But why not use real bricklayers? No expense spared, eh? The palace are footing the bill; a bill can be padded. Or are we actually debiting the palace for proper bricklayers?'

'What a sharp son you are suddenly. Be careful you don't cut yourself.'

'We don't want the core to collapse through incompetence. Slump and slide.'

'It won't slump. See how my architect keeps an eye on the placement of bricks.' Gibil indicated a little figure clambering aloft, shadowed bobbingly by a parasol his servant held.

Muzi shaded his keen hunter's eyes. 'Are those little pipe things the bones of the building? They're rather birdy bones . . . hollow. I'd have thought having a bunch of hollow ducts running throughout isn't exactly –'

'Those,' interrupted Gibil, 'are to fan the fire with air from inside. They also act as expansion joints. As the bricks heat up and expand, those collapse to take the strain.'

'Really?'

Lord Gibil sweated. 'I'm surprised you noticed at all.'

'I can spot a fox skulking half a mile away.'

'Yes, well, very good.'

Thessany said, 'Why doesn't Muzi see if he can calculate how many more donkey-loads of bricks are required before we can safely let the heap run down to nothing? Meanwhile, the rest of us can take a closer look.'

'Good idea. That's your task, Muzi. And look after the chariots, will you?'

'The slave can hold the reins.'

'No, we need him with us.'

'What for, Dad? I don't get why Thessany's dancing master is with us, either. Is he in charge of some dancing at the funeral?'

'Not exactly. Look, Muzi, I have a lot on my mind.'

'I'm trying to be helpful, Dad, but how can I help if I don't know what's going on?'

'You've been a great help these past few days. I'm

proud of you, Son. It's important to know the right number of bricks. We have to clear any excess away. That's where the audience'll be standing.'

'Yeah, but you hire folk to count bricks.'

'Son, if you ain't willing to take a personal interest in humble bricks now and then, you can kiss shekels goodbye.'

'You're a banker, Dad, not a builder.'

'A banker has to know what he's funding, inside out. Will you stop arguing with me?'

Gibil mopped his brow and climbed down; likewise Gupta and Thessany, who tossed her reins to Muzi. Fretful but obedient, Muzi steered two chariots side by side towards the brick dump. The rest of the party headed for the rear of the construction, with Alex tagging anonymously behind.

Of course, the real reason for using a corvée gang was that genuine bricklayers might have puzzled about certain features of the brick core. As it was, only the supervising architect needed to be bribed. No officials from the palace came to inspect a mere brick interior. They would turn up when the expensive decorations began to be installed: the golden ship-prows, the gold-wreathed torches, the golden bulls and centaurs. These would be fixed to a thick outer skin of combustibles: resinous timber and reeds which were destined to be soaked with oil. When that stage of the work was reached soldiers would set up camp to guard the valuables, and to control sightseers who trekked out from the city. By then Lord Gibil might well relax; the conduits for molten gold would be safely hidden . . .

Finally the day and the sunset hour of the funeral arrived. The rays of the dying sun ruddied the golden tiers which earlier that afternoon had gleamed so brightly that they seemed to boom like gongs, dazzling the massing crowd which by now amounted to – what? – a hundred thousand people? The shadow of the festival temple cut a lengthening black wedge across the fields, a great pointer for latecomers still pouring from Sin Gate.

Soldiers had drawn a cordon round the golden pyre and round the throng of dignitaries who stood closest to it. Gentry mingled with magi, courtiers, 'ambassadors' from Babel. Dominating this select though far from scanty assembly was a lone elephant, staked to the ground by all four legs for security. In the purple-curtained howdah on its back sat, no doubt, the king in private mourning.

Up near the summit of the pyre the row of golden sirens sang laments, the voices of the choristers within the hollow statues amplified through trumpet-mouths. Behind this choir servants were busily pouring stored barrels of flammable oil down the inside skin, soaking the wood and reeds. Above sirens and servants, topped only by heaven, stood the catafalque bearing the embalmed body, presumably of Hēphaestion: a remote waxen nakedness, a recumbent athlete. Earlier, the catafalque had been borne through the crowds and might indeed have carried a waxwork figure; though everyone must soon see it burn like flesh rather than melt like a candle.

Early stars were pricking through the deep-blue satin which now shrouded Babylon, as though those stars were vying to translate Hēphaestion's soul upward into one of them.

The mahout, who had been perched astride the elephant's shoulder, suddenly scrambled up and pulled the royal purple drapes aside with his hooked stick, disclosing . . .

. . . Alexander sitting there in the howdah. A lantern

hung alongside, illuminating him for all to see in the growing dusk.

Yes, he was the same Alexander: the same torpid, flabby figure of a man with heavy jowls, rouged cheeks and lips, hair in ringlets. Silken-gowned, bejewelled. The king wept copiously, tears pouring down his cheeks, mingling with the rouge so that soon he seemed to be weeping thin watery blood.

Yet as he wept he seemed to grow not weak, but stern and strong – as if it was a poison which those tears bled from his system. His flab appeared to harden into muscle, so that soon no soft mortal sat grieving there, but rather a marble god.

The king raised a hand in farewell; and by way of a signal. Hastily the sirens fell silent. Within a minute torches were touched to the base of the pyre. Flames raced up the ornamented tiers, licking golden lions and centaurs, leaping out from amidst serpents and centaurs. All the precious figures seemed to dance. Quickly the whole edifice was engulfed in fire.

Alexander pulled rings from his fingers and tossed these in the direction of the blaze, whose heat now smote the spectators. With hands thus bare, the king ripped the silk gown from himself and rose amidst its tatters. Beneath the silk he was wearing a bronze cuirass and a kilt of iron-studded leather thongs. In his right hand, now, he was flourishing a sword. All of a sudden he was valiant power incarnate.

Or was he about to kill himself? No. He stabbed his weapon towards the flames, then towards the sky . . .

A hand closed on Alex's arm. Before he could even see whose hand, he was being dragged sideways through the throng in the direction of the tethered elephant. He had to hop to avoid falling over.

A Greek officer was hauling him. It was the ruffian,

250

the make-believe beggar. Within moments Alex was face to face with Aristander.

'Sir, it's the man who told you about the scroll – then became a slave of Marduk's daughter.'

The futurologist poked his nose at Alex to sniff him out. 'So it is!' On this occasion his nose wasn't dripping. 'You disappointed me, fellow. You missed an appointment.'

'Should we take him in for interrogation, sir? Nobody noticed me grab him. Everyone's gawping at the bonfire. Say the word; we'll whisk him off.'

The inferno roared deafeningly. Above the city the darkening sky stormed with even blacker smoke as though a whole district was burning down.

Terrified, the elephant curled its trunk up and trumpeted. Swaying convulsively, it tried to tear its feet loose. Drool dangled from its mouth. The mahout beat it over the skull with his stick to no avail; then ran nimbly out on to its head to hook at its trunk. King Alexander stood laughing victoriously, still saluting with his sword the raging blaze which cloaked the melting of hollow bulls and centaurs.

'Hēphaestion, goodbye!' he screamed. 'Farewell, best of friends!'

Alexander paid no heed whatever to the mahout, who capered like a monkey. But the elephant paid heed to the jabbing, iron-pronged stick. Twisting its trunk about, it seized the mahout's arm and dashed him over its head to the ground. It wrenched one forefoot free – the chain snapping at a weak link – and stamped this pile-driver down into the earth within half a cubit of the stunned man's head. The elephant lowered its tusks; however, these had been sawn short and capped. Again it lunged forward. The stakes restraining its other front leg began to tear loose. The thunder of the foot descending a second time made the mahout, still half senseless, jerk and hop aside like a frog before collapsing again.

Panic spread outwards. Aristander crashed into Alex as Greeks shoved and fought clear of the immediate circle around the beast; while élite Macedonian guards thrust inward to take whatever action they imagined best. Though buffeted this way and that, Alex couldn't tug himself from the officer's grasp.

'You stay put!'

The elephant hurled its weight sideways and succeeded in freeing its other front leg, complete with chains and uprooted stakes. The howdah started to tilt. The king at last deigned to heed his own safety. Grinning ferociously, sword still in hand, he scrambled out of the back of the howdah. Before he could lose his balance he launched himself from the elephant's buttocks. How reckless to leap clutching a sharp blade; but his luck was in, his life was blessed. He hit dirt, sprawled, recovered himself. How his soldiers cheered to witness the old heroic Alexander once again; though amidst such din of flames, cries of alarm, and screechy bellowings their cheers were but hollow rounded mouths. Trying not to look shaken to the marrow by his impact with the earth, the king retreated in Alex's direction, hobbling.

Now that their king was clear – and before the crazed juggernaut could wrench its hind legs free to rampage through the crowd – the boldest (or most bloodthirsty) Macedonians attacked. Their swords either bounced off the beast's hide or else cut slashes which were too shallow to do anything except madden it more. A couple of spear thrusts in the body were mere wasp stings, vicious but survivable. The howdah slumped further askew. It had been well strapped and did not upend itself under the elephant's belly, but the lantern broke, setting fire to the purple curtains. The air reeked of must and elephant shit.

Unexpectedly a blond quarterback broke through into the centre field. It was Muzi.

He snatched a spear. He darted and feinted, dancing before the stamping, lurching monster. The elephant reared ponderously. Blazing fabric brushed its back. Its front legs crashed back to earth. At last the rear stakes ripped loose.

In that moment, when the animal was grounded solidly with head bowed, Muzi dashed in. Using all his force, he drove the spear through the elephant's left eye. Deeply, deeply.

The elephant lurched. Muzi bounded clear; and the great beast slumped forward in an ungainly heap. He had scored true. Despite skull bones, his point was buried in the brain.

Panic subsided. Away from the immediate vicinity, few had noticed.

Muzi had ended up close to Alex. Panting, he stared at Alex and at the officer holding him.

The king limped over, flanked by guards. He seemed at once exhausted – and transfigured.

'You're a true Herakles,' he said to Muzi. 'What's your name?'

'Muzi, son of Gibil, Your Majesty.'

'Ah, the Lord Gibil who built the pyre?'

'The same, sir.'

'And you would have sacrificed your life to stop a mad beast from spoiling this ceremony . . . What shall I give you in return? Ask anything.' As Muzi hesitated, the king added, 'You must ask. Modest refusal will only anger me.'

Muzi scratched his neck, then pointed at Alex and the officer. 'Well, sir, your man there seems to have grabbed a slave of mine. I would like to have my slave back.'

'This man's in custody, Majesty,' protested Alex's captor. But already Aristander had turned away, distancing himself from events.

The king flushed. 'Is that your request?' He scrutinized Alex, pursed his lips. 'A slave, a one-time runaway, whom you already own?' The king's gaze lingered long.

'I may own him, sir, but right now your man has him. He's my wife's favourite slave. That's my request, Great King.'

'What did the slave do?' asked Alexander. But before the officer could answer the King held up his hand. 'No! That doesn't matter. The request is granted. The slave is pardoned. Release him.' And the king turned away.

'You lucky bastard,' hissed the officer, before propelling Alex briskly at Muzi.

Muzi said nothing till they were midway through the throng between the dead elephant – with its own little funeral pyre now guttering on its back – and the place Alex had been abducted from.

Then he halted Alex forcibly. 'So why did I help you out – when you're screwing my wife?'

'Master?'

'Think I'm a fool? Not as big a fool as you imagine. Let me tell you something, boy. I saved your bacon from whatever roasting it was gonna get because I've been studying Thessany and you. Oh, I've seen her attitude to you: all this pretence of couldn't-care-less, and you're-just-a-menial. I've seen through it. But more, I've been studying *her* ways – with quite a lot of admiration, I might add. Then there's my dad, who admires her too. He wants you to screw her, doesn't he? That's what all this dragging you around with us was really about. You're my dad's insurance policy to keep Thess satisfied.

'Well, I'm damned if I'm going to screw up this little game – 'cos I'm learning games now, and I want Thess to play this one just as far as she pleases. Surprised you, eh? This game for sure has one thing going for it: it lets me take off hunting with the boys. But that ain't the most important. The most important is, it amuses Thessany – and I'd hate for her to be bored or unhappy. I sincerely mean that. I guess my dad feels that way too, specially now that he's getting such hot business tips from her.

'Listen: one day Thess is gonna learn to love me, in *her* way. Then she'll realize that I knew all about this caper; and she'll love me twice over.

'*Nor* am I kicking up any piles of shit while she's pregnant. But I'll tell you one thing, fellow.' Muzi held Alex by the throat, firmly though not too constrictively. 'If anything goes wrong for Thess or my dad, or if that Indian fakir or you create any smartass Marduk-style capers which drop shit on our house, then I'll strangle you personally. Yeah, capers like whatever prompted that officer to collar you; and what was all that about, eh?'

'A misunderstanding,' croaked Alex.

'You can dip your cock – till the day comes when Thess admires me sufficient that I can cut it off of you. But you'll keep your nose clean in other respects. Got it?'

Alex gurgled, 'Yes.'

'Listen: I just became a guy of some note by giving that old elephant a fatal headache. The king might have been a bit put out that I didn't ask for a title or something. But *now* he knows me. I intend to keep his respect, honourably.'

Muzi released Alex. 'Right oh, slave; back to your mistress.'

How right Muzi was; and at the same time how wrong. Right about the lovers; wrong about Lord Gibil knowing. Right about a conspiracy; wrong about a Marduk plot. Wrong about the family honour when his own dad was about to rob ... correction, about to clean up gold which would otherwise have gone to waste.

In a way the situation was pathetic. Here was Muzi trying to join in on intrigue, as he viewed it. Instead he produced a parody of intrigue. He was an oaf of honour.

Yet for the first time Alex felt respect for Muzi; respect mixed with fear, not least fear of where the clumsy apprentice subtleties, the would-be guile of an honourable man, might lead.

Really, this was all Gibil's fault for the way he had let his son grow up: as a sort of mental virgin, a worthy innocent. Maybe that was because Muzi was indeed rather stupid; if brave-hearted. Unfortunately he wasn't sufficiently stupid to survive unscathed and unbewildered. He had begun to think for himself.

Or maybe it was Gibil's fault that his son's initiation into the business of life was so long overdue; because he had treated Muzi in this manner not out of indulgence, nor even out of contempt at the contrast between father and son, but so that the son should *redeem* the father. Muzi should be exempt from the finaglings which had brought Gibil riches; the family heir should not inherit wickedness (or its kid brother, unscrupulousness). Yet without a certain wicked streak, how could Muzi ever steer the family fortune? So therefore he had to be initiated. This process had been left far too late. In the matter of the proposed robbery Muzi's education was still being neglected.

The money baron required a prince with unsoiled paws to succeed him. That was the real reason why Gibil had readily agreed that Muzi should be excluded from the scheme to steal the gold. Gibil had decided that his daughter-in-law was perfect for the role of wicked anti-conscience to his son.

Alas, Muzi already possessed a conscience and a sense of destiny of his own.

Or did he? Was that really so? Perhaps Muzi's wish for princely respect was precisely what his own father had implanted in him.

And maybe this whole sorry imbroglio was Thessany's fault for playing lioness games with her young husband's emotions.

Thessany, Gibil, Gupta and Alex revisited the scene of the cremation late the following afternoon, by which time the brick core would have cooled.

Gibil drove the party out in a big four-wheeled carriage. As procurer of the pyre Lord Gibil had a perfect and logical excuse to inspect for any structural damage which the intense heat might have caused that core, which was going to be clad in white marble to the eternal memory of Hēphaestion. Equally, Lord Gibil must needs dissociate himself utterly from any pilferage, should Gupta be caught staggering away with ingots of gold. This might present a problem, given the involvement of Gibil's own daughter and his daughter's slave . . .

Gupta pointed out reassuringly that no one else — save for the bribed architect — knew anything about ingots being there. Maybe there weren't any! Or not as many as expected. Maybe the gold had been vaporized by the furnace heat and deposited as faint gilding on the city wall and adjacent rooftops.

If caught, said Gupta, they should swear that all

along they had been intending to return the gold secretly to the palace, as a loyal gift of which the king must never hear; but hadn't wanted to raise false expectations at the Treasury. The treasurer would surely be delighted and relieved; and wouldn't blab.

When they arrived, by way of the Marduk Gate, they found perhaps a score of sightseers ambling in the vicinity of the blackened ziggurat, its tiers amorphous with drifts of carbon. Soldiers stood guard. Other soldiers might be sleeping in several military tents nearby, where the standard of King Alexander flew: a simple purple pennant on a spear stuck in the ground, the butt a carved pomegranate.

On Gupta's instructions Gibil brought the horses round in a circle and halted them so that the carriage was just out of sight of the soldiery round the corner of the eastern wall. Alex hammered in a peg for the reins, and the four accomplices walked boldly to watch from the corner.

Soon they had mapped out the routine of the soldiers. At each corner of the extinct pyre a guard was stationed. Every three or four minutes a soldier would set out for the next corner clockwise, taking about a minute to reach it. For thirty seconds or so there would be two guards on that corner and none on one of the other three. Then the 'relieved' guard would proceed onward, clockwise; and so forth.

Gupta drew a grid in the sandy dirt and x-ed in different combinations of single soldiers, couples, and empty stations. He stared for a while, then stood and erased the pattern.

'Better than I hoped for! We should have regular blind spots. Rotating the guard doesn't keep the chaps on their toes at all. It accustoms them to novelty. Let us proceed.'

Lord Gibil sauntered off, swinging a walking stick

pompously to distract attention. He headed for the remains of the elephant, a hummock of huge bones and torn hide which several cats and curs and carrion birds were quarrying. The good meat and offal had already been carted off.

Thessany, being in an advanced state of pregnancy, would stay with the cart. Alex took a couple of leather bags. Gupta donned a many-pocketed patchwork coat of nondescript confusing monochrome materials – he looked like a mass of clotted cobwebs. He and Alex wandered idly towards the ex-pyre.

The south face was in shadow; that was where the different ducts debouched into brick moulds, hidden behind what one hoped were still loose bricks.

Gupta halted, close by the city wall, and with his heel carved a circle in the soil. 'Here's the psychological boundary point – between guards ignoring you, and feeling curious. Don't pass beyond. When I go, sit down in the circle with your back to the pyre.'

The westering sun was dazzling except in the immediate lee of the blackened brick mass. (Gibil had suggested an approach under cover of darkness, but Gupta had poured scorn. What would they be doing lurking outside the walls by night?)

The soldier at the south-east corner left his station and headed for the south-west corner. Gupta jigged his limbs and his coat of confusion, dislocatingly, and . . . what did he do next? What did he become? His shadow flitted away from Alex, who quickly sat down facing the opposite way.

Minutes passed: ten, fifteen, an age.

Then: 'Open a bag!'

Ingots descended.

'Now the other.'

More bars of gold.

'Go; and come back.'

Scrambling up, Alex heaved a bag in each hand towards the carriage as fast as he could. He tumbled the contents in for Thessany to cover with straw.

Three trips later, Gupta's voice said, 'Don't come back.'

This time Alex simply dumped the bags in the carriage, then unpegged the horses and climbed aboard.

They waited.

'Thess?'

'What?'

'I once heard it said that the whole universe exists only as a thought in the mind of a god. It's a pattern like a *holographos* – real to us, imaginary to the god. People who become aware of this can work what seem to be miracles.'

'Like Gupta becoming invisible?'

'Something like that, but what I'm thinking is . . . has it ever crossed your mind that maybe the whole of Babylon, us included, exists only as a pattern in the mind of some piece of *tekhnē* at the Akademia of the Future? How could we tell if that was so? When we possessed the little scroll – when you called it a control scroll – I thought for a while that maybe it was part of what controls our reality. I thought it was a part which somehow had materialized inside Babylon – the way a god might reach into the world he imagines, and insert a miraculous object. I thought that maybe Babylon is a *holographos* visible to all the Akademics; and right now maybe they're stepping right through our ghosts, observing how we steal the gold!

'And maybe only an invisible man or woman can spy them watching us. Only someone who is full of clarity and detachment. Only someone who can trick the eye and mind.'

Thessany knit her brows. 'That . . . sounds like a

most delicious kind of intrigue. But Alex, what's this Akademia of the Future you're talking about? Is this some secret society Gupta has told you of?'

'The Akademia at Heuristics, Thess.'

'At where?'

'I know it's against the law to mention it! Surely we two can talk about it privately?'

'If I only knew what we were supposed to be talking about! I've never heard of a place called Heuristics; or of this Akademia!'

'But Thess . . . ! Look, you came to Babylon with your dad – what is it, five, six years ago? Where do you think you came from?'

'I . . . yes, we did come from elsewhere. From another country, I forget which one. How remote it seems.'

'You came from *America*.'

'I've never heard of such a place.'

Alex shivered despite the heat. 'Thess . . . something has altered. Something in you; something in the city. Something has been changed.'

'Of course I've changed. I'm pregnant.'

'I don't mean . . . ! Answer me this: where did the piece of *tekhnē* in the temple come from? And the one in your chapel at home?'

'Some Greek scientist crafted those. Aristotle . . . or was it Archimedes? Maybe it was Archimedes. With a name like Archimedes his ancestors must have been princes of the Medes, and magi. No, I think it must have been Aristotle, the king's tutor.'

Alex gripped her hand. 'Thess! Think of Greeks: thousands of Greeks arriving as visitors! How do they get here? They come in a *tekhnē* carriage that floats on air. The carriage comes from Heuristics.'

She laughed lightly. 'I think the strain of our current exploit is telling on you. Lots of Macedonians and other Greeks came with Alexander's armies and settled here in the city. But not recently.'

'They arrive at the Ishtar Gate every day in that hovering carriage.'

'You have my leave to go and stand at the Ishtar Gate for a week to try to spy this strange device. You won't ever see it. There's no such thing. People come to Babylon in coracles, with donkeys. Or on foot, or on horseback.'

'Are you being honest with me, Thess? You aren't teasing?'

Again, she laughed. '*You're* teasing *me*.' A puzzled frown crossed her face. 'I seem to remember . . . some kind of dream I had. Something like this fancy of yours. No, it eludes me. Dreams always do. They don't mean much.'

Something had indeed shifted in the pattern of the city and its people, but it hadn't shifted in Alex . . . He remembered how he had once suspected his own sanity. Had he once, in fact, been mad? A visionary who dreamed of the distant future?

No. He struggled now to recall the *tekhnē* of that future. If Thessany wasn't japing him – and she certainly didn't appear to be – then surely what had occurred was that sometime during the past half-year the pattern of the city had reached completion. Before, fresh information, fresh personae were still being input into the system. Personae had to be interfaced compatibly. Each carried a kind of key to open the locked city and fit into it. The city pattern had to be able to accept the influx. Now Babylonia was full up. The keys – logical connections to what went before – had been deleted.

Not from Alex, though. He still knew. He still remembered.

Why not from Alex? Was he a sort of cursor, a mobile marker threading the web of Babylonian life? Maybe he had merely been overlooked.

Had others been overlooked? How about Gupta, the invisible man?

Or was the explanation simply that the city had by now accumulated more than a half a decade's worth of events? Babylon's processing capacity had begun to overload? Unnecessary memories had been dumped; or stored?

But not his.

In Thessany's womb a foetus was thinking foetal thoughts, hearing mysterious sounds of unknown speech vibrate through the drumskin of her belly. Child within mother: one dawning new consciousness, taking up extra space in the pattern of Babylon ... Therefore the mother had lost part of her memory? Could that be why Thessany had forgotten America except as a faded, irretrievable dream?

Perhaps all these explanations were true, and together summed up to the change which had occurred.

Could his love, who carried his child, be persuaded to remember what she now, to his horror, denied?

'Here I am!' Gupta, in his dingy cobwebs, hauled himself aboard, laden with more ingots.

The gold seemed stupid: fool's gold. The real gold wasn't any function of this feat of invisibility which Gupta had just pulled off, this hidden act of stealth. The really golden prize would be *to see what was invisible.* To behold what had vanished. To spy the secret onlookers.

Maybe there were no invisible onlookers strolling amidst the Babylonian ghosts, admiring, amused, intrigued by their antics. In that case the golden prize would be to perceive the *tekhnē*-mind which was the true god-creator of Babylon: the mind which contained analogues of human beings whose originals lived out their lives elsewhere in places such as Oregon and New York and Calcutta.

'All's done that can be. Let's collect your father.'

Thessany flicked the reins. 'Gid-up!'

'Gupta?'

'What is it, Alex?'

'I'm troubled.'

'I need to relax. Tell me later.' And Gupta commenced a breathing exercise.

In the disposition of the gold Alex played no part. It was another seven days before he could get a chance to talk to Gupta alone, at the end of the Indian's weekly visit to train Thessany in subtle arts – a week during which worries about Muzi almost succeeded in distracting Alex.

Muzi had noted with the keenest interest the mysterious excursion undertaken by the four on the day directly after he had both saved, and challenged, Alex. Yet he pressed no questions upon Alex, nor in Alex's hearing did he press any upon Thessany, or upon his father. (Lord Gibil now radiated contentment, with the merest thread of anxiety attached.) However, Muzi watched like a hawk and harked like a hare.

Alex had decided not to tell Thessany what Muzi had said to him, particularly since what he had told her while they were waiting in the carriage had struck her as so fantastical. In the house he avoided meeting her eyes and tried to be inconspicuous, cultivating his own version of invisibility, even though such behaviour was susceptible to a number of false interpretations.

One such misinterpretation, on Thessany's part, might be that he was virtually quarrelling with her; that his words to her in the carriage had been wayward, sick inventions, pretexts to distress both himself and her, thus to stretch and even sever the emotional tie between them for reasons perhaps not unconnected with her coming labour. In which case in a sense he was deserting her, withdrawing moral support at a time when she would need it; for remarks which he heard exchanged between Thessany and her father-in-law indicated that Dr Cassander still loomed in the wings, along with the threat to cut Thessany's baby out of her belly when the time came. Thessany appeared to be doing her best to combat this threat by reminding Lord Gibil, via allusions to Hēphaestion's funeral, that she had some sway over him; that she held a lever in her hand. However, Lord Gibil – complacent with success – showed signs of fending off this lever, and resisting this sway, in the matter of the family heir at any rate.

A possible misinterpretation on Muzi's part might be to suppose that Alex either misconceivedly considered himself warned off by a jealous husband, or else was deliberately disobeying Muzi's overt message: to keep Thessany content. Thus to save his own neck; and his cock.

Fortunately, though Thessany was distracted by the prospect of Dr Cassander's interference, she also appeared to note Muzi's new watchful mood and to try to parry this nonchalantly. Perhaps she suspected Muzi of brooding equally about the supposed need for surgery, but in a proprietorial, gung-ho fashion.

A week after the robbery, Alex lurked along the lane with his water-barrow.

Gupta came out of the gate. A few dozen strides brought him to where Alex waited. 'Ah, my troubled friend! Have you overcome your moral anxieties now that there is no aftermath?'

'That isn't why I was troubled.'

'Anxieties about Thessany, then? I think my exercises may help her in childbirth.'

'Meaning that she'll be able to vanish and give birth somewhere far from doctors' knives? Are you a midwife too?'

'Be careful what you say. Who knows but Irra might be skulking on the other side of this wall?'

'Or Nettychin.'

'No need to worry about Nettychin.'

Alex whispered, 'Are you and Thess planning something? Are you going to spirit her away to safety? Is she going to give birth invisibly and silently in the garden? With nothing known until the infant wails? She must have asked you to help out – to use invisibility somehow!'

'It's easier to steal a heap of gold than to do what you're suggesting. I won't talk of this.'

'Muzi has guessed about me and Thess. But don't tell her that! He's suspicious of you too; he's watching.'

'I had noticed. Alex, you think too much. Excessive thinking can sometimes weave illusions.'

'Does that mean Thess told you what I said to her during the robbery?'

Gupta raised an eyebrow. 'I'm afraid, if you told her something momentous, it has been eclipsed by a big belly. She has pressing concerns. They press from within, where your penis pressed. So it isn't the theft or the birth that oppresses you?'

'No. Listen to me and hear me out. First I want to ask you one question, Gupta. Have you heard of the Akademia of the Future at Heuristics, in Arizona, America?'

After he had listened carefully to Alex, Gupta said, 'Be quiet a while.' He shut his eyes and stood still for all of two minutes without breathing. Then he opened his eyes again.

'Alex, I feel I once knew something about this. Before we both became Babylonians, in the belly of Babel . . . yes.'

'But no longer?'

'A man of invisibility co-operates with the world. He doesn't stand silhouetted on a skyline.'

'What on earth does that mean?'

'It means that you are standing on a skyline. You can still see both ways: into one valley, or into the next valley. The first valley is like the vale before we were born; the other valley is our present life. This is a terrible thing you have suggested to me. Ha ha! Of course I can be invisible – if it is only a matter of masking part of a pattern! Of course I could steal gold invisibly. If this is true, then I am invisible to myself. I do not know who I am.'

'Months ago,' said Alex, 'while I was still staying at Kamberchanian's inn, I went to the Greek Theatre one afternoon. I saw a play by Euripides, about Andromeda. Andromeda spoke these lines:

> "Like the real Helen who never sailed to Troy
> So that men and ships followed a ghost
> And Priam's son loved a ghost in bed,
> A hallucination sent by gods to craze men . . ."

'There's an old legend that the real Helen never travelled to Troy at all. She went somewhere else – to some island, or to Egypt, I dunno – and hid herself. A double, a false Helen went to Troy in place of her. A phantom, says Euripides.'

Gupta slapped his brow. 'Are we all false Helens here? False Alexes, false Guptas? Here is where we came into existence first of all, with borrowed memories?'

'As so many *elektronik klōnes*, made by *tekhnē* . . .'

'So many amber shoots?'

'No, *elektronik* as in lightning and, and . . . damn it.' Frustration gripped Alex. 'I think future *tekhnē* is able to copy a person's mind and memory. Many persons'! Babylon's the pot where we all stew together.'

'Why can't I remember these things?'

'Because now that we've all become functioning Babylonians, some of our original memory-wax has been erased. What was wanted here was true models of human behaviour. But behaviour springs from real-life experiences. To start with, we had to remember who we were. Now that we've been in Babylon long enough, experiencing new events, the yarn of our personalities has all been spun from the original spool on to a new spool.' Alex sighed. 'Spools, indeed! I can't describe this future *tekhnē* except in Greek, badly. I suppose in Anglika you would say . . .' Ice gripped his heart as he sought for English and found only scattered words. Many words, oh yes! Not just a handful. Words such as 'nuclear' and 'rifle' and 'computer'. 'Christ' and 'David Copperfield' and 'sociology' and 'drop-out'. A whole gang of words. But they wouldn't join together. They had no syntax, nothing to set them in order.

'I've lost my native tongue, Gupta.'

'I . . . so have I. Maybe that is because of the *hypnos* we underwent to learn Babylonian? A *hypnos* undergone not by ghosts, but by real flesh-and-blood people!' Gupta frowned. 'Flesh and blood, hmm. That doesn't quite accord with my philosophy. The universe is only a veil of illusions spun by time, using energy as its fabric. Is the false Helen – the *elektronik* avatar – any less real by virtue of being energy locked inside a piece of *tekhnē*? The actual Helen herself is just a pattern of energies.'

'That hardly resolves our dilemma!'

'I must think about this carefully, Alex. I must meditate.'

'And I must wheel this water home.'

'Yes, do keep lots of water in the house for the confinement.'

'Canal water. Ditch water.'

'Safe enough, if boiled.'

'The baby isn't due yet. It'll be another five or six weeks.'

'Unless Dr Cassander sharpens his knife prematurely.'

'Can't you help her at all?'

'Yes, with my yoga.'

'What's the use of yoga, if Cassander is going to operate anyway? You wouldn't even mention yoga — unless you two had other plans!'

With sudden briskness Gupta said, 'Of course there is an alternative. A potion to induce rapid early labour before the baby is too enormous. That's what she wishes me to procure: a potion of ergot. I'm reluctant. Ergot is a hallucinating poison: and she would need a strong dose. There, I've told you after all; may I be forgiven.'

'We illusions must stick together, eh?'

'Hmm. How much easier — more comforting, even! — it is to talk about birth and ergot, knives and ditch water . . . than about the other matter. But: pain suffered by ghosts is perfectly real to the ghosts. The death of a ghost is real to the ghost.'

Just then a Macedonian soldier on horseback hove into view at the end of the lane. He cantered along till he reached Nettychin's gate, where he reined in and hollered.

Alex resumed pushing his barrow homeward.

* * *

After prayers that evening, Muzi made an announcement:

'Listen, everyone. I got a message from the palace today. Two weeks from now I'm invited to hunt with the king himself. He feels vigorous. He wants to see some blood shed. We'll ride out to the wild beast park and camp by Olympia Spring: the king with me, and General Perdiccas and Antipater. Along with soldiers and attendants. Irra will squire me, 'natch. I figure on having a slave with me too; with my wife's say-so. For the looks of it. It's a question of prestige.' Muzi directed his gaze at Alex. 'You, boy, are the only household slave hereabouts.'

Thessany exclaimed, 'What a great honour, Muzi! I'm so proud. Of course you must go; and of course you must borrow Alex.' She sounded entirely delighted and sincere.

'I surely intend to go; but it's gracious of you to let me deprive you of Alex. I appreciate that.' He laid his hand on the clay idol of the dog-headed warrior. 'I promise before our home-god that your slave won't come to any harm a-hunting.'

Harm, such as what? A mauling by an enraged lioness? Or perhaps a javelin in the back . . . ? Muzi had given his word, though. Honour was uppermost.

While on the top of Thessany's mind, perhaps, was Gupta and ergot and two or three days' liberty . . . Muzi and Alex would return from the hunt to find a baby prematurely born and Thessany safe from Cassander's knife. Or else to find Thessany poisoned and Alex's child dead inside her; or born dead.

The baby: product of two ghosts who together had created a third ghost quite as real and alive as they were. The babies of Babylon would have no originals anywhere else, of whom they were only copies and *klōnes* . . .

Irra grinned at Alex as they were heading out of the chapel. 'Can you ride? Or would you rather run alongside us?'

'I can ride,' said Alex. 'I used to live in the country. Somewhere once upon a time. It wouldn't look very prestigious, would it, if I arrived at camp hours late like some beggar, all flaked out, coated in sweat and dust?'

'Oh, you'll get coated in sweat and dust, whatever happens. Boy.'

Mama Zabala had been cooking apricot pastries; and Thessany, swollen with child, steered herself to the kitchen in pursuit of the sweet aroma which now drifted through the house. She emerged along the corridor with a pastry in each hand, her mouth crammed with the remnants of a third.

Other odours contended but failed to conquer. During an intrusive house-call the day before, Dr Cassander had delivered many little bags of crushed myrtle flowers and knobs of asafoetida gum which he insisted should be strung up all over the place as prophylactics against any invisible imps of sickness. (Muzi, of course, concurred.) Everywhere, that is, excluding the kitchen. Mama Zabala rebelled at the prospect of asafoetida tainting her cuisine with its reek of garlic; and perhaps she had embarked on her pastry crusade in retaliation. Certainly she had lured Thessany and beamed as her pregnant mistress stuffed herself.

'Just the thing! Don't be coy. Your body knows what it wants.'

Mama Zabala had sent Alex packing from the kitchen on an unnecessary errand soon after Thessany arrived, as though his presence might spoil the complicity of the two women, thus diminishing the cook's victory over the male doctor's prescriptions. Alex had hung about within earshot of the reed door.

Out at the back he could hear Tikki barking excitedly, and the voices of Muzi and Irra. Two maids were giggling distantly. Anshar had been despatched to the palace with a message about some detail of the following week's expedition.

Now Thessany emerged, and he had his chance.

'Thess!'

'Mmmm,' she munched. She nodded at the door, still rustling from her exit.

'I must talk to you.'

She swallowed with several gulps.

'Not here. Now now.'

'Gupta's due tomorrow. Maybe bringing ergot.'

Thessany looked not so much annoyed as puzzled. 'Why did he tell you?'

'Because I told him something. Do you remember what I said while we were waiting in the chariot for Gupta?'

She looked blank.

'About the Akademia.'

'Oh, that.'

'Gupta and I talked about it. If a real intrigue's to your taste, ask him whether he thinks Babylon genuinely *exists*.'

She wagged her pastries at him. 'These are to my taste.' She stuck out her inflated tummy. 'Here's my intrigue, occupying all the space there is. For the moment.'

'Ah, but the maids will care for our baby after it's been born – '

'Shhh!'

'If you aren't to get depressed, you'll need an intrigue that's worthy of you.'

She grinned. 'Oh Alex, you're inventing an intrigue

for me, so that I shan't risk poisoning myself! That's what this is all about.'

'No, it isn't. No, I'm not.'

'I must make a choice: between Cassander's knife and his stitching needles – and you-know-what. You-know-what seems a lot safer. You wouldn't do me a service by dissuading me. You'd only avert the crisis by a fortnight or so.' She cocked her head – 'Someone's coming' – and waddled past; in time to meet Muzi returning by the front door, while Alex slipped quickly back into the kitchen.

'Dr Cassander said you oughta rest up in the afternoons.'

'I got hungry.'

'You'll give yourself bellyache.'

'I'll have worse bellyache soon.' Noise of munching.

'I don't think that Gupta guy ought to visit till all this is over. When Anshar gets back here I'll send him wherever Gupta hangs out to say that – '

'No! Gupta guru teaches exercises to relax me.'

'You ain't gonna need exercises, Thess.'

'I know. But indulge me, Muzi my love, my lion; and I will love you.'

'Well, okay.'

Only at this point did Alex realize that Muzi had never actually accused him of being the baby's father. On the night of Hēphaestion's funeral he had charged him only with screwing his wife, not with bastardizing his heir.

Did Muzi naïvely assume that his first coupling with Thessany must instantly have made her pregnant? Surely not. Lady Gibil had touched on the facts of life at that dinner party a while before the wedding.

It would have been pointless, in this city of Ishtar and sacred love, for Thessany to simulate virginity on her wedding night, say with a sachet of beast blood, leading Muzi to assume that he was the first one to bite the peach.

Surely the plain truth was that Muzi himself couldn't conceive ... of the baby not being his. His wife might behave like a whore, but at least her womb had to be faithful; honour demanded this. Muzi imagined erroneously that Lord Gibil winked at Thessany's adultery because it kept her content; obviously Gibil couldn't countenance his own grandson being the product of a slave's loins. But probably Muzi's reasoning never proceeded as far as this. Emotionally, in his soul of honour, he knew that he must be the sire. Otherwise the whole world came unstrung.

He was willing to study and accept devious chicanery – even unto his wife in bed with a slave – but at this one central hurdle of paternity he must have baulked, without even letting himself perceive it.

It was even possible that Muzi *was* the father. What price the few nights' advantage Alex had enjoyed? Maybe those had made no difference. Upon what magical intuition, what transparency of her own womb, was Thessany's certainty based? Why, upon wishful thinking.

Not until now had the possibility occurred to Alex that he himself *mightn't* be the father. He refused to consider this. Any more than Muzi would believe the opposite.

Following Gupta's next session, Alex managed to catch him in the street again.

'Did you bring ergot?'

'I shan't tell you. Let's talk of the other matter.'

'Why shan't you tell? Does the guru obey the disciple now?'

'In this case maybe he does! When the disciple is almost a saint.'

'Did Thess ask about the other matter?'

Gupta shook his head. 'Should she have done?'

'I should have thought a saint might be interested in her own reality.'

'Ha ha, how little you know of saints. Especially very pregnant saints.'

'What about their legendary clarity? Their clear perception of truth and illusion?'

'Hmm. If what you say is true, what would happen if you tried physically to leave Babylonia? Would some intelligence take heed? Would soldiers ride forth and drag you back? Would you reach the edge of the pattern and evaporate?'

'Maybe the answer isn't at the *edge*. Maybe it's down below Babel.'

'Waiting for your Deborah to discover it, in a few months' time?'

'Waiting for Zarpanit. I'm not interested in any Deborah.'

'Whatever is in the Underworld beneath Babel must be part of the pattern of Babylon. Surely, Alex? How could it lead elsewhere?'

'Maybe there's some kind of *tekhnē* interface between our world . . . and another world.'

Gupta frowned. 'Too mechanistic an approach, my friend! You talk as though you might find a key in the street which unlocks an actual door to heaven. Key and heaven are of different orders of existence.' He hesitated. 'Maybe my own tricks with visibility might reveal something. I might become invisible to the pattern of Babylon and thus, as it were, independent . . .

'Perhaps not I! Thessany perhaps; if she becomes what I hope for – a saint. Water, Alex, cannot be ladled with a spoon made of water. Air can't be trapped in a box made of air. Fire will not burn fire. Ice will not melt ice. Clouds do not knock stony mountains down. If we're ghosts, we can only grapple with other ghosts. Yet perhaps a saint may succeed . . . I hear that you're going hunting next week?'

'That's right. Will that be when the ergot gets used?'

Gupta's only answer was: 'Remember: the ghost of a lion can kill the ghost of a man.'

'Don't worry about that. Muzi has guaranteed my safety. I wish you could guarantee Thessany's.'

'I wish so too. I think we do need a saint – even if her métier is seven veils of semblance, six sorts of deception. Perhaps especially such a saint!'

8

In which a lion hunt goes too far

The hunting camp was located a good twenty minutes' walk (or five minutes' ride) from Olympia Spring, which was one reason why campers became – and stayed – grimy. Olympia was the only water source for miles around, but camping at the spring itself could have deprived shy beasts and provoked fierce ones.

Animals themselves observed a kind of waterhole etiquette: slaughter did not take place at a spring – and hunters obeyed the law of Babylon as to how many trophies might be bagged. To the eye of the rider the game park seemed boundless – it numbered half a dozen widely scattered oases – but an orgy of killing could clean out the stock of lions and tuskers within a year or two. Sometimes hunters, who paid a fat licence fee to the palace for the privilege, only counted coup rather than scalping big game; which was why Muzi had been pleased at the gratuitous chance to spear an elephant which berserked.

Half a dozen grand tents – one of these royal purple – were pegged out on the shorn pate of a low hill amidst a horseshoe of other hills furred frizzily with mesquite and paloverde and creased by little meandering canyons. Here and there rocky debris spilled on to the flats below, where creosote scrub soon yielded to cactus. On this, in the distance, wild goats grazed. A solitary jackass would utter its high-pitched bray; a quartet of pronghorn antelope would take fright and bound.

Babylon – Babel Tower principally – was visible on the horizon amidst the double haze: a faint mist of smoke, a green fuzz of fields spreading from southwest to north-west. Much further west was Arabia Deserta, uncrossable parched tracts. If you stood on the topmost ridge of the horseshoe hills and looked east, instead, you would certainly fail to see even the tips of the distant arid Zagros Mountains of Persia . . .

Since this was the king's first sportive outing in two whole years or more, the party was licensed – by Antipater, the king's Inspector of Game and Superintendent of the Royal Parks – to kill both a lion and a lioness.

Tradition demanded that actual kills, as opposed to coups, should be achieved on foot, preferably by near-nude champions; so it was possible that no lions at all might succumb. Given the significance of this occasion, with Alexander newly vigorous and lively, it seemed a necessary omen that the quota should be at least partly filled.

Servants had scouted out on horseback in the cold lavender half-light of dawn; now an hour later they returned to camp as shadows drew strength from the climbing sun. No pride had been spotted anywhere near Olympia, but Irra reported sighting, from the far side of the hills, buzzards circling away across the eastward plain.

The hunting party soon rode forth; and Alex remained in camp with other slaves and servants.

The sun ascended, baking that hilltop. All tasks were soon done; on the royal menu for that evening were salted fish, ox-tongues jellified in jars, celery and cheeses, beer and wine. The shade of an awning around the royal tent was sought; an intricate grid was scratched in the ground; knobs of quartz of various hues were collected; dice and a big bundle of differently dyed threads appeared – and the Game of Babylon commenced, to while away the day.

The rules were thus. Each player became one or other of the gods; Marduk or Ishtar, Shamash or Sin or whoever. Each god set out from his or her temple, the object being to touch base at each of the other temples (minus one) – but without crossing any part of the route traversed by the god whose temple the player had elected to visit first – and finally to occupy the summit of Babel.

Each player tossed the dice, then shifted his knob of quartz a corresponding number of thumb-widths along the streets and laid a trail of coloured thread behind to mark his course. As soon as the first target temple was reached – as soon as Shamash reached the temple of Ishtar, say – Shamash then had to consider the implications of the route Ishtar had chosen so as to avoid his own route being blocked by her future moves, moves which she would make with an eye to impeding him and if possible to boxing him inside a single district; though he could not impede her.

She, however, would have to touch base at another temple – not Shamash's, now that he had reached hers first, but Marduk's, for example – and whilst Ishtar was trying to impede Shamash she would also be aiming to chart a route which brought her to all other temples (save Shamash's) but avoided the route of Marduk. Marduk, meanwhile, might be attempting to block Ishtar while he himself avoided the manoeuvres of Sin, whose temple he had visited first of all.

Meanwhile, of course, Shamash would need to pay attention to Marduk's route in so far as Marduk might assist him by blocking Ishtar – which also involved watching Sin's route, since this would constrain Marduk.

It was the first time Alex had played the Game of Babylon, which he had glimpsed people huddled over in games rooms, squatting around wooden mapboards. Yet, moving his knob of amethyst quartz which represented Enlil, god of the air, he felt that he had been playing in reality for the best part of a year. Fiercely intent silence was punctuated by oaths, chortles, and squeaks of chagrin.

Quite often in this game – so the palace servant who spelled out the rules for novice Alex had explained – no god ever reached Babel. Masters in the Game of Babylon – grand mnemonists – would play without memory-threads to mark the routes, with umpires recording these out of sight on beeswax boards; and master players disdained the chance element introduced by the dice, moving one finger's length on each occasion.

The first game ended in stalemate shortly after noon, though Alex had been boxed inside the Zababa district some while before, reduced to shunting back and forth aimlessly. Since the spider's web which he wove inside his box of streets might yet impede the god who had visited Enlil's temple first, resigning was forbidden.

The players refreshed themselves from water-skins and ate some fruited barley-bread. They debated a siesta, but began another game. This also ended – faster – in stalemate.

So did a third game.

The fourth, however, spun out longer and longer as the afternoon wore on till remarkably all but two gods were boxed in, and the two who remained free were Ishtar, played by Alex's earlier counsellor – and Enlil, played by Alex himself.

By now Ishtar and Enlil had a veritable maze of overlaid threads to negotiate; and both were about to start their final circuitous march upon Babel, Enlil from the Borsippa Gate, Ishtar from the Ishtar Gate.

With the two dice Alex threw a nine.

Just then drumbeats thudded faintly from the flat below.

'Single rider coming,' observed one of the slaves. 'Carry on.'

The noise of hooves quickly grew louder, and then scrabblingly lost rhythm as the horse began to ascend the slope. Alex moved his piece of quartz away from the Borsippa Gate, wishing he could use the sewer tunnel as a secret route to Babel.

Half a minute later a lathering horse snorted to a halt by the tent. A hot, dusty Anshar dismounted.

'Alex! Where is Master Muzi?'

'What's happened, Anshar?' Alex feared that he already knew.

'Mistress Thessany goes into convulsions! Her body tries to give birth. Mama Zabala says the contractions come too early. Not normal at all! Mistress is ill. Dr Cassander is summoned.'

'Is she in pain?'

'Her body is racked. It can't expel the baby. Horrible!'

'Is Gupta guru there?'

'Him? He visited yesterday. Why today? Where is Master Muzi?'

'Over the hills,' said the Shamash player.

'Bound to be back by dusk,' said Ishtar. 'Stay here or you might miss them.'

'I'm sorry, I can't play any longer,' said Alex. 'I can't concentrate.'

'You're almost there,' protested his opponent. 'You could be a good player.'

'Could I? It seems life's just thrown me a double nothing.'

'What d'you mean? There's no nothings on these dice.'

'On mine there are, today.' Alex stared at the sketched-out grid littered with threads, wishing he could leap into the reality of the city and be back home in a trice. Though what use could he be there?

'Oh damn it, damn it,' he snarled, and swept his palm across the board erasing a whole district, tangling memory-threads.

'*Hey*,' growled his opponent.

Anshar looked sympathetic but puzzled.

The hunting party returned an hour later, lion-less and disgruntled.

'Wine for the king! Wine for us all!' bellowed General Perdiccas. Slaves and servants scurried to take charge of horses, to serve refreshments. Dogs cocked their legs against tent stakes unbaptized since morning, then flopped with lolling tongues.

Anshar had run to black Galla and gripped the saddle, blocking Muzi's descent.

'Master, you should ride to Babylon tonight! Your wife is in labour, sudden and terrible!'

'*What?*'

'She is convulsed and racked.'

'Oh gods. When?'

'Her pains start at noon. Contractions soon become excessive.'

'Who sent you? The doctor? My father? Who's there?'

'Both are summoned. I rode of my own accord.'

The king had already dismounted and lurched inside the purple tent, followed closely by Antipater. He looked as dark with anger as with dust. General Perdiccas, still in the saddle, trotted his steed over.

'Some trouble, Master Muzi?'

When Muzi told him, the general frowned. He was a

stub-headed man with grey hair cropped close as could be, but very little forehead. He wore a squared-off grizzled beard.

'That's very unfortunate, Master Muzi. And no trophy to show for today. Tomorrow we must ride harder and farther.'

'It isn't Irra's fault that the lions skedaddled.'

'He was *your* scout, sir.' So Muzi was responsible by proxy for the lack of a dead lion. Some ridiculous piece of hunters' etiquette; a matter, thought Alex stupidly, of pride . . .

'I . . . um . . . oughta ride back to the city.'

'Back?' barked the general. 'You can't abandon the king's company.'

'I can crave his permission.'

'Pah! He's in a mood, till he drains a few cups. And then he may be in a different sort of mood. You listen to me: your being invited along was a great honour.'

'I appreciate that, General.'

'Riding off would ruin all that. D'you hear, young fellow? It might have been a different case if you'd speared us a lion. You didn't. No one did. We need to have at least one lion in the bag. Till we do, you may *not* resign your part in the chase – and weaken us. I advise you for your own good, as a father would.'

'But my wife – '

'Has likely given birth already. She started hours ago. It'd take you another double hour at least to canter back. You couldn't force that hoss unless you wanted to burst its heart. Don't be an idiot. Come to the king's tent. Wine will ease your worries.'

'What would she think of me? What would anyone – ?'

'Your wife's too busy to think. What would the king think? That's more to the point. If she's any sort of wife I'll tell you what she'll think if you quit here. She'll think you're an almighty fool.'

'She could *die*.'

'Then she won't think a thing.'

'She's Marduk's daughter!'

'And this is the *king's* camp.' The general slid down from his saddle. 'Don't disappoint us, Master Muzi. Once before you slapped the king in the face, in a manner of speaking.'

'I didn't.'

'Matter of opinion.'

Muzi pushed Anshar aside and dismounted. The general clapped Muzi on the back, and together they headed for the royal tent.

Inside the purple tent, as first the hills turned purple, then the whole sky from zenith to western horizon, a drinking bout commenced. This went on for a whole double hour till long after the bruised blood of evening had become clotted darkness, hardly dispelled by feeble lanterns which acted more as navigation markers to those picking their way around camp. A mound of uprooted creosote bushes, now sun-withered, had been built up the day before; but this bonfire would be lit only if lions menaced the camp – it would quickly consume itself. A half-moon arose.

At last the cold feast was called for, and Alex was summoned inside to be one of the waiters. Now he could see what he had been listening to intermittently.

Muzi, Antipater and General Perdiccas sat on fat cushions upon the carpeted ground. The king would alternately sprawl out on his own low couch like the sick voluptuary he had once been – and then suddenly swing himself upright to perch on the edge, alertly studying whoever was speaking, swinging his gaze sharply onward to bring in another opinion, like a magistrate or a judge at a rhetoric competition. Alex soon realized that themes were being set by the king for his three guests to discourse upon amusingly, inventively, and in firm strong voices whilst keeping pace with the drinking. Every so often the king wearied of a subject and cut across whoever was speaking to proclaim a new topic – the real riddle of the Sphinx, the habits of crocodiles, the secrets of the pyramids – which he would enlarge on with boisterous intensity and tipsy rodomontade before lolling back limply again, his wine-cup wavering in his hand.

Muzi looked glad of the distraction and ballast offered by the viands.

'I warrant,' said the king, seizing a stick of celery, 'that a slave could discourse as well as a free man! Eh, Antipater?'

Gaunt but sinewy Antipater said diplomatically, 'Some slaves in Greece are well educated, sire. Some are used as tutors. But it would surely be a false syllogism to suggest that therefore all slaves possess this capacity. Generally slavery is a sign of inferiority. Perhaps only through the happenstance of fortune! But equally the condition of slavery provides a natural niche for life's donkeys, as opposed to life's stallions or life's lions. Thus slaves must labour – and some of them may even bray persuasively. One surely would not wish to abolish slavery any more than one would wish to make lions eat grass. Democracy often tends towards weakness because all voices are heard – and many are the voices of asses.'

'How would one test my proposition? Why not at random? I shall wager with Master Muzi here one golden talent that a slave can best me in argument, thanks to that slave's own native talent for wit and logic.'

Muzi looked up anxiously from his ox-tongue.

'I challenge Master Muzi,' continued the king, 'since I see that we have here with us a slave whom he prizes highly. There must be something special about such a slave, eh?'

Alex had become a focus of attention.

'Your Majesty,' Muzi said hastily, 'would a slave *dare* defeat you in argument, even if he could?'

'Good point,' growled Perdiccas. 'The really clever slave might aim to lose. His victory might embarrass his master.'

The king clapped his hands. 'I make a decree! Just as there is truce at the Olympic Games and at the Oracle of Delphi, so this slave shall be a free man for tonight. He shall join us at table. Give him my chaplet of golden laurel leaves to wear.'

A palace servant hastened to the royal travelling bag, and Alex found himself crowned with metal which bit into his brow.

King Alexander patted the couch. 'Come sit by me. I like the look of you, as much as I've liked the look of any man since my beloved Hēphaestion departed into the heavens. Your face even seems familiar, as though I glimpsed you during the fever dreams of my illness.'

So that's the score, thought Alex.

The king hadn't been flying a kite about the possible abolition of slavery; as feared perhaps by Antipater, who now smiled wanly.

Nor was this some spur-of-the-moment scheme to embroil Muzi in public shame, for one reason or another.

The king fancied Alex.

'If this free man – free for tonight – pleases us,' King Alexander enthused, 'why then he shall ride to hunt tomorrow as a reward.' The king slipped an arm round Alex and cuddled him briefly. 'He seems muscular enough to dare death or glory. Do not tremble so, free man! Tonight you are almost my equal.'

'Sire,' said the general doubtfully, 'Lord Aristander might doubt the wisdom of a new Hēphaestion ... from the ranks, as it were. Hardly even from the ranks.'

'We are miles from Babylon, my General. And I am drunk, am I not? So watch your tongue. Yes, yes!' The king stabbed a finger at the mound of ox-tongue. 'Eat it! Eat your great bovine tongue!' He giggled crazily. 'If only we had killed a lion today, how different I might feel!'

Perdiccas obediently carved a slice of tongue; but now the king snatched the laden plate towards the couch.

'You eat his tongue, free man! Put a burly tongue in your hand before you become an orator! Devour it, gobble it down.'

Several sorts of misery haunted Alex. He picked a whole tongue up in both hands and began to gnaw his way through, hoping that bad table manners might disqualify him as King Alexander's bed-warmer. The king only laughed and drank deeply.

He wiped his lips. 'Bolt it down! I can't wait to find if your mind also is muscular.'

Alex soon sickened of this surfeit of tongue and laid the stump down. Muzi had hitherto refrained from uttering Alex's name; nor had the king enquired it. In the monarch's current volatile mood Alex rather feared the consequences – hostile or affectionate – if King Alexander learned that his namesake sat by him.

'Are we ready?' cried Alexander. 'Best of three. I choose the first topic, Master Muzi selects the second, and our free man makes the final choice. The first theme shall be: the Size of the World, according to

Eratosthenes. I shall argue in favour of the Greek sage.'

'Not born yet,' muttered Perdiccas.

'Never mind! According to an oracle book, thus it shall be.' The king shuffled his buttocks and farted. 'Eratosthenes will visit Egypt. He will observe that the sun stands directly overhead at noon on the summer solstice in the town of Syene. Whereas at the same time in my own city of Alexandria, several hundred miles north, the sun is seven degrees away from vertical . . .'

The king expatiated for a while. When he concluded, all eyes turned towards Alex.

He was expected to argue against *this*? It sounded as though Eratosthenes had calculated the size of the world correctly!

The only opposing argument Alex could think of was that the world which he and King Alexander inhabited was actually an *elektronik* pattern within a piece of future *tekhnē*. Babylonia was the whole of the world, and no bigger than the box which stored it.

Wouldn't this be blasphemy? Blasphemy punishable by impalement?

'Well? We wait, agog.'

Alex opened his mouth with no idea what to say. He was saved by a commotion outside.

Outcry. A crackling roar.

A guard ducked inside the tent. 'Pardon me, sire! General Perdiccas – '

The general rose, seized a sword, and hurried out. While the tentflap was open it was plain that the pile of creosote bushes was blazing; red firelight enflamed the night.

The king chucked Alex under the chin. '*Argumentum ex machina*, as the well-shaved Roman barbarians will phrase it!' He too rose and grasped a spear. As he did so, a martial transformation came over him. 'Perhaps the lions have come to us!' he roared, and strode swiftly out.

Muzi armed himself and followed. Antipater too, and servants. Alex, still chapleted with golden leaves, also took his leave of the tent.

Near the bonfire Anshar was wailing and beating his breast. A strange horse stood quivering, streaming in the sudden heat. By the horse stood Nettychin.

The general intercepted the king: 'It's another messenger for Master Muzi, sire. The fool thought wild beasts were chasing him. At the bottom of the hill he lit a brand. To alert us he threw the brand into our wood.'

'What news by night, fellow?' bellowed Alexander.

Apparently Nettychin did not recognize his king, or else he was too distraught to care. He stomped forward and addressed himself to Muzi.

'Dire tidings, Master! Your daughter is well. Your wife is dead.'

Muzi gaped. 'What daughter?'

'Dr Cassander cut a baby girl from the Mistress. The Mistress died from loss of blood.'

Thessany, *dead*? Alex could hardly comprehend. At that moment all hopes died, all love froze over. All futures ceased to exist.

'Lord Gibil came to our house. I offered to follow Anshar, who had told me the way and the landmarks. Distracted, Lord Gibil agreed. I owe the Mistress a shekel for ever. I am her good and faithful servant; and will be so to her daughter. I borrowed a horse; I rode. Night fell and wild dogs howled in the wastes. The land was as dead as my heart, poisoned by snakes and scorpions. The dust of dead bones clogged my nostrils. The horse ran wild as if to dash itself from a cliff in sacrifice. Each rainbow hue of day was extinguished for always. When the moon rose, its light was feeble and leprous. I heard a dragon pursue me, to sting me in the heart. I came to this place.'

That bloody butcher, Cassander!

Alex's rage focused upon Muzi – Muzi who had dragged him from the city on this stupid expedition of prestige which bid fair to end in Alex becoming the king's catamite for a night.

'You useless prick,' he snarled at the husband, who stood in shock. 'You honourable hero. Lioness-fucker.' (Muzi's eyes widened.) 'And now the Pandar of your wife's slave!'

Almost on Alex's lips: 'Whose baby do you think it is?'

Muzi bared his teeth and jerked his sword towards Alex. 'Arm yourself! If Thessany's dead, then so are you. Get a weapon, slave.'

'Kill me unarmed,' said Alex. 'Run me through. Screw your sense of honour and your promise to the dog-god. I don't care.'

'Stop this at once!' shouted Perdiccas. 'For shame!'

The king seemed stimulated by the quarrel. 'What passions run riot here!' he exclaimed, somewhat squeakily. He hawked to clear his throat, and continued in firmer voice. 'You shan't fight this fellow, Master Muzi! A fine way to win a wager, by killing the object of it. I was already tussling with this man – I have prior claim.

'I am, of course, deeply sorry about your wife,' he added. 'I knew the grief of Hēphaestion's death. Aye, knew it – and overcame it.'

Muzi lowered his weapon. 'May I ride away, sire? Will you accept this slave as a gift to my king?'

'He isn't yours to give tonight. And tomorrow we must all hunt together. A king – like a god – must soar above mortal sorrows. Likewise those who serve him. There exists only one immortal tragedy, of which all human misfortunes are but reflections warped in the glass of life. That tragedy is the death of empires – in the broadest sense. It is that doom which a king forever fights.' A tear squeezed from Alexander's eye.

Muzi dropped his sword on the ground, and approached Alex. 'We've all got our sorrows, boy. So it seems.'

'I just can't believe she's dead,' mumbled Alex.

The king discarded his weapon. He draped an arm across Alex's shoulder. 'I begin to perceive the true tender nature of your grief – shared so exquisitely with your master. Let me console you.' He began to pull Alex towards the royal tent.

'Is the debate to continue?' asked Muzi in confusion.

'Bugger that,' said the king. 'I've quite lost interest in words.' He hauled Alex inside the tent. No one followed.

When King Alexander reached the royal bedding, however, he sprawled across it. Drunkenness triumphed. He passed out.

Alex sank down on the carpet. For a time he regarded the abandoned feast, then he crawled from one wine-cup to another, draining them all. Dizzily he curled up.

Tomorrow, he thought, *I shall die*.

And then he thought: *My daughter. O my daughter*.

The thought had little substance. Daughter was only a word, which soon became meaningless.

Alex had won no contest of wits, nor even shared the king's bed, yet Alexander still insisted on including him in the next day's adventure.

The following morning the hunting party rode like the wind across the scrubby plain beyond the hills, with Tikki and other hounds bounding alongside. Alex was mounted on Irra's mare; Irra had been left behind at camp.

The riders startled goats grazing on the sagebrush and the grey-green creosote shrubs. Antelope, nibbling at owl's clover and mallow, scampered off; but no lions were spied. In brakes of mesquite and brittlebush big cats had left no scent lingering for the dogs. Eventually they reached a hillocky ridge, laced with wandering minor canyons, and cast around for a while; but only a lone fox slunk away. Noon came and went.

By mid-afternoon they came to an oasis of a thousand trees where a family of elephants were feeding. Here the hunters watered their mounts and rested while the horses packed grass into themselves, the party keeping a watchful eye on the great grey cows and the bull lurking deep in the foliage. No lion contours rippled the long grass. When they set out again, Antipater spotted a buzzard spiralling lazily down. Two miles on, they found the remains of an elephant calf. Wild dogs fled at their approach. A few buzzards bounced aloft. The corpse wasn't yet reduced to bones and hide; flies festered on remnants of meat which weren't yet dried to jerky. Nearby they found lion spoor. The hounds chased off to the east, but after another mile they checked and cast about in vain.

'On! On!' cried Alexander. 'To the end of the earth, where Oceanus flows!'

And they rode on.

They had ridden like the wind before, but now the farther eastward they went the more did a wind from the east oppose them, fitfully at first then ever more gustily, stirring up devils and snakes of dust. By late afternoon the terrain ahead looked like a hazy mirror of the land behind which their horses' hooves had just beaten.

Now they were riding into the sun, which bloomed

redly as it sank behind dust veils. Perdiccas called a halt. The party reined in. The general drank water from a flask and spat.

'We've come too far, Majesty. The gods thrust us back.'

'The very story of my life,' the king commented sourly. 'Will no one ride on?'

'Into Apsu?' asked Antipater. 'Into the abyss?'

'Pah! We are Greeks, you and I.'

'This is Babylonia, with its own gods.'

Was this place really near the edge of the world? Was there an actual edge, a great plunging crevasse boiling with fog? Alex strained to see ahead, but now the air was a dirty distorting glass.

'I'll ride.' He thumped his horse with his heels.

As he urged the mare onward she whinnied and shied. He persevered but soon felt nauseated. The ground seemed to become a mass of separate dots which moved further and further apart. The mare's hooves were sinking. She had to pluck her feet free with each new step; she snorted with terror. Alex could hardly breathe. Emptiness rose up from the interstices of the world, suffocating him. He felt sucked dry, hollowed out, a husk. Soon, helpless, he wilted over his mount's neck. The mare struggled about and carried him back.

When he rejoined the others he could feel himself fill out again with substance.

'He fainted,' remarked the king. No one else commented.

The party finally arrived by moonlight at the ridge, and could urge the horses and themselves no further. After sharing the rest of their food with the dogs they dossed down on the ground under saddle blankets.

In the dawn light a roar awoke them.

Down on the creosote flat walked a full-maned lion.

Hastily they organized. They armed. They rode down in two groups, with the hounds whistled ahead to harry and block. The riders spread out till the lion, snarling at the dogs, was inside a loose circle. Perdiccas, Antipater and Muzi dismounted and threw off all clothing but their loincloths. The king stayed seated, watching.

'You too, faint-heart!' Muzi shouted at Alex. 'You *too*.'

So Alex slipped down from his mare and soon stood naked but for a strip of cloth and a sword.

However, he faced no real danger. For it was Muzi who dashed wildly and rammed a spear through the lion's throat, killing it.

9

In which Alex waxes eloquent, and the lady vanishes

Where to end? Where better than with the death of a lion and the death of a lady?

A death which at first seemed to equate with the death of love and even the death of meaning. Of love, arrived at by a strange route yet arrived at none the less and now lost. Though never really lost. Always with Alex now, like an arrowhead lodged non-fatally in his chest near his heart — which would throb and twinge for the rest of his life, or perhaps for five or twenty years until it worked its way out, reminding him whenever it pained that he was still alive, that Thessany had been alive, that they had touched.

Alex is writing this in Greek upon waxed boards; many of them. If this were an orthodox tale it should end in catharsis or in celebration — a great discovery might be made.

But death alone ends our own rambling stories, and will end the world's history. We can never know our own death, thus we can never know the end; nor the whole. When a person is dead they cannot look back and survey the terrain of their life. Likewise when a culture is dead it cannot look back on itself.

For a while after Alex's return to Babylon he thought about suicide. This was perhaps a salve for his soul, a consoling indulgent elegiac tune which he played upon his heartstrings: a threnody for Thessany, requiring the player to remain alive so as to be able to continue playing.

Should he walk by the waters where the Jews wail? Should he hurl his body from Babylon Bridge to drown himself amidst the spinning coracles?

If he did so, would he wake up elsewhere?

This sort of death by drowning – as opposed, say, to being butchered by knives or torn apart – presupposed that you might possibly wake up elsewhere; that there existed somewhere else, such as some different plane of being, where you might revive.

No doubt you wouldn't wake up at all. No doubt you wouldn't know anything more about matters or about yourself, ever again, than you knew when deeply asleep in the dead of night.

Thessany had written a will and had it witnessed by a magistrate, and in her will she had given Alex back his freedom; which seemed a dubious gift when he felt that he was her slave for ever, should he choose to go on living. The will meant that Muzi had no hold over him; nor any obligations. Alex was cast out of Muzi's house without ever setting eyes on his daughter, if the baby was indeed his.

Gupta met him and took him back to Kamberchanian's inn, promising that he could live there free for as long as he liked, till he felt able to help out with business at The Eye of Horus next door; the Indian hinted that he had squirrelled away a few ingots from the robbery of Hēphaestion's tomb.

Before long it occurred to Alex that if Hēphaestion deserved a memorial, why, so did Thessany. And this memorial – of words, not marble – would take months to make, and make well, so that through it Thessany could come alive again.

Soon he began to write; a process which Gupta observed indulgently, then laughed at somewhat.

With the death of not-yet-sainted Thessany Gupta seemed to have withdrawn his emotional support for Alex's suspicions of Babylon as a phantom of future *tekhnē*, a brothel of *elektronik klōnes*.

'Who are you writing for?' Gupta asked him. 'When you finish your labour of Herakles, will you have finally delivered a report to someone somewhere else?'

Sporadically during his labour Alex felt that he was a mad program fulfilling itself in a mad machine, which itself mimicked the mad machine which was the world, the universe . . .

Alex was Andromeda chained to the rock of Babylon, stalked by time the ravager.

Andromeda. Prometheus. Christ. The holy trinity – beauty, science, soul – nailed to the stony trunk of time as the storm of years swept onward. And from all their wounds, suffered or yet to be suffered, blood dripped to paint the shape of history.

The idea of suicide as an escape route to somewhere else now shrivelled away. If what Alex wrote in Greek on boards was merely an account of an imitation of reality, whereas elsewhere a more authentic world existed, in what way did his work differ from most writings – even histories – which established other, more deeply envisioned worlds into which the reader might escape? Obviously Babylon the fabulous must be more real – in the sense of being more ideal, truer, more determined to endure – than any other world which had given birth to it, from which Babylon's inhabitants had fled, leaving behind perhaps originals of themselves who might come to feel in time that *they* were the echoes and copies.

One often wants to believe in another, more heightened world – without any evidence whatsoever, or only tenuous, suspect evidence. Hence the origin of faith.

But here in Babylon was life. This was life; no other. There was nowhere else but here, but Babylon; just as for the original historic Babylonians there was nowhere else. Likewise for a Roman in Caesar's Rome. Or for an American in America. Where you are, is the only place. Is life itself.

Life sometimes seems to consist of a set of symbols and analogies, as though life is the key to some other reality elsewhere. But life is all there is. Now that Thessany was dead, Babylon was the only place for Alex to be. His mistress now was Babylon. He was the slave of Babylon, the whore.

He wrote on waxed boards for the sake of dead Thessany but also for the benefit of Thessany's daughter, who was also his own daughter. Their daughter was a child of Babylon and of nowhere else. In the years ahead there was time enough to discover how best to see her, how to meet up with her eventually; how to present her with his own and her mother's story. She would grow up. Alex would keep his eye on her. In sixteen years or so she might go to the temple of Ishtar and he might meet her there; though not to commit incest. Unless she was as capricious as her mother had been . . .

He wrote to inform his daughter about the past, which is the future. If she believed his tale; if she had any way of understanding it.

Meanwhile, farewell to foolish notions of throwing himself from Babylon Bridge.

On the contrary, perhaps he would visit the temple of Ishtar – tomorrow! – to renew contact with the reality of Babylon.

But first he would end; first of all. For in Babylon, where time is trumped, the end is always the beginning.

Here.
Now.

Not the end.

As I approached the gateway to the courtyard shaded by its cedars of Lebanon, no guard was keeping watch outside. I could hear the faint chatter of both guards, within. The lane was deserted.

A voice from behind called out, 'Alex!'

I turned; there in the lane stood Thessany.

Hadn't she died after all? Had the whole agony only been a cruel – or necessary! – intrigue? Had Muzi and Lord Gibil been fooled as well as me? Had Marduk in his temple needed to be duped by tragic final news? Had the baby girl who remained in Muzi's house been a child of beggars, bought new-born? Procured by Gupta, who had indulged me while I wrote my tale? Who had smiled knowingly, well aware that Thessany and her daughter were living somewhere in the city incognito?

Had Dr Cassander been bribed with some of the ingots which Gupta had failed to present to Lord Gibil? I never saw Thessany's corpse. Did Muzi or Gibil ever see it? Or did they see a dead slave girl, her face recontoured with wax? Or a body entirely made of wax?

What about the terrible convulsions witnessed by the household?

I ran to Thessany to clasp her.

My hands passed through her body. My body passed through hers.

I nearly fell. I staggered back. She still stood before me, smiling wryly now.

'You're a *holographos*,' I accused.

'No I'm not. It's me, all right.'

'Of course you're a *holographos*. There's a glass eye somewhere near. Close by Ishtar's gate: obvious location! Marduk is showing you to me. Or someone is. *Why?*'

'If I'm a *holographos*, dear, then either I'm an image of somebody alive and kicking in another part of town – and why should I hide my physical self from you? – or else I'm just a memory-image stored in some little scroll, in which case we could hardly engage in repartee. So I can't be a *holographos*, can I?'

'What are you?'

'I'm a ghost. A genuine ghost.'

'But . . . ghosts don't exist. Not that sort of ghost!'

'In Babylon one ghost exists. That's me. As I lay dying I remembered what you said in that chariot, when we were robbing the tomb, and I suddenly knew how to become invisible. I realized how my dead body could stay there on that blood-soaked pallet – and how my pattern could continue on. I knew how I could store myself within the pattern of Babylon; how I could hide and stay free without the pattern knowing I was there.

'And I did it. Oh, what a wondrous intrigue this is! Though it's dodgy too, and perilous. I have to keep on the move. I have to jink and duck, and mimic not being here at all. I have to find empty corners and nooks. I have to be a chameleon. I have to be a pane of glass. I've spent ages learning the tricks of staying invisible so that Babylon doesn't know I'm here. I shouldn't really appear to you – but I must! Because you love me; and I love you. Besides, shouldn't a ghost appear now and then? Else she wouldn't be a proper ghost! Alex, you must – ' She hesitated, glanced around.

I must what? Take lessons from Gupta, then kill myself? So that we might lurk together evermore as two mischievous ghosts within the pattern of Babylon?

Was hers the voice of my unfulfilled suicide calling out lamia-like to me?

She didn't say what I must; or mustn't.

'Oh, I can tell you such delicious secrets! But not right now. I must go.'

'Wait, Thess! Have you appeared to Gupta?'

'Just to you.'

'Will you appear to both of us together?' Thus I could be convinced that she wasn't a private hallucination, an imaginary person who had formed in my mind during all the months of scribing — formed with such total conviction that now suddenly here she was projected into ghostly reality.

'Please, Thess?'

'I'm not sure if I can safely appear to two people at once. The pattern's more concentrated then. It's denser. It could notice me and trap me. I think I'd better appear only to you, when I can. Maybe you'd better not even tell Gupta about me. I don't know; I'll think about it.'

'But it's true that Babylon's just an *elektronik* model?'

She laughed. 'Otherwise how could I be a ghost? Ooops — !'

And she vanished from before my eyes, just as a man turned the corner into the lane. A tall, robed, black-bearded man wearing a beehive of a turban. Swinging a jaunty stick, he strode towards me and the temple gate. It was Shazar, come to sample the wares of Ishtar; though not to find another bride for Marduk.

It must be three months now since Deborah-Zarpanit had gone to the Underworld, and a new Zarpanit had married Marduk. Procuring the replacement Zarpanit had been none of Shazar's business; nor would finding the next one be.

Shazar was merely intent on paying a fraternal

visit, of Sin to Ishtar; just as in the Game of Babylon, the timeless game.

The guard had resumed his post outside the gate. Hastily he drew himself to attention. As Shazar passed by me he paid scant heed to someone whom he had never personally met. Besides, my hair was bushy once more. I hadn't needed to shave my skull to remain true to Thessany. Her lion mark would always stay printed on my cheek, like a kiss which had bitten deep.